Garrett in
Wedlock

Garrett in Wedlock

Paul Mandelbaum

𝓑

BERKLEY BOOKS, NEW YORK

THE BERKLEY PUBLISHING GROUP
Published by the Penguin Group
Penguin Group (USA) Inc.
375 Hudson Street, New York, New York 10014, USA
Penguin Group (Canada), 10 Alcorn Avenue, Toronto, Ontario M4V 3B2, Canada
(a division of Pearson Penguin Canada Inc.)
Penguin Books Ltd., 80 Strand, London WC2R 0RL, England
Penguin Group Ireland, 25 St. Stephen's Green, Dublin 2, Ireland (a division of Penguin Books Ltd.)
Penguin Group (Australia), 250 Camberwell Road, Camberwell, Victoria 3124, Australia
(a division of Pearson Australia Group Pty. Ltd.)
Penguin Books India Pvt. Ltd., 11 Community Centre, Panchsheel Park, New Delhi–110 017, India
Penguin Group (NZ), Cnr. Airborne and Rosedale Roads, Albany, Auckland 1310, New Zealand
(a division of Pearson New Zealand Ltd.)
Penguin Books (South Africa) (Pty) Ltd., 24 Sturdee Avenue, Rosebank, Johannesburg 2196, South Africa

Penguin Books Ltd., Registered Offices: 80 Strand, London WC2R 0RL, England

This book is an original publication of The Berkley Publishing Group.

This is a work of fiction. Names, characters, places, and incidents either are the product of the
author's imagination or are used fictitiously, and any resemblance to actual persons, living or
dead, business establishments, events, or locales is entirely coincidental.

Grateful acknowledgment is made to the Ohio Arts Council, the California Arts Council, and to James Michener and
the Copernicus Society of America for financial support of this project and also to the magazines where the following
stories, in somewhat different form, first appeared: to *DoubleTake* for "Pendant"; to *Glimmer Train Stories* for "Yoga Is
a Personal Journey"; to *Harvard Review* for "The Explorers"; to *The Massachusetts Review* for "The Omelet King"; to
New England Review for "Changeling"; to *New Letters* for "Several Answers"; to *Prairie Schooner* for "Garrett in
Wedlock" (published as "Eclipse") and for "Parni's Present"; to *The Southern Review* for "Virtue."

PRINTING HISTORY
Berkley trade paperback edition / December 2004

Library of Congress Cataloging-in-Publication Data

Mandelbaum, Paul, 1959–
   Garrett in wedlock : a novel-in-stories / Paul Mandelbaum—Berkley trade pbk. ed.
      p. cm.
   ISBN 0-425-19637-2
      1. Remarried people—Fiction.   2. Stepfamilies—Fiction.   3. Divorced men—Fiction.   I. Title

PS3613.A53G37   2004
813'.54—dc22   2004046319

PRINTED IN THE UNITED STATES OF AMERICA

10   9   8   7   6   5   4   3   2   1

for Elena

Acknowledgments

I owe a special debt of gratitude to my kind and insightful agent, Betsy Amster; to my editor, Allison McCabe, whose ideas and enthusiasm have been inspiring; and to Tom Lutz, Nancy Schwalb, and Elena Song for their careful reading and longtime support. My heartfelt thanks also to Frank Conroy for the education; Nicole Yasmeen Daya for sharing her childhood; Kristen Fabiszewski, versed in the ways of IVF and midwifery; Alan Sea, Baltimore's foremost mortician/grammarian; Dr. Miran Song for all that free medical advice; and to Robin Bartlett, Terence Cannon, Jamie Diamond, Beth Gylys, Charlotte Hildebrand, Carol Holstead, Maryjane Krasnoff, Ginger Russell, Eric Savage, and Laurie Winer for their knowledge of the world and how it works. For some of my impressions of kuru, I'm grateful to Richard Rhodes for his book *Deadly Feasts*.

Garrett in Wedlock

"Why all this marriage, marriage?...
The human race would have become a single person centuries ago if
marriage was any use."

—*A Passage to India*, E. M. Forster

"'Oh, well,' said Brave Orchid.
'We're all under the same sky.'"

—*The Woman Warrior*, Maxine Hong Kingston

Contents

one

Garrett in Wedlock

From behind the kitchen door frame, Garrett spied on the children. The little boy, Turpin, sat cross-legged in front of the TV, dropping crayons one by one into an old coffee tin. Each crayon landed with a small *plunk*. Next to him, his older half sister, Lynn, clicked through TV channels, pausing for a second on each station before twisting the dial back, fast—like a roulette wheel. When the coffee tin was filled with crayons, the little boy turned it upside down. Wax shavings fluttered to the floor.

"TRIAL TODAY OF A SOUTH BALTIMORE WOMAN IN CONNECTION WITH—" *Click.*

"IF YOU'RE OUTSIDE, JIM, YOU WANT TO AVOID—" *Click.*

"DAMAGE ESTIMATED AT FOUR MILLION DOLLARS, INCLUDING THE MUSEUM'S TREASURED GUTENBERG BIBLE—" *Click.*

"BLOCKING MOST OF THE SUN'S *VISIBLE* SPECTRUM——" *Click*.

The children seemed unaware of Garrett, and he took turns focusing on each of them through the wedding ring, a simple gold band, he'd be soon giving their mother. Garrett studied the boy, then the girl, through the ring's small hollow—as though using a telescope to examine distant and exotic life forms.

"INSANITY PLEA——" *Click*.

"LITTLE HOLE IN THE CARDBOARD, LIKE SO, JIM——" *Click*.

"IMPALED THE POPULAR MIDDLE-SCHOOL VICE-PRINCIPAL WITH A FIFTEENTH-CENTURY AUSTRIAN HALBERD——" *Click*.

"SAFE AND FUN——" *Click*.

Already, Turpin was wearing his tuxedo vest. He'd wanted to sleep in it the night before, he was so eager to dress up. His head was covered with the blondest hair, virtually white, inherited from his Norwegian father. When backlit by the sun, the boy's head nearly disappeared behind a fierce halo. There was something mysterious about him, and he seemed to know more than a six-year-old was supposed to. Possibly because his mother and father had divorced. Divorce imposed a special shadowy wisdom on children.

The boy turned toward Garrett and smiled, then held up a piece of paper covered with dark cryptic circles.

"What's that?" Garrett asked, stepping out from the kitchen.

"Mygg."

"Turp, speak English, please."

"Bugs."

"That's terrific!"

"No it's not."

"AVOID THE TEMPTATION TO STARE——" *Click*.

"IRREPARABLE TOLL——" *Click*.

"TRULY A GOLDEN OPPORTUNITY——" *Click*.

"'KEPT TO HERSELF. WHO KNOWS WHY A HEART GOES DARK?' SUMMED UP ONE NEIGHBOR, WHO WISHES TO REMAIN——" *Click*.

Garrett sighed and looked over at the girl, who was still abusing the television set, a bygone black-and-white Zenith. "Lynn," he asked her, "could you wake your mother, please?"

"What's in it for me?" She shook her sleek black hair and raised her round nose in the air. She bore little resemblance to her brother. And, of course, she looked nothing like Garrett, but a lot like her father, the import-export dealer M. Parni Ghazal.

This felt like some kind of test. A coded message he was supposed to decipher.

"My sincere gratitude?" he tried.

She glanced at him and away.

"A Gummi Bear?"

No response. They could be rugged little customers, these kids. In the year since he'd met them, they were always coming up with new ways to rattle him.

"Never mind, sweetie," he said, deciding not to make a big deal of it. That was probably best.

The bedroom was peaceful, quiet, and striped with sunlight, and the air smelled sweetly of General Tso's chicken, which they'd eaten the night before. Garrett opened a window and sat on the edge of the bed. As May-Annlouise slept, he watched her delicately chiseled nose quiver with each light breath. She was a fitful sleeper, and most of the blanket had fallen off her. She usually flailed in the middle of the night—"sleep jumping" she called it—sometimes knocking Garrett with her hands, her feet, or even her elbows, waking him with a knee to the kidney, semiclenched knuckles against his jaw, the random cuff and chop. He had tried several protective postures over the months since moving in—lately, a fetal cringe.

He sat still, watching her body twist. Her nightgown had slid above her waist, and he put his hand on her belly, her beautiful pale belly with its faint, white lines that rippled like the luminous waves inside a seashell.

"Oh, God." She bolted upright and looked past him. "I had that dream."

"Which dream?" he asked, taking her face in his hands. "The one where you're auditioning for the Baltimore Ballet and your slippers catch fire?"

"No, the bicycle dream."

"The one where your brakes fail or the one where your naked rump is sticking up in the air?"

Shaking her head, she shut her eyes. "The rump one."

"And your first husband is running beside you, holding the handlebars?"

She nodded vigorously against his palms.

"And your second husband is hanging on to the book rack?"

"Yes, yes, yes." She stared feverishly now at Garrett and demanded, "What does it *mean*? Do you think it's some omen, about today?"

Garrett looked over to the closet door at his rental tux hanging quietly like a third person in the room and felt suddenly claustrophobic. He said, a bit sharply, "You've had that dream three times this month; you must really love it."

"I hate that dream, Garrett. You know I do. Don't tease me."

She looked at him imploringly, and so he took her in his arms and gently rocked her, whispering moist *clucks* into her ear. Back and forth he rocked her, petted her, held her tightly and jiggled her and kissed her earlobe, stroked her auburn hair and nuzzled her warm neck, and wondered, as he did all this, if the dream was indeed some sort of sign. Lately, he'd been looking for a sign to tell him whether they were doing the right thing. He could not find the answer inside himself.

After showering, Garrett unveiled his rental tux from its protective cellophane. The collar was faded from overuse; so many other men had summoned the courage to wed before him.

Facing the mirror, he struggled to knot his bow tie. It flapped in his fingers like a small bird caught on his shirt. Starting over and over again, Garrett soon broke into a sweat. He stared at his reflection and wondered if this business with the tie was meant to tell him something. Just as he'd wondered about the eclipse due shortly after noon. Just as he'd wondered absurdly about that expired date on the cottage cheese.

Finally, he managed to control the fluttering silk long enough to tie it. He then pocketed May-Annlouise's wedding ring for safekeeping; Turpin would be the ring bearer, but Garrett preferred waiting until the last minute to entrust the boy with that burden.

May-Annlouise returned from her bath, radiating heat.

With her back to him, she climbed into her wedding dress—essentially a gray cocktail dress. May-Annlouise was adamant about not wearing white, and Garrett had to admit, with a twinge, that white might be the wrong color.

"Let's take a picture of us," she said. She positioned their little camera on the dresser, set the timer, and rushed to her place beside him. As he wondered whether they were in frame, May-Annlouise squeezed his hand with her fingertips, still puckered from the bath, and Garrett suddenly imagined her old, her hand still in his, and was pleasantly surprised how much this thought consoled him.

Just as the blinding flash went off, Turpin flung open the bedroom door. He ran in and clutched his mother.

"Look at *you*," May-Annlouise said. She bent over the boy and rebuttoned his vest, which he'd done askew. His gray tux was a miniature version of Garrett's, except for its short pants.

"When do I get to bear the ring?" he asked, and she smiled and told him soon, at the courthouse.

"Garrett's going to keep it for now, so you don't have to worry about it."

"I won't worry," he insisted. She laughed and pinned a boutonniere to his jacket and sent him on his way.

"Where's yours?" she asked Garrett.

"I can do it," he said and aligned the red rose tip and sprig of baby's breath with his lapel. The rose's tough stem resisted his efforts to fasten it, and then yielded so suddenly that Garrett pierced his finger to the bone.

"*Garrett,*" yelped May-Annlouise. Quickly she passed him some tissues.

Grinning nervously, he pressed one to his injured finger. Instantly a red spot seeped through, and it seemed strange he wasn't aware of more pain.

May-Annlouise sank onto the bed and stared at the ceiling.

"My parents have never seen me get married," she said and handed Garrett another tissue, taking one for herself because she was beginning to cry. She'd been orphaned at eighteen. When she'd first told Garrett (calmly, gravely, and over a candlelit dinner of her own painstaking creation) that her folks had died in a natural-gas explosion at the motel where they were pursuing a second honeymoon, he felt a flood of protectiveness toward her. He made love to her that night for the first time and with greater tenderness than he'd ever made love to anyone in his life. She'd been traumatized, after all—though she didn't act it. In bed, she maintained an acute focus. And generally, she wasn't one to dwell in self-pity, though every now and again a gust of sorrow would flatten her. "Do you think two people can be truly married if their parents aren't at the wedding?" she asked now, through her tears.

Please, no, Garrett thought, *not again.* He *couldn't* invite his parents; he was barely able to *tell* them he was getting married. The rare, dutiful phone call, the rarer visit to each of them in their separate retirement havens—even these tied his stomach in knots.

"It's funny," May-Annlouise was saying, between sobs, "I doubt I would—have married Parni—if my parents were—still living." She passed Garrett the box of tissues, taking three more for herself. "And with Tor—it felt—I wasn't thinking about—"

Garrett stared at the growing pile of crumpled red-and-white Kleenex, a field of carnations. His own blood was deserting him! Much as he wanted to comfort May-Annlouise, he kept thinking of William Holden, who'd died a few years earlier kind of like this—they found his house overflowing with used tissues, each with a red stain on it. "This isn't normal for me," he told her. "My blood pressure must be high or something."

"But this time," she said, regaining her breath, "I—really—really—*wish* my mom and dad were here. With us. Somebody watching—it makes life so much more—*real*."

"Your boss will be there," he offered.

"Yes, dearest," she nodded heavily, her damp hair swaying. "I adore her, but it's not the same. And no one will be there from your side."

Immediately her brow furrowed as though in worry she'd pushed the point too far, had hurt his feelings even. And so—maybe to make it up to him—she took his hand, stuck his finger in her mouth, and stanched the bleeding with her tongue.

A spring afternoon, some two decades earlier.

The moon edged across the face of the sun, and tiny crescents twinkled in the shadows of the dogwood leaves. Garrett wanted to ask his parents why.

His father stood on a ladder, reaching a glove-covered hand into the second-story gutters, pulling out fistfuls of rotting leaves, while Garrett's mom dutifully held the ladder's base.

She wore a sleeveless housedress and closed her eyes to face what sun remained.

"Don't look at it," his father said from above.

"Yes, I know," she said. "My eyes are closed."

"Don't even do that. Garrett, don't look at it."

His father reached after more sludge, the bandana around his forehead drenched with sweat, the back of his T-shirt one dark stain.

Kneeling before a row of azaleas, Garrett picked at the previous fall's debris, trying to make room for new growth, or so it had been explained to him.

"What's making these shapes?" he asked, meaning the twinkling crescents.

His mother turned, adjusted her footing.

"Steady," his father grumbled.

Garrett watched, dumbstruck, as her bare heel stepped toward the metal ridge of a flowerbed border. A shadow of pain crossed her face, and she recoiled, her shoulder bumping the ladder. He was surprised how quickly it fell, bouncing playfully against the side of the house, leaving a pair of marks on the white wall, his father landing in the bushes.

"Damn it to hell!" His dad's voice blared with the annoyance of someone not seriously hurt. Which was *good*, Garrett reminded himself. But now, he knew, his parents would start arguing that much sooner.

He fled into the house and to the basement, where he decided to hole up in the crawl space where the sump pump lived. It was cool in the crawl space, and dark, and thoroughly out of the way. He waited for his eyes to adjust, but there was no light for them to adjust to. Even though he had to relieve himself, he was determined to stay hidden. He heard footsteps above him and the muffle of his parents' voices. "IT WAS AN ACCIDENT!"— plaintively from his mother. "THAT WAS NO ACCIDENT!"—his father now. The pressure built against his bladder. In desperation, he lifted the trap door that covered the sump pump well, and into this pit he aimed and emptied himself—his fear. The pump would take it somewhere else, he hoped, far from the house.

When he emerged several hours later, he found his parents in the den, his father scraping at spots of mold that had sprouted in one corner of the floor and his mother training a flashlight beam on the area. They seemed forever occupied with home repairs.

"Are you hungry?" she asked. "I'm going to make dinner soon."

Garrett shook his head.

She set her flashlight down and looked him over, touching his forehead with dry lips and then fingertips—her own eyes puffy, scanning him for signs of damage, as though he'd been the one to fall off the ladder.

Garrett went to his room. It was dark outside—night. But he assumed instead the eclipse wasn't over. And as he lay awake, he had no idea when it was supposed to end. . . .

He shuddered now over this memory—ashamed of his child-hood ignorance and impotence—and fidgeted against the front seat of a yellow taxicab as he and May-Annlouise, Lynn, and

Turpin sped down Maryland Avenue toward the courthouse. Garrett held up his wounded finger, and every so often he'd lick its tip and stick it out the window; he appeared to be continually testing the wind.

May-Annlouise and the kids sat in back. He glanced at them and saw Lynn cup her hands and whisper in her mother's ear. May-Annlouise explained: "She says you look handsome today."

"Thank you, Lynn," said Garrett, suspicious of the translation. "You look especially beautiful this morning." She giggled and hid behind her mother's shoulder.

The cabdriver, wearing a jade earring and several days' growth of beard, flipped through the stations on his radio.

"ANCIENT CIVILIZATIONS BAFFLED BY THE CELESTIAL RIDDLES—"

"HER SUDDEN, INEXPLICABLE FURY—"

Finally, the driver settled on some foreign song that sparkled with the clink of finger cymbals. What was this guy—Turkish? Maybe Armenian. Garrett ought to know, having worked at the city's Office of Neighborhood Enhancement for the past six years. He kept tabs on the Poles, the Lithuanians, the Greeks— each group inhabiting its own little pocket of Baltimore. Maybe the cabbie was some kind of Slav. *Clink clink* went the finger cymbals. Garrett had always felt himself to be *without* ethnic heritage—or heritage in general really—even his features were a kind of Americanized puree: a Cheez Whiz of a face.

The finger cymbals put him in a kind of trance, and he began to count the bus-stop benches painted with the mayor's name—COURTESY OF WILLIAM DONALD SCHAEFER AND THE CITIZENS OF BALTIMORE—municipally sanctioned graffiti, that

was. Such a ham, his boss's boss's boss, the mayor, always com-
mandeering an audience. The cab now drove past the Chicken
Little where Garrett often ate his lunch, and he wondered out
of the blue, who *was* General Tso anyway? And what was his
connection to chicken? *Clink, clink, clink.*

They arrived to find the courthouse besieged by TV cam-
eras. News vans, each with a transmitter dish craning above its
roof, were parked in front on the sidewalk. Wires snaked dangerously across the stairs.

"What's going on?" Garrett wondered aloud.

"A carnival," said Turpin.

"Woman stab her lover," the cabbie said, slapping off the
meter.

Garrett remembered reading about the incident: she had
gone berserk at the Walters Art Gallery and destroyed some
exhibits and then impaled a guy. And now, as he handed the cab
driver a twenty, Garrett found himself murmuring, "Why?"

The driver merely shrugged and pointed to—the sun? the
coming eclipse? the interior light of the taxicab?

As they climbed the courthouse steps, past cables and cam-
eras, Garrett wished he and May-Annlouise had chosen a different place to marry in. A house of faith. Or some shady glen
by a stream. Not this office of punishment. Inside the front
door stood a canopy of sorts, a metal detector really, with a security guard on either side. Garrett paused at the threshold,
sure that he would set off an alarm, that the guards would turn
him away. He took a step forward. The security guard on the
right shifted his slouch and said: "She'll bust your balls, man."

Garrett froze, unsure if he'd heard correctly, and peered into the guard's calm face. Perched on a stool, his belly bursting out of a deep-blue uniform, the guard seemed to be looking right at Garrett without seeing him. *Who are you?* Garrett wanted to ask. *Strange messenger!* But just then, the other guard, the one on the left, laughed and said, "Long she don't stab me with no fifteenth-century hell bird."

"Garrett?" He felt May-Annlouise tapping his arm. She put her mouth next to his ear. "He wasn't talking to you."

Garrett nodded and walked through the metal detector, his hands trembling. On the other side now, he watched as his future family passed through the portal to join him. Turpin stepped across cautiously. May-Annlouise handed her purse to the guard with the calm Buddha-like face, who gave it a cursory glance. In the end it was Lynn who set off the alarm. Both guards leaned forward, and the little girl let loose a shriek that echoed along the cavernous foyer.

"It's all right, lamb," said May-Annlouise, and soon the little girl quieted. Poking through the pockets of her daughter's dress, May-Annlouise turned up nothing. Then she unclasped the thin chain around Lynn's neck and pulled out a silvery locket the size of a smelt. Lynn opened it and showed the guard a portrait of her father, M. Parni Ghazal, the import-export dealer, baring his teeth. Garrett had never seen this talisman before and wondered why she'd worn it today.

Lynn inched her way across once again, holding her hands over her ears. Pleased not to have set off any alarms this time, she collected her locket and ran ahead with her brother.

"Why did you assume that guard was talking to you?" May-Annlouise asked. "*Who's* busting your balls?"

"I didn't assume that." He laughed expansively, trying to cover his guilt and embarrassment. To have imagined that security guard was trying to pass along a message, some sign about today! *Am I losing my mind?* Garrett patted her hand and said, "Goodness."

"I *adore* your balls. I'd like to roll one around in my mouth right now." Her breezy flirting, the very ease with which her tongue formed sexual words, never failed to arouse him.

"Which one?" he asked, his own weak attempt at banter.

"I love them equally."

They caught up with Lynn and Turpin, who were playing hopscotch on the floor's black and white squares. Lynn looked up at Garrett and whispered to her mother, "Why is he blushing?"

"He's overheated, sweetheart."

Turpin announced he had to use the bathroom.

"All right," said May-Annlouise. She looked at Garrett and said, "Could you take him, please?" Oddly enough, this hadn't come up before. Before, Turpin had always followed his mother into the women's room. Now she was saying: *Take him. He's your kind.*

Garrett and Turpin looked each other over.

"Do you really need to go?" Garrett asked.

The boy nodded solemnly, and the two of them hiked down the hallway in search of a men's room. Dark oak doors towered forbiddingly on either side, none of them promising a john. One pair stood open, however, revealing a small courtroom so crowded with spectators they bulged into the hallway.

"Is it fair to say, ma'am, that you know right from wrong?"—the muffled boom of a man's voice from within the courtroom.

"Not at that moment, sir. It's not fair," came the scratchy reply.

"Can we watch?" asked Turpin, who was lately keen on the subject of right and wrong.

"No," said Garrett, hustling the two of them around a corner and into the men's room. He prayed the boy was old enough not to need help. They parked now in front of two urinals, the old type that ran down to the floor, and Turpin asked if he could stand inside his.

"No," said Garrett again, with a shiver of revulsion. Though, come to think of it, hadn't he once asked his own father the same curious thing?

Garrett tried now to lead by example, without actually exposing himself before the boy. And after a bit of fumbling, Turpin seemed to figure out what to do. The two of them stood there in their gray tuxedos, waiting for the rain of relief.

In no time, however, Turpin had zipped back up and begun running around. Staring at his own urinal's pink disinfectant bar, Garrett wondered, *Why can't I pee in the same room with this kid?* Some shame, vague as memory, clamped his insides.

"Wash your hands?" he called out, a tourist with a phrase book in the land of parenting. Turpin was too busy activating the air dryers, four of them, which together sounded like a jet engine over Garrett's shoulder. Unsure whether the boy had managed to pee either, Garrett felt too awkward to ask. They began to head back, rounding the corner and then passing the open courtroom doorway.

"So—are you or are you not responsible for your own actions?"

"Some more than others," said the scratchy voice.

"Are you saying before this court, before God—"

"God." She coughed. "God ain't been watching out for my best interests lately."

Turpin suddenly left Garrett's side and ducked into the crowd of onlookers, burrowing between a tweed skirt and khaki slacks, the top of his pearly head becoming lost in a crush of crotches.

"Turpin!" Garrett hissed. "Come back here!" He excused himself as he wedged his way into the throng. There must have been at least fifty people standing in that aisle, and their body heat began to smother Garrett. At last he caught up to the boy, who stood at the front of the gallery, restrained only by a red velvet rope.

A dozen yards ahead, a woman sat on the witness stand— thirtyish, haggard, with lank hair tied back from her ashen face. Arms crossed, she avoided eye contact with the prosecutor in front of her.

"I'm just a substitute teacher. Scarsville trash," she said. "Ask the vice-principal if he knows right from wrong. Ask him about bad faith!" She began to wheeze, choking on her own breath. "He's a pillar of the community!"

"She's hyperventilating," said the judge and asked the bailiff to find a paper bag. The woman on the stand now laughed convulsively. She stared straight at Garrett, who found himself leaning back into the crowd.

"I LOVED him," she said, waving the paper bag she was meant to breathe into. "Do you understand?" the woman cried. She spoke directly at Garrett—conspicuous in his gray tuxedo—a game show host and she its forlorn contestant. "I got BLINDSIDED!"

Turpin squirmed against his legs.

"Your Honor," said the prosecutor. "This sort of emotional mayhem is not helpful."

As she continued to stare at Garrett, some kind of strange current seemed to flow between them, like they were two distant shores of the same river. From their separate banks, they watched a languid stream of hurt and disappointment float by. They shared, her pale gaze insisted, a morbid understanding. He didn't know about what exactly, and he didn't want to.

Garrett glanced toward the ground, then plunged his hands in his pockets and felt for the ring he'd put there, but found instead: a hole. A hole in his rented pants.

Alarmed, he scanned the floor for any glimmer of gold. Then he looked at the people standing near him, studied their hands to see if someone might be palming a ring. They all seemed to be wearing wedding bands of their own. He tapped the elderly woman to his left and, when she turned toward him, pointed at his naked ring finger, a vague pantomime that inspired only a shrug. Looking toward the man beyond her, Garrett pointed at his ring finger again and was ignored. He turned to his right, saw a gentleman in a charcoal suit, whose face registered a deep disgust over the proceedings. Garrett touched him on the arm and whispered, "Have you found a wedding ring?" The man shook his head, then gave Garrett a tight smile, but only—and this took a moment to realize—with the far half of his face. The near side remained palsied in its grimace, as though cast in wax.

With his hand clamped on Turpin's shoulder, Garrett began retracing their steps, withdrawing through the crowd, out to the hallway. He loosened his collar to send some air down his neck. His first steps were wobbly, and as he walked, Garrett listened to his shoes click on the marble and felt aware of his every itch and pore.

"Why are we going back in here?" Turpin asked, as they reentered the bathroom.

Garrett studied the floor, glanced queasily into the basin of each urinal. Found nothing. Was sure the ring had been in his pocket during the cab ride.

"What's Scarsville trash?" Turpin wanted to know. Back in the hallway now. Large squares of black floor tile alternating with white.

"What's Scarsville trash?"

"Um, Scarsville's a nickname," Garrett answered at last. Looking to either side, he moved along a column of tiles one at a time like a pawn.

"For what?"

"A neighborhood." Deep in the heart of the city's Appalachian underbelly—only a mile or two from downtown. Garrett, a nice middle-class boy from Towson, had never set foot there.

"What's Scarsville trash?"

"She was just—disturbed," he said, trying to forget the woman's morbidly knowing gaze. "Can we talk about this later?"

The boy quickly fell silent.

Black square, white square, black square, white square, all the way back to the main entrance now, where Garrett was about to explain to the security guards—

"There you two are," said May-Annlouise, taking his hand. She turned him around and led him down a different hallway now. The bare walls put him in mind of a hospital, and he imagined himself being wheeled into some very experimental surgery during which he'd be fitted with a wife and two children. A family transplant, to replace his old damaged one.

They entered a judge's chambers. Where Garrett saw, standing next to Lynn, his fiancée's boss, wearing her pantsuit uniform and that blazing red beehive of hers.

"Dorothy!" cried May-Annlouise, running to hug her. May-Annlouise had worked at the Fiske Travel Agency all her adult life. She'd known Dorothy Fiske before having any children, before marrying either husband, even before losing her parents. In fact, Dorothy Fiske had helped her through that painful time. May-Annlouise often called Dorothy her "rock" or her "guardian angel."

"Hello, sugar," said Dorothy, returning the embrace. "Garrett," she added with a nod. Maybe it was because May-Annlouise had been married twice before to men who'd failed her, but Garrett always felt scrutinized by Dorothy Fiske. Though he must have passed some preliminary test to get this far, he feared that at any moment, she could peer at him, shrug her shoulders, and say, "Nope. Forget about this one, sugar." And May-Annlouise just might, so in awe was she of her "fairy godmother."

The older woman now produced from her vast purse a cluster of grapes for the kids to snack on while they waited. Lynn ate just a few, then gave the rest to her brother and began combing her fingers through his hair. Garrett had never seen her take such care with him before, and the two children seemed in that moment so completely innocent and fragile. How were they to endure his bungling attempts to raise them—to become a second father to Turpin, and a third father to Lynn. Her third in eleven years! The math alone was dizzying. How were they to bear it? he thought. All this *learning* at their expense? A wave of pity suddenly rose in Garrett. But before he could go to them, offer them some words of comfort and affection, a back door to the chambers opened, and to Garrett's amazement, in walked the man with the palsied face. He smiled his half-smile at everybody and introduced himself as Judge Cantrell. He looked a little distracted. Maybe he was still contemplating the nearby trial.

"Tom," said Dorothy Fiske from the back of the room.

"Dorothy," said the judge. "You're looking lovely as always."

"They know each other?" Garrett whispered to May-Annlouise, before remembering Dorothy had arranged Judge Cantrell's services as a favor. *My judge,* she'd called him.

"What's wrong with your face?" Turpin asked, his own cheeks bulging with grapes.

"Turpin," May-Annlouise said.

"Well, young man, it's a strange disorder, but I assure you it's not half so bad as it looks." He laughed with part of his mouth and the children laughed with him. "Now let's get you nice people MARRIED!" he said with sudden gusto. "Have you prepared vows, or should I do the honors?"

"We're—we haven't prepared," May-Annlouise said.

"That's fine," said Judge Cantrell. "It's my pleasure. And this way I don't have to listen to yet another reading of Khalil Gibran." He waited for a response to this little joke before cracking his own lopsided smile. "Would you like the short version, or shall I go on a bit about my personal views on marriage?"

"Oh, we'd love to hear what you have to say, right, dearest?" Garrett bobbed his head.

"Okay then," said the judge, glancing at their license. "May-Annlouise and Garrett. . . ."

While Judge Cantrell spoke, Garrett marveled at the man's face, not knowing whether to trust the side that assured them everything would work out fine, or to believe the cringing half, aghast at all it saw.

Outside, the shadows grew darker and darker; the eclipse had begun. Through the chambers window, the leaves became a grayer green and the birdsong grew panicky. Judge Cantrell's voice ("Dorothy, dear, could you flick on a few of the over-heads?") seemed to fade, as light switches throughout the courthouse *click click clicked*—a plague of crickets.

Garrett's mind, like a ball of string thrown high in the air, began to unspool. He imagined an eclipse from some previous era—peasant farmers, convinced that their world was at an end, running from their homes and falling on their own pitchforks. . . .

Now dark moments from his own past intruded, things he'd prefer left forgotten: the godless unease he'd felt standing in the back of that Pikesville synagogue at his best friend's bar mitzvah. . . . A telephone moan from a girl he'd briefly dated in high school, then let down—Susan, her name was Susan—his first real kiss, and she was, he later learned, schizophrenic—institutionalized, someone said. . . . Tennis with his newly divorced father, a topspin winner, hit by Garrett so angrily that it injured one of their doubles opponents, wrenching the man's vas deferens. . . .

I can't come to your wedding? His father's voice, blaring with familiar annoyance, but also, this time, injury. *Is your mother invited?*

No one's invited, said Garrett. *It's a small civil ceremony—in and out. You'd feel cheated coming all that way.*

May-Annlouise on his case about it, as well. His struggle to explain: *It would be like inviting trouble.* He pictured it as a brawl, so bitter had been his parents' divorce. *Why invite trouble?*

Concentrate, he told himself now.

Today, his new life already tainted: he vowed to make it up to May-Annlouise for the lost ring, to Turpin for being cross a little while ago. That fragile look on the boy's face! Garrett vowed to be faithful, to have faith—of all things, faith. To pay *attention.* And he realized, his stomach clenching with regret, that he'd missed most of what the judge had been saying, though, just now, the word *ring*, yes?

May-Annlouise nudged him.

"Did you wish to exchange rings at this point?" Judge Cantrell said.

Garrett wiped his palm on his pants leg. His shoulder blades itched. Most of the sun had vanished, and the room pulsed with every available watt of fluorescence.

"There's a problem with the ring."

He glanced over at Dorothy Fiske, expecting a dramatic sigh or some angry shake of her beehive—the dreaded veto. But if Dorothy Fiske objected to this marriage, she was keeping it to herself. Her silence only terrified Garrett more. *Say something,* he wanted to tell her. *Do something. Help.*

"Ah yes, your ring," said the judge. "You were looking for it in Courtroom 101 a little while ago." Neither side of his face was smiling now. "I'm sure it will turn up."

May-Annlouise cocked her head. "You lost the ring?"

While Garrett tried to gauge the amount of disapproval in her voice, Judge Cantrell forged ahead and pronounced them a family. "I wish you all the happiness there is."

Garrett looked at his bride, leaned toward her smiling lips, and paused.

Footsteps echoed from the hallway. The crackle of walkie-talkies. Soon a crowd began to pass the open doorway of the chambers: a pack of guards and yapping reporters, and trapped in their midst, like cornered game, was the woman with the ashen face from the witness stand. The woman who had stabbed her lover with some medieval weapon. Allegedly. A halberd. Or "hell bird." "*Who knows why a heart goes dark?*"

She stood tall but graceless, her shoulders bowed as though something heavy pressed against her chest. Her wrists were cuffed in front of her, and her fingers fluttered stiffly like broken wings. Garrett immediately noticed a glint from her left hand. Was that a ring she wore? Did they let prisoners have rings? Garrett seized on the idea that this woman had somehow found May-Annlouise's wedding band and was now wearing it. He held up his own left hand and pointed to his ring finger— a question, a plea.

Nearly past the open door, the woman peeked inside at their little ceremony, stalled in her tracks, and smiled wanly at him. "Lotsa luck, hon!" she called out. Dabbed her glistening eyes on her sleeve.

The entire wedding party stood quiet, shocked by her attention. Turpin was first to respond: "Go way!" he shouted. A squeaky, helpless cry.

"Garrett," May-Annlouise whispered in his ear, "does that woman know you?"

"Go way!" Turpin repeated. The boy's face reddened, and his hands plunged deep into his pockets as a stain bloomed across the front of his gray shorts. A few drops fell from their hem, just as all the lights wavered, then shut down.

The courthouse fell into complete darkness. While out in the hall, there followed a scuffle—"Get the fuck off me!" shouted the strange woman—the jangle of metal, bursts of walkie-talkie static.

When emergency lights came on seconds later, the prisoner, her guards, and the pack of reporters had drifted farther along the hallway; everything else seemed the same as before.

Except Turpin was gone.

"Turpin!" cried May-Annlouise. A trail of urine droplets retreated deeper into the judge's chambers toward the back door. "Turpin!" she screamed, and sprinted through the doorway into a narrow service corridor, with Garrett right behind her, his body moving spontaneously, beyond thought or will, powered by sheer urgency.

The corridor led to a stairwell, and he could hear the echoing scamper of footsteps.

"Turpin!" May-Annlouise called, climbing the stairs. "Stop!"

"Mom!" the boy called back, still running, his light feet pattering like rain.

"Mommy!" cried Lynn from behind.

"Turpin!" shouted Garrett. He moved his stiff limbs as fast as they could go. Sweat gathered in the folds of his flesh. His lungs were burning, and he could feel the painful beating of his heart.

"Garrett!" rang the small, faraway voice. It surprised him: as though he hadn't expected Turpin to know his name. "Garrett!" called the boy again. How fresh it sounded. Garrett had never heard his name said that way—with so much depending on it.

"Don't be afraid, Turp!" he called up. He liked the sound of his own voice saying that, so he said it again: "We're here! Don't be afraid!"

The stairwell windows revealed the dim spring day outside, and Garrett saw, as he climbed higher and higher, the sky turning brighter, the leaves greener, and he was amazed, in some stubborn recess of his soul, how fleeting the eclipse had been. The day flowered before his eyes, and the moon seemed to tug on the tide of his very own blood.

The names, a thick clanging chord of names, echoed back and forth, tolling like church bells—Turpin-Garrett-Mommy-Lynn! Turpin-Garrett-Mommy-Lynn!—as the four of them continued to race up the stairs.

Garrett pushed himself onward, to another story, then another. Outside, the trees now swayed below him. Suddenly there were no more stairs. Only an open door that seemed to lead to the very sky.

In the middle of the roof—wind and light playing through his hair—stood Turpin. The boy idly palmed a fistful of gravel. May-Annlouise rushed over and covered him with a hug.

"Turpin, what's gotten into you?" she scolded, smearing his forehead with kisses. The boy gurgled laughter and offered no explanation.

Lynn had caught up by now and squirmed into her mother's bear hug. May-Annlouise planted kisses over Lynn's beaming face, too. She was so ripe with love, May-Annlouise was, in the sweetness she lavished upon her children, and so often upon Garrett as well, that to doubt her, he sensed, would be like telling fate: *I don't want love.*

And I do want love, he reminded himself. *I absolutely do. Absolutely and truly I do.*

He walked over and embraced them, as much of them as he

could wrap his arms around, and kissed the top of his wife's head. His *wife!* A crisp breeze tickled his face as he admired the view from the roof. In the harbor, sailboats bobbed contentedly at their moorings, and this sense of well-being lapped inside him as well.

"The sun!" Turpin crowed, gesturing toward the newly bright sky.

"Don't look at it," said Garrett and, after glancing at Turpin's mischievous smile, he saw a gold stripe on the boy's finger. "What's that?" he wondered and held the youngster's hand. A plain fourteen-karat wedding band.

"Did I give this to you?" he asked the boy.

"Arryggggh," Turpin said and made a silly face.

"May-Annlouise, let's see your hand."

"Oh," she said, looking up at him, "you put that so romantically." She let him gently slide the ring onto her beautifully pale finger. The fit seemed looser than he remembered.

"Is this ours?" she asked skeptically. "It's a little loose."

"It *has* to be ours," he said, "doesn't it?"

"Yeeaa!" the children screamed. "The ring!"

"I guess we could get it tightened," she proposed cautiously, handing it back to him.

"You don't believe it's ours," he pressed.

"It's just looser than I remember."

"Arryggggh!" the children screamed giddily, and May-Annlouise ushered them toward the stairwell, then down into the building.

Garrett lingered on the rooftop. He took a last look at the view of bobbing sailboats, hoping to reclaim the well-being they'd inspired just moments before. His eye was soon drawn, however, to that region south of the Inner Harbor, the city's underbelly, pocked with crumbling warehouses, tattered billboards, and an elevated freeway ramp abandoned in midconstruction. And he thought of the woman from the witness stand—who lived in one of those gray neighborhoods—recalled the tearful way she'd gazed upon his new little family, wiping her cheek on her sleeve and, as he remembered now, ruefully shaking her head. Maybe she was struck by how different, how much better, life would be for them than it had turned out for her. Maybe she longed for the lasting happiness that so clearly would be theirs. At least, as he hurried back inside, Garrett surely hoped that's why she'd been crying.

two

The Explorers

Her belly glowed at him through the bathwater, the silky belly he would feather with kisses every night as she slept. He wanted to join her in the tub, and began removing his shirt, when she started to say something, then stopped.

"What's the matter?" he asked.

Finally she said, "My ex-husband called."

"Which one?"

"Tor."

"When?" Garrett asked. "When did you talk to him?"

"Yesterday." May-Annlouise sighed. "He said he has to see us tonight. Something important. He wouldn't say why." She shook her head and tucked a strand of auburn hair behind one ear; rising steam clouded the expression on her face. "I know it's Husband's Day Eve," she continued. "But I'll make it up to you, I promise."

Garrett stared at the water, placid and clear, covering his bride's body. "So he's coming?"

May-Annlouise nodded, her chin breaking the surface and sending ripples across her breasts, her arms, that beautiful belly.

At eight-thirty, as Garrett unlocked the deadbolt, he hoped that Tor Undset, geographer and explorer, a man who had traveled to Attu, Zuqar, and the Mergui Archipelago and had written books about all of these islands, was not as imposing a presence as his photo implied. But in fact the man was huge, filling the open doorway.

He wore a sheepskin jacket that smelled faintly of mutton. A duffel bag hung from the plateau of his shoulder. He was holding a large box, and he looked happy doing so. Garrett offered to take it from him, but Tor just smiled and shook his head; Garrett hated him immediately.

After the visitor laid his package on the creaky dining room table, the two men locked hands. Tor set down his duffel bag in a corner of the room and surveyed the apartment.

"Taking in the lay of the land?" Garrett joked, and then allowed himself to realize an obvious fact he'd happily repressed: Tor used to live here. This apartment had once been his home. Glancing now at the duffel, Garrett wondered if Tor was on his way to the airport.

Just then, the children raced into the living room, seven-year-old Turpin screaming, "Papa!" The boy's older half sister, Lynn, called out, "Daddy," because she referred to her own father as "Papa."

Tor picked up his son and stepdaughter, one in each arm, and kissed them through his bushy blond beard. "Hello, land urchins," he crooned.

May-Annlouise quietly entered the room.

He put the children down. "Hello, Em."

Turpin began spinning like a top in front of his father.

"What's in the box?" said Lynn, nestling her cheek against the plush flesh of Tor's jacket.

"Well, it could be a present for you and Turpin," he said.

The boy demanded Tor remove the plain wrapping paper. Underneath: a fish tank, gizmos attached, half-filled with water and some pebbles along the bottom.

"It's empty," Turpin said. But already Tor was pulling from his coat pockets small plastic bags, each containing a brown-and-tan-striped fish.

"Lion fish," he explained, after all four bags lay on the table. "Fairly venomous, so be careful never to touch them, children."

"Oh, for crying out loud," said May-Annlouise.

"Where'd you get them?" Turpin wanted to know.

"Let us say their natural habitat is the Philippines and other warm climes." Tor winked at Garrett, who sensed evasion in this answer, and also that Tor had turned to him because Garrett, above all people, could understand why a man would try so hard to impress these children. "I think they are hungry."

"What do they eat?" Lynn asked.

"Guppies," said Tor, pulling another plastic bag from his pocket.

"Tor," May-Annlouise said, "don't scare them."

But the kids insisted they weren't scared and wanted to watch.

"Lead, Turpin," said Tor, hefting the aquarium. He and the children marched into Turpin's room. Garrett stayed behind and rubbed his wife's shoulders, stiff as slate.

"He's a child!" she said of her ex-husband, with less rancor than Garrett expected. "A child, a child." She laughed gently. Garrett stopped rubbing her and went into the kitchen to get silverware and plates. The knives clinked together in his palm.

"Pistol-handled," he said to himself, setting the table around May-Annlouise.

"What?" she said.

"Pistol-handled. Isn't that what they call this pattern?"

"I don't know."

"Was this silver a wedding present?"

She nodded. Garrett laid down napkins. *Which wedding,* he wondered. "Do you own anything that isn't a wedding present?"

May-Annlouise laughed. Garrett went along and smiled at her. It was an ugly thing he'd said, and he was glad she didn't call him on it. In general, his wife was charitable that way, and Garrett tried not to take it for granted.

He went to check on the others. Turpin, Lynn, and Tor surrounded the aquarium. Tor held the bag of guppies, and every so often he would reach in and toss one into the tank.

Turpin and Lynn screamed, a mixture of fright and glee,

whenever a lion fish inhaled a guppy. It was as though the smaller fish simply ceased to exist, except as part of the larger fish. When Tor asked if he should stop, Turpin said, "One more." After that, the children asked for another. They were resentful when Garrett told them it was bedtime, and they wouldn't go until Tor promised he would come see them the next day.

After the children were tucked in, and Garrett had made sure to get the final kiss goodnight, he joined the other adults at the dining table.

"You needn't feed me," their guest said.

"We may as well eat," May-Annlouise snapped. "Dinner's all prepared."

"If it's all prepared," he said, and gave Garrett another wink.

After dislodging an especially tight cork, Garrett poured some wine into each glass. Tor took a long quaff and then announced he was dying.

No one moved as Tor described an incurable disease called kuru, which ate holes in the brain, releasing a torrent of crippling symptoms. He claimed to have been infected on one of his early expeditions, to New Guinea in the 1950s, some thirty years ago. Although the disease often took a long time to incubate, once awakened it could finish its victim in a matter of weeks. In hindsight, said Tor, he now believed that his brother and fellow explorer Lokke had died from it after descending, during his last days, into a spiral of dementia.

May-Annlouise repeatedly smoothed the tablecloth in front of her. "How did you get this?"

"I ate some bad brain," he confessed. "There was a tribe that used to feast on their deceased relatives, and Lokke and I were invited to partake."

Garrett put his hand over his wife's and felt the tautness in her fingers.

"We did not wish to appear rude," Tor said defensively. "You know, these people would customarily greet their loved ones by saying, *I eat you*. Partaking was an honor. And an expression of respect."

The three of them sat in front of their food, Tor at the place usually occupied by his son.

"This disease," he added, pushing a meatball onto his fork with a crust of bread, "it's in the mad cow family. Are you no longer vegetarian, Em?"

"Just a little," she said.

Garrett was surprised to learn there'd been a time when May-Annlouise ate no meat.

"Are you sure?" she asked. "That you have it?"

"Oh yes. Or some variant. I have already suffered the occasional spell. The world's leading authorities are courting me to participate in their research," he said proudly. "But I feel I cannot." He paused and delicately dabbed his napkin to his lips. "Em," he continued, "I know I don't deserve to ask anything of you, but I need your help. I would like to spend time with my children."

Her eyes locked on his. "Sure. Well, what do you mean?"

"Em, I would like for you to watch over me while I die."

"Tor—what are you asking? To stay here?"

"A man should die at home," he said tentatively. "Which presents something of a problem for a vagabond like myself. Let us say I have a history here as nowhere else. There is not a soul alive who knows me better than you do, Em. I realize the two of you are less than a year married, but I promise not to be any interference."

At that point, his jaw seemed to unhinge and the most ghoulishly mechanical laughter spilled forth. It must have lasted five seconds. Bringing his fingertips to his mouth, he murmured, "I am so sorry. The laughter is merely a symptom."

"What about the children? They'd have to witness this?"

"There is nothing unnatural about children watching their father die," Tor said, his voice deepening. "Except possibly to Americans. I know I'm supposed to check into a nursing home and sit in front of the TV, while some high-school flunk-out changes my intravenous—"

May-Annlouise stood up, tipping her chair. She ran to the bathroom and shut the door. As Garrett moved to follow her, Tor grabbed his arm and said, "I would never do *anything* to hurt the children. I love them."

His wrist enclosed by Tor's grip, Garrett could feel the struggle of his own pulse. Yanking free, he went after his wife and found her leaning against the sink. He stood behind her and studied her reflection. Water frothed into the basin to drown out her sobs, and Garrett knew she was simply too merciful, too good, to send Tor away.

May-Annlouise dreamt Tor was dead. Not entirely dead, but dismembered, his parts scattered throughout the apartment: His head spoke to her from the refrigerator's lettuce bin; his arm—lodged inside the trash can—kept prying open the lid; his penis lay throbbing on the bathroom sink where the toothpaste should have been.

She awoke confused, and she nestled within the shelter of Garrett's arm. Dizzy from the dream, she filled her lungs with the bracing smell of his armpit and waited for her head to clear.

"Dearest," she said, when he stirred. "Did I do the wrong thing?"

He stroked her shoulder. "You have to be able to live with yourself."

"I need to be able to live with you, too."

"You do," he said. "We will."

He could be tremendously accommodating, her new husband, not at all like the previous two. She felt an extra guilt pang that Tor was intruding on Husband's Day, the third Sunday of each month, when she made an extra effort to pamper Garrett. The festivities typically began the night before—after the children went to sleep—with sex of Garrett's choosing. May-Annlouise believed that men needed to impose their will in the bedroom sometimes, or at least to believe they were imposing their will, and in the case of Garrett, who could be accommodating to a fault, this provided a growth opportunity. He'd yet to demand anything she wasn't glad to abide.

"So, a rain check on the Husband's Day sex?" May-Annlouise sighed.

"Sure," he said. "We'll just postpone the holiday this time."

"How can you be so wonderful?" she asked, a little plaintively.

"Did you—" he began a question of his own. "Did you used to celebrate Husband's Day—before . . . ?"

"No," she said emphatically, shaking her head against his armpit. "It's a new holiday." As a token of her sincerity, she reached down and gave his cock a healthy squeeze.

There came a soft tap from the door.

"Breakfast is available," said Tor's muffled voice.

"Just a minute," May-Annlouise called out.

She strained to hear him leave. For such a big man, he had light footsteps.

She kissed Garrett's ear and whispered, lewdly, "But I was going to make you a Dutch Baby." Still holding on to him, she felt a rude itch to make love right then and there; the idea excited and then immediately shamed her. How long, she wondered, would Tor be staying with them?

May-Annlouise climbed out of bed. She put on the slacks and shirt that had been draped across her chair, but when she realized they were yesterday's clothes, she told Garrett to go on without her.

She took off the blouse and held it to her nose. She'd been so nervous, her body had sweated an overpowering distillation of her usual smell—a scent that had evolved over the years. She remembered how it had seemed to alchemize after her first nights of intimacy with Tor. At the time she'd viewed the pungent change as proof of their love chemistry. And this more or less was the scent she'd maintained (like basil it was, with walnuts and iron); she kept waiting for it to change again in response to Garrett's arrival on the scene.

In the dining room now, her kids were eating grapefruit, and Tor laid a plateful of scrambled eggs on the table. To May-Annlouise, the eggs looked like brains, and she thought of her dream and was so nauseated she wondered if she'd be able to sit still.

"Mommy," said Lynn. "Daddy just told us about Yom Kippur and Muharram."

"Yes," said Tor, ladling out the eggs with a flourish. "I thought they should know a little about the religions of the world." He swept into the kitchen and returned with a platter of pancakes.

"That's nice," Garrett said and told Turpin to take the hollow grapefruit half off his head.

"It's a yarmulke."

Lynn turned to Garrett and said, "Uncle Lokke is reincarnated."

"That's right, if you're Hindu," said Tor cheerily as he flipped pancakes onto the children's plates. "Lokke is still among us, in some form or other. That's what Hindus believe."

"Let's change the subject," said May-Annlouise. It chilled her to see Tor standing over Turpin, their white hair so similar that for a moment they seemed like two ages of the same person. She wished it weren't Sunday, because she wanted to call a doctor, a few doctors, and find out more about this kuru business.

After breakfast, she stared at headlines while Tor flipped through the world atlas. When they'd been married, he used to read it on those few evenings when he stayed home. He studied maps the way musicians see a score: they hear the music in their heads. One winter night she'd found him perspiring over a map of the Congo.

To him, she'd been a place as well, part of his empire, though merely an outpost. On his wanderings around the world he'd carried his headquarters with him, returning now and then to plant his flag in her.

When Garrett finished washing the dishes, Tor suggested a game of croquet in the courtyard behind the building. "I noticed one of those old mallets in your closet, Em," he said with a wink. The croquet set, a deluxe model from Abercrombie & Fitch, had been a wedding present from Lokke, a detail May-Annlouise hoped wouldn't surface.

"I don't feel like it," she said, but the two men hauled out the long wooden case anyway. They carried it together, one at either end, with the two children lending support. The four pallbearers advanced slowly out of the apartment and to the elevator.

Soon, from the kitchen window, May-Annlouise watched them plant wickets.

Her children took the first shots. Before long the men raced ahead, clacking their balls together whenever possible. As Garrett stood hunched over his mallet, grasping its handle, the instrument seemed disturbingly phallic to May-Annlouise, and it looked as though the two men took turns pissing on the courtyard grass, marking their territory.

Soon her husband and her ex progressed to that late phase of the game called "poison." The idea was to hit your opponent's ball before he could hit yours, and even though May-Annlouise hoped Garrett—her beloved and accommodating Garrett—would prevail, she found part of herself rooting for Tor, because he was a petulant sport, and it would be easier on everyone if he could simply win.

Garrett's next shot rolled long and slightly to the left. Tor's effort veered wide and settled at the base of the oak tree. Back and forth, back and forth, the two men stalked each other, until Garrett's ball landed inches short and lay vulnerably in the shadow of Tor's. Her ex aimed carefully, brought his mallet back, and delivered the final poisonous tap.

As Tor bent forward to pick up the two balls, he stumbled. It was unlike him, and though he regained his balance in an instant, May-Annlouise couldn't take her eyes off the divot made by his knee.

"Em," said Tor, one afternoon, "I was hoping to take the children to the National Aquarium. When they come home from school."

As he spoke, May-Annlouise watched his mouth twitch under his beard like a small animal flitting inside a shrub. His speech was halting—or did she imagine this?

"What if you should feel ill?" she asked, recalling his stumble from a few days before.

"I am monitoring my condition," he said. "I should be able to weather the afternoon without incident."

"But Baltimore has changed so much since you lived here. You might get lost. With the children."

He gazed at her, clearly hurt.

"I could come along," she suggested. "I don't have to return to work—"

"No," said Tor, pushing back her words with both his palms, and suddenly it was May-Annlouise who felt hurt. She kept the memory of her anguish within such easy reach: the jealousy she'd suffered during those long nights he'd be away and warming himself with indigenous tramps from many lands. Of course, she could never prove it, but she was certain—having lived through her first husband's betrayal—that Tor was cheating on her. And so, to retaliate, she'd briefly taken a lover, a temp from the office. May-Annlouise never told a soul.

"I am capable," Tor continued. "Perhaps next week it would pose some danger. Have you explained my situation to the children?"

"Not yet," she admitted. "I haven't figured out how."

"That is one more reason why I need time alone with them."

May-Annlouise gave in and told him how to get to the new subway station nearby. She began to sketch him a little map on a paper napkin.

"I don't think that will be necessary."

"Listen, Tor," she said. "Just in case. If you have to, you can give it to a cabdriver or someone. OK?"

The ink bled into the napkin, and he seemed to wince with each cruel stroke of her pen.

"There you go," she said, guiltily, sadistically pressing the map into his hand.

Ha! What were a few city blocks compared to the places he'd been? Deception Island. Pukapuka. Were they not more treacherous than the Inner Harbor? The very idea made Tor laugh out loud as he walked, and he threw the napkin with its bloody directions into a trash can. The children laughed with him. "Your mother thinks I will lose us!" Ha ha ha!

He paid their admission, then ushered his children past the tiresome exhibits about crabs and algae directly to the center of the aquarium. There they stood surrounded by an enormous tank that held butterfly fish, squirrel fish, surgeon fish, triple tails. . . . Tor had no trouble recognizing and naming each species, as though acknowledging old friends at one's club.

"You know everything," Lynn doted. She kissed him, and Turpin kissed him as well. A school of lookdowns swam by— the light sparkled geometrically off their silver bodies, and the music of harps whispered such peace! His two children, solid and small, squeezed him, and the child-oil smell of their hair was gratifying.

"I want to cook for you," he told them. "Couscous."

"What's that?" they asked.

"It's a Moroccan grain. I once ate it in Fez. Fez is a city. And a hat."

Tor felt alive with wisdom. "If not for Islam," he added, "the West might have lost all trace of its own greatest ancient thinkers. We might never have heard of Aristotle."

"Oh," said the children.

A massive grouper swam past, and Tor saw in the fish's patient expression a resemblance to his own brother Lokke. Uncanny! The fancy that this grouper might in fact be Lokke reincarnated sprang in Tor's breast. "Look, children, your Uncle Lokke!" he blurted.

"Where!"

They waited for the stately fish to come around the tank full circle.

"Is he that one?" Turpin pointed.

"Here he comes," said Tor. "Wave." The children waved, but when the grouper passed, it showed no awareness of them, no glimmer of recognition, and although the children did not seem to mind, Tor felt disappointed. Perhaps he'd been mistaken. Perhaps Lokke was reincarnated elsewhere. Perhaps there was no such thing.

The children now took Tor by the hand, and as they led him away, he suffered the distinct sense of leaving something behind. He reached into his coat pocket for the map May-Annlouise had drawn. Not to look at it, just to touch it, to know it was there, and then he remembered it wasn't.

They arrived at the deepest level of the aquarium, reserved for sharks and other of the most roughneck species. Turpin and Lynn ran to the glass, caressing it with creamy fingertips. Giant predators floated along in the dim light, while one especially fat specimen lay on the sandy bottom. A sandbar shark? A Caribbean reef shark? To his irritation, the name escaped him.

"Whoa! A dead one!" said Turpin, pointing to the shark.

Its gills were obscured by a large rock, and so Tor could not tell if the creature was breathing. Nonetheless, he spoke out with confidence: "It's not dead," he said. "If it were, the other fish would be feeding from it."

"Oh, gross," said Lynn, who just the other night had condoned the sight of lion fish inhaling guppies. Poof! All evidence gone! But the eating of a creature larger than oneself, mused Tor, involved wounds, blood. There was little dignity in the act.

A nurse shark? Would its dorsals be so blunt? Tor decided it was indeed a nurse shark and yes of course it was alive, because elsewise the other fish would be nibbling from it, and, yes, that was gross.

Tor had always envisioned himself a swallower, not a nibbler. Majestic. The pinnacle of his food chain. A grand accumulation within the borders of his sovereign Self. "Wake up, Mr. Nurse Shark!" He tapped on the glass. "Wake up, before they start nibbling you!"

"Wake up!" cried the children.

But the shark ignored them. Maybe it wasn't a nurse. What then? A bull shark? A porbeagle? Surely he knew this!

The name continued to elude him, and Tor's self-doubt grew deeper. He had nibbled after all, he had to admit—eaten from creatures larger than himself. And then of course that one experiment with cannibalism. But gracious! For him, the point had little to do with eating a dead New Guinean villager. As far as Tor regarded it, the rite was most about the honor of his own inclusion. Everything revolved around him! Ha ha! Though possibly that unfortunate villager had once believed so, too.

"Wake up now!" He tapped on the glass.

Disgusting really—the man's rugged old head split open like a coconut, and his mind's meat apportioned according to the grip of his widow's fingernails. Then they all nibbled. . . .

Tor was a Christian.

That's right, a Christian. He didn't talk about it—aloud he preferred to entertain other, foreign faiths. He was an explorer of faiths. But when it came to his own death—his own Christian death—Tor was counting on resurrection. He even entertained some vague idea of coronation. But decapitation! Dispersal, disintegration. Disgusting! He preferred to banish such thoughts, but now they intruded upon his peace of mind.

"Wake up!" The side of his fist hurt.

A Caribbean reef shark after all? The name seemed lost to him forever. *Good-bye,* he said to himself.

"Daddy?" Lynn whimpered. The children stared at him fearfully.

Good-bye.

He realized with a shiver: the moment in his life when he would know as much as he would ever know—that moment was behind him. Maybe it had passed upstairs as he gazed upon the school of lookdowns. Maybe it had passed weeks ago.

He now knew less.

And now, less still.

This is definitely good-bye.

Tor became aware of all the surrounding water, all those fiercely selfish appetites. Soon, he would be consumed in turn, by his own family; they would digest whatever they could of his life, discard the rest, until finally he would reside exclusively within the marrow of their memory. And that, if he was lucky!

"Turpin, Lynn," he uttered. "I have something to tell you." His voice sounded baffled. But one ought impart whatever wisdom one still could. "Everything," he said slowly, "everything eats everything else. Eventually."

He returned his children's stare through the brine of his own tears. The aquarium glass seemed to be melting all around them, the water level rising, drowning his words, his thoughts. His jaw unhinged, and great belches of laughter washed out of his mouth as he felt his sovereign Self continue to drift away, one cell at a time, one memory at a time, one guppy, ha ha, at a time.

A crowd had gathered. Someone escorted him out of the building. Rather brusquely. Tor reached into his pocket for the map, just to touch it.

When Tor hadn't returned by twilight, May-Annlouise compulsively straightened the apartment, just as she would on those long-ago nights when he'd roamed wild, beyond her reach, abroad.

Now, hearing the homey jingle of Garrett's keys, she ran to the hallway.

"I've done something stupid," she confessed and quickly explained. "I'm afraid they're lost."

"How long have they been gone?" Garrett asked.

"Only three hours, but he's been acting strange and light-headed. I should never have said yes. I'm going out to see if I can find them."

"I'll go," Garrett offered.

"No. Stay in case there's a call," she said. The long-thwarted desire to seek Tor out—to corral him—overwhelmed her. "I love you," she reminded Garrett and kissed his cheek.

Outside, the air felt moist and heavy against her face. She walked the nine blocks to the subway station and then another six for good measure and began her search, casting her dragnet in progressively tighter circles, though really Tor and the kids could be anywhere. She called his name.

Pulling the grille across his storefront, a shopkeeper looked at her sharply, as though she were some pathetic housewife, hounding her stray husband. *It's not like that!* she wanted to announce. She tried calling the children's names. No response.

May-Annlouise was strung out, having spent much of the week trying to reach neurologists. When they finally did come to the phone, they were often aloof and generally stingy with information when they learned Tor wouldn't submit to examinations.

As for any risk passed down to Turpin, a nightmare she could barely voice, none of the doctors would guess, though one assured her it seemed extremely unlikely. Even he would make no guarantees. Though he did suggest her "obsession" over Turpin was displaced grief over the more certain loss of her husband.

"My ex-husband," she said.

"Whatever. Any risk to your son, or to you for that matter,

seems virtually unthinkable," the neurologist said. "Just don't eat the man."

She disliked doctors. She *wanted* to believe in them, but they made it so hard. They were always patronizing her, judging her.

Her face wet from an invisible mist, she felt a headache massing now above her left eye. She cursed herself for not bringing an umbrella, or a watch, and wondered how long she'd been gone. Time had behaved oddly these past few days.

After maybe another half hour, she saw in the distance an old apartment building, stone gargoyles jutting from the wall, and a figure slumped on the stairs, his head bent. Steam rose from his hair as though the drizzle were dissolving him.

May-Annlouise instinctively began crossing to the other side of the street until she realized the figure was Tor. Turpin and Lynn huddled behind him, and she called out their names.

"Mom!" They ran to her, their young faces creased with concern. Her children fell against her so hard they knocked her back a step. Once safely within her embrace, they wept. She held them fiercely, and Turpin slid his slender forearm up the sleeve of her coat. When Lynn asked in a whisper if Tor was truly dying, May-Annlouise had no choice but to tell them.

"Wake up," Tor's voice called from the steps.

"You had some sort of spell, Tor?"

"Wake up." He said each word slowly.

"We couldn't get him to move," said Lynn.

"Come with me," May-Annlouise said, bent to help him.

"Em?" he asked, when they'd made it to the bottom of the stairs.

"Yes?"

But he didn't add anything.

"Are you able to walk?" she asked.

"Glad you came, Em." He draped a heavy arm around her shoulder and pulled her to his chest. She could smell his odor and noticed how much it resembled her sweat from the other day—her basil-walnut-iron scent. She wasn't sure what it meant that their two smells had kept pace over the years, but it disturbed her.

"I was thinking—" he said, as they walked.

"What?"

A few yards ahead of them, the children advanced slowly, silently. Tor's hand wrapped halfway around her head, and he pressed her close. "Glad you came, Em," he repeated.

"Of course I came."

"I wish we could make love," he whispered and kissed her forehead.

How she had wanted that at one time—many times. And the memory was so strong it confused and frightened her, because it felt a little—under her ribs, along her neck—like wanting him now. Her pleasure at hearing him say those words made her seem unfaithful. And she so wanted to remain faithful to Garrett, especially since she hadn't been to Tor. Her fling with the temp still haunted her at times—the banal cowardice of it—never mind that Tor had practically driven her into the young man's arms!

"Can we make love tonight?" Tor asked now. "When he leaves?"

"What do you mean, 'when he leaves'?"

"When he goes home."

"He is home. It's Garrett's home now."

Tor smiled, the same sickly, confused, denying smile that was on his face the day she'd announced she would no longer put up with his "wanderlust."

"Garrett is probably worried," she said and tried to pick up their pace.

❧

The four of them stood in the doorway, hair soaked and eyes feverish, the whole family unit—apart from Garrett.

"So what happened?" he asked.

"Tor had trouble finding us." May-Annlouise exchanged a blurry glance with the big man that made Garrett think of sex.

"Good-bye," mumbled Tor, shedding his sheepskin jacket. He stared at the coat hanger May-Annlouise was offering. Finally, she just took the jacket and hung it up herself, then led Tor to his duffel bag, where he crouched precariously, pawing through its contents for a dry change of clothes.

"Kids, why don't you get into your pajamas?" she suggested.

Garrett motioned her into the kitchen.

"So is this it?" he asked her, as he checked on the large pot of chili he'd been stewing. "Is this what he was talking about?"

"This is what he was talking about," she said in a distant voice that was mildly infuriating.

Everyone claimed to have no appetite, so Garrett ate a bowl of chili by himself in the kitchen.

He found himself visualizing what he might ask May-Annlouise to make for next Husband's Day. It was a sweet holiday she'd created, a way of paying attention, which he'd grown to relish over the past year—and now, suddenly, miss. Maybe stuffed peppers, he thought. Or pork medallions with mashed potatoes and green beans. The White Sox were going to be in town for a doubleheader, and Memorial Stadium was sponsoring Cal Ripken, Sr., Seat Cushion Day, which the kids would like. He should stop by Barnes and Noble and browse the erotica section for some new Saturday night moves; maybe visit a Superstore this time. Chicken enchiladas?

He spooned the rest of the chili now into pint-sized plastic containers—four modular meals for the freezer. The apartment was quiet, almost as quiet as when he'd been alone, waiting for the others to return. Feeling restless, he decided to check on Turpin.

The boy sat on the floor of his bedroom, toiling over his jigsaw puzzle, a ten-thousand-piece portrait of a sea turtle. Jigsaw puzzles made Garrett nervous: the idea of putting so much effort into building something that, when finished, would be torn apart. Still, he'd bought this jumbo model when Turpin had asked for it, and the seven-year-old immediately showed a tremendous aptitude for shapes and patterns; already he'd put together much of the underbelly.

"Do you, um, want to talk about today?" Garrett squatted beside him.

"No, Mom already talked about it." The boy glanced at him narrowly so that Garrett began to question his own motives for being there. Initially he'd imagined himself dispensing comfort but now wondered if instead he'd come on an intelligence mission and somehow the boy had picked up on this.

Garrett's legs began to ache, but when he stood to leave, Turpin said, "Help me."

"How, Turpin? How would you like me to help you?"

"Help me find his head."

Garrett sat down and sifted through puzzle pieces identical as grains of sand. He found what might have been an eye, but turned out to be a segment of coral reef. Turpin studied the pieces in his hand with the concentration of a fortune-teller, before exchanging them for a fresh handful, then another after another. Throughout this process, from their tank in the corner of the room, the lion fish stared out, less hale these past few days, but still menacing.

Turpin and Garrett worked together in silence—clicking into place two pieces of tortoise shell and a stretch of border—until eventually the boy leaned against the side of his bed and fell asleep, a green tri-pronged piece of seaweed clutched between his fingers. Garrett stayed on the job for another half hour; he was close to completing the neck and wanted Turpin to wake up to that bit of progress in the morning.

In homes where father and mother speak different native languages, paternal dominance ranges 1.5:1 to 3.3:1. . . . So began the demographic language report Garrett had brought home from work. He reread the first sentence and flipped ahead to the charts. Across from him sat May-Annlouise, who hid behind a mystery novel. Tor, in the blue chair normally used by Garrett, clutched a map of his native Scandinavia. In the two days since his getting lost, Tor's general disorientation seemed to have worsened. His eyes pointed now to a spot beyond the atlas, somewhere near his feet.

"Tor," Garrett asked, but got no response.

The atlas began to slide down the big man's lap. His right hand had let go, but his left held on to a single page, which was tearing slowly—the sound of an old record, badly scratched.

The book crashed against the floor, leaving Tor with the page in his hand.

May-Annlouise knelt beside his chair. "Are you all right?"

He shook his head slowly.

"Do you want to go to the hospital?"

Slowly, but firmly, he shook his head.

May-Annlouise turned to Garrett. "We should give him our room."

Garrett suppressed a grimace. "Can we even lift him?"

They each took an arm and pulled Tor out of the chair. But when they tried to lead him to their bedroom, he stepped backward.

"Tor," May-Annlouise asked. "Wouldn't you be more comfortable in our room where you'll have more privacy?"

Our privacy, thought Garrett.

Tor nodded but then took another step backward. Eventually, they turned him around, and led him, step by backward step, to the master bedroom.

Over the next few days, Garrett brooded over the fact that his marriage bed had been commandeered for Tor's likely deathbed.

At work he reread the language report without comprehension. Sometimes, he imagined May-Annlouise and the children speaking Urdu around the house or Norwegian and himself unable to follow a word of it. "Yama," he blurted out loud. "Dabu." He tasted the foreignness of the made-up words.

After a particularly unproductive day, Garrett came home and found everyone in the master bedroom watching *Wheel of Fortune.*

"I'm home," he said from the doorway.

"I EAT YOU!" Tor saluted him. On the TV, lovely Vanna White revealed an X.

"Oh, I didn't hear you come in!" said May-Annlouise. She sprang from her chair and took three steps toward Garrett. But before she could reach him to offer a kiss hello, Turpin had begun whimpering, and she reversed course to swoop down on her son. "What is it, Turpin?"

"Does everything," the boy asked, his eyes riveted to the X, "eat everything else?"

"No!" Garrett barked. He felt a surge of fury at Tor, and at Vanna White, too. "Now listen up, everyone," he ordered the room in general. He'd never issued a family edict before, and this one was coming out a little crazy: "There will be no eating of anyone in this house. Is that clear?"

Everyone remained quiet as Vanna White turned over a first, then a second M.

"Em," said Tor, seemingly oblivious to Garrett's announcement. The big man stared vaguely in May-Annlouise's direction. "All my travels. Never."

"Yes, Tor? In all your travels—what?"

"Never anyone. Else. Only you."

May-Annlouise clicked off the TV—banishing Vanna White—turned now to her ex-husband, and said softly, "That's good of you, Tor."

"Only you."

"Thank you."

"Em," Tor continued. "Only me?"

She glanced helplessly at Garrett, then back at Tor and stammered, "Yes, when we were married. Yes, of course."

"Only me?" Tor repeated.

Garrett couldn't bear any more of this, and so he walked over to his wife and gently took her by the elbow. "Excuse us a minute, Tor," he said and ushered May-Annlouise into the living room.

"What was that all about?" he demanded.

"He must be deluded," she said, her arm still trembling in Garrett's grasp. "He was on the prowl the whole time we were married. I know it."

"What difference does it make now?"

"He had to be," she insisted. "He's just forgotten."

"Or chosen to forget," Garrett offered.

"The man has a disease, for God's sake! He doesn't choose anything anymore!"

So this was how it was going to be. Everything the man said or did from here on out would be excused, elevated even, by the authority of the dying. Garrett's heart sank. But his wife looked so tired and disheartened herself he didn't press the point and even, later that evening, made an effort to mask his distaste when she said: "He needs a bath."

They helped Tor stagger to the tub and lowered him into

three inches of warm water. May-Annlouise soaped her ex-husband with a washcloth. She worked suspiciously fast, as if she were afraid to linger, Garrett thought, in front of him.

"OK," she said, his cue to turn on the flexible showerhead.

"Only me?" Tor mumbled, his eyes closed against the water trickling down his face.

They drained the bath and dried him while he was still sitting, then guided his legs over the edge of the tub and, together, eased him up, then slowly backward toward the master bedroom.

"Lokke?" he asked, studying Garrett.

"Lokke's your brother," said Garrett curtly. "I'm just the new guy on the night shift."

May-Annlouise sighed miserably. "And you were being so nice."

At work the next day, Garrett found himself looking up airlines in the phone book. He called to ask the price of a one-way ticket to Oslo.

"What date would you be flying, sir?"

"Tomorrow?" Garrett said.

The ticket agent quoted a fare of $875.

"This is for a relative of mine who is somewhat incapacitated. Would he have to change planes in New York?"

"Yes."

"Could I pay to have someone lead him from one plane to the other?"

"We offer our Sky Nurse wheelchair service, which is free of charge."

"What kind of name is that?" demanded Garrett, who was put in mind of some rest-home aide mercy-killing her patients. The Sky Nurse. Flustered, he hung up.

That evening, as Garrett walked in the door, May-Annlouise gave him a dry distracted kiss and said, "He hasn't eaten all day."

"Who hasn't?"

"*Tor.*"

Garrett imagined hearing the same news about Turpin, or about another, unborn child of theirs, a child with no allegiance beyond them, no blood other than theirs. If this child ever refused to eat, Garrett would be devastated. But about Tor, the news was good. Wasn't it?

Shortly after dinner, he found the children in Tor's room, where they'd unrolled sleeping bags by the foot of the bed. "What's this?" Garrett asked from the doorway.

Turpin looked up at him. "We're on an expedition."

"Our rations are dangerously low," Lynn added bravely.

"Correct, Commander Rygh!" Tor crowed.

The children wore their nightclothes, and Garrett realized they were planning to camp in the master bedroom with Tor. The idea seemed morbid and faintly taboo. Did they think Tor was playing? Was he? With the room's gamy scent still in his head, Garrett went to tell May-Annlouise he found the expedition unwise.

"He's not supposed to be contagious," she said, from some far-off land herself, "not like that."

"Maybe not," he allowed but insisted nonetheless.

The children cried when May-Annlouise led them to their

own rooms, and they didn't want anyone to tuck them in or kiss them good-night.

Garrett rolled up the sleeping bags and was about to turn the lights out in the master bedroom when Tor beckoned him. Glancing at the extra pillow on the night table, Garrett had a sudden vision of placing it over the big man's face. The Sky Nurse. It took him several long moments to banish the thought. He sat on the edge of the bed, his bed; the springs creaked.

The dying man's breath was shallow and slow. "Lokke?"

"Um, yeah?" Garrett might even have said, "Ja."

"Who was that beautiful woman?"

"Excuse me?"

"With the auburn hair? Just now? Beautiful."

Garrett pronounced the four syllables of his wife's name.

"Has someone arrived there first?" Tor asked, clasping Garrett's forearm and trying to pull himself higher in the bed. "Am I? Too late?"

"Too late for what?"

"Is she wed, brother?"

Garrett blinked at the gruesome splendor of this opportunity: Tor handing over the cracked canvas of his memory, entrusting Garrett of all people to restore it—or, as he was more inclined, to paint over it. *Yes, she is wed,* he wanted to say, *to her only and ever true love; they have two enviable children together; she's your nurse; patients often become infatuated with their nurse.* Oh, how he wanted to say that! But couldn't bring himself to; the entire notion seemed suddenly like vandalism.

"That's a good question," he said at last, backing away from the bed. "I'll try to find out."

In their stuffy living room, Garrett lay awake on the sleeper sofa and thought about the ravenous past, especially his wife's past, and hoped it might consume itself before completely devouring their marriage.

By his side, May-Annlouise nibbled her chapped lips. "We won't have to watch this again someday, will we?" she asked. "With Turpin? Tell me we won't."

"We won't," Garrett assured her.

"That's right, we won't," she announced willfully. "It's virtually unthinkable. I virtually won't think it."

He worried, not for the first time, whether she was truly over her ex-husband. Turning toward her, he quietly slid his hand underneath her nightgown and along the soft bank of her thigh.

"Garrett," she whispered. "I don't want to—scare the kids."

"Scare the kids? What about Tor scaring the kids?" Not a great argument, not very mature of him or relevant, but how long was he supposed to go without? "My rain check," he added.

"Not now," she said, moving his hand.

He was determined, however, and his fingertips made their way through the brush of her pubic hair and began pressing their claim in gentle circles. He took pleasure in the growing raggedness of her breath. She clasped her hands over her mouth, and when she next opened her eyes, she stared morosely at the ceiling.

"So I'm weak," she said, to his bewilderment.

Already his sense of triumph was waning. He felt the need to make her come again, and maybe again—to evoke wave after radiant wave.

Waves of fever, waves of forgetting, his own hand at the center.

three

Pendant

Having flown halfway through tomorrow, Lynn desperately wanted to arrive.

Tired and dirty, she stood in the airport line, leaning against her stepfather like a sapling against its stake. The din of travelers was hypnotic, and each of the many loudspeaker announcements reverberated in Hindi, then English, equally incomprehensible. Wearing her *salwar kameez*, bought with three months' allowance, Lynn hoped to be mistaken for native, though there was little chance of that with Garrett at her side.

"Your purpose here?" demanded the officer at the head of the line.

Lynn looked to her guardian.

"Holiday," said Garrett, handing over their passports. "School vacation. Pleasure."

"Valuables?" the officer asked suspiciously.

Lynn clutched the locket that hung beneath her *kameez*. She unfastened the clasp, pulled the heavy pendant along her breast-bone, and handed it to the officer for his consideration. He ran his fingers along its edge to prize it open and peered at the picture inside. Her papa, her *real* father, whom she hadn't seen since she was three, squinted in this photo, smiling handsomely.

"No, no valuables," said Garrett, taking the locket and returning it to Lynn.

"Pleasure," she repeated, hopefully.

From an airport pay phone, Garrett listened through the distracting hiss for his wife to answer. Her hello was faint and groggy. Though midmorning in Bombay, in Baltimore it was still last night.

"Honey? May-Annlouise?" he shouted. His own voice boomed in his ear. "We're still at the airport."

"Will you call me . . . from her father's in a day or so . . . dearest?" she asked, or something like that. Not all the words were audible, though her concern was. "Do you know . . . how much . . . trust you?"

She meant her trust as a compliment. Still, he felt defensive and wanted to remind his wife that the main reason he'd agreed to chaperone was that she herself had refused. Plus, he saw in this trip the chance to score some fatherly points with Lynn by taking her. He *wanted* the girl to meet up with her real father instead of idealizing the man in his absence. And frankly, Garrett hoped to look good in comparison. These were very mild ulterior motives, as Garrett saw them; there was nothing not to trust him about.

"We're holding up fine," he said in response. The crumbly phone connection frustrated him, the way it chipped away at his wife's voice. He told her he loved her and not to worry, and then handed the receiver to Lynn, who with great animation recounted her view from the airplane window, while Garrett fished around the purple daypack strapped to his waist for Parni Ghazal's phone number. Suddenly apprehensive about making that call, he allowed Lynn to talk a while longer with her mother. All too soon, however, he found himself dialing Parni's apartment. After six rings a woman picked up and squealed excitedly. This had to be Nazar, Parni's first wife— whom he had not divorced or even disclosed before marrying May-Annlouise.

"Yes, yes, pass me the telephone," said a man in the background and then, on the line: "Mr. Garrett? Are you at the Surudar station?"

"Our flight was delayed," Garrett explained. "We're still at the Bombay airport."

"That is fine," he said. "That is not a problem." He told Garrett to call again from the Surudar station. "My driver will come for you. Kindly describe yourself to me."

The word *upright* occurred to Garrett; he felt an urge to describe himself as *upright*. Aloud, though, he supplied his height, weight, and hair color.

"More specifically, if you please," insisted Parni Ghazal.

Garrett looked down at the marsupial pack bulging from his waist and described it to Parni Ghazal, who seemed satisfied

("Purple neon belly pack, excellent"), but the exchange left Garrett feeling diminished.

He gave the receiver to Lynn, who chattered gaily as though she'd last talked to her father yesterday and not a decade ago. She couldn't possibly have much memory of those couple of years when Parni had brought his Indian wife stateside and May-Annlouise had felt obliged to share her husband under the same roof, just so that he might remain in Lynn's life. Garrett pictured Parni on the other end of the phone line, lounging regally in a silk smoking jacket.

Pointing to his watch, Garrett whispered to the girl that this call was costing them, and she reluctantly told her father she'd see him in a few hours.

They made their way outside, hailed one of a swarm of yellow-and-black taxis, and set off into the turbulent streets. The driver honked in continual proclamation of their existence—for whose benefit, Garrett couldn't tell. Stopping now at a red light, the driver cut his engine, as though he intended to camp there. In a shop window, a carcass twirled in the putrefying heat. A motor scooter pulled alongside Garrett. Its riders, a family of four, kept their balance and smiled at the curious sight of him. On Lynn's side, a ragged teenage girl was holding an infant through the open window and demanding, "Rupee. Bee-bee. Madame."

Lynn gasped.

She thrust her hand into her pocket, pulled out some coins, and virtually threw them from the cab, as though they burned her. While the mother bent out of sight to collect them, Lynn frantically rolled up her window and, hiding her face between her knees, began to wheeze. The beggar soon reappeared on Garrett's side, where she pressed her infant's face against the glass, tapped metronomically with an American quarter, and repeated, "Rupee. Bee-bee. Hungry."

Garrett hurriedly unzipped his belly pack and, having nothing but traveler's checks and hundred-rupee notes, pulled out an opened package of Ho-Hos he was carrying for emergencies. He rolled down his window and held one toward the girl, who backed away and eyed the turdlike cylinder warily.

"Bee-bee," she reminded him. "Rupee."

"Ho-Ho," he explained, pointing to his mouth. To demonstrate, he showed her the inside of a Ho-Ho he'd begun somewhere over the Atlantic. He took another bite from it now and pushed the uneaten one toward her. Before she could be persuaded, the taxi sputtered to life, and only then, through a veil of car fumes, did she extend a bony hand. Garrett leaned out the window, but she was already too far away, and so he sank back into his seat and passed the Ho-Ho to Lynn.

"I thought she was selling her baby for a rupee," she said, having recovered enough to take a bite.

"No," he said. They finished their Ho-Hos glumly.

To his growing dismay, at each succeeding red light, a different girl with a different baby approached the cab. Garrett could only look away and marvel at this dreadful repetition.

Finally at the train station, he found a seat for Lynn and settled her with their bags before taking his place in the ticket line. He stood underneath a sign that declared CLEANLINESS IS NEXT ONLY TO GODLINESS, while nearby a sweeper stirred up a year's worth of dust with her bunched straw. By the time he reached the head of the line, his depression had been replaced by churlishness.

"No, not Sudapur, Sar-un-dar," he shouted over the piercing efforts of a street musician.

The cashier, an elderly man in whose huge ears rested a pair of antiquated hearing aids, blinked stubbornly behind thick glasses and asked, "Are you possibly mistaken?"

"It's Sarundar. Sarundar, for God's sake," Garrett shouted. He had just heard Parni Ghazal pronounce it a half hour ago, and would have dug into his daypack for proof, but he'd taken the annoying thing off and left it with Lynn. Fortunately, the cashier, having looked through his timetables, smiled in congenial recognition and sold Garrett two second-class tickets to Sarundar.

Eight hours later, the train in which he and Lynn had been standing since Bombay ground to a halt for the hundredth time. There was no station, just a wooden sign nailed to a sprawling banyan tree. A tall young woman walked along the tracks, proffering leather goods through the train's windows. He asked the man pressed against him: "Sarundar?"

"Yes, yes," said the man, smiling.

Garrett and Lynn grabbed their bags and hurried toward the door, the only passengers to do so. As they stepped off the train, it began moving again, and Garrett stumbled briefly when his feet hit the ground.

There was no sign of Parni's driver, and now that Garrett's eyes had adjusted to the twilight, he saw nothing even resembling an actual street. In the distance stood a cluster of huts—a few of them glimmered with light. He looked above for wires, and saw only one loosely strung pair, sagging with crows.

"I wonder if there's a phone here?" he said and glanced down the railroad tracks in time to see the last train car disappear around a curve. Suddenly exhausted, he fell into a brief reverie about fancy hotel bathrooms, each with a telephone by the can, and fluffy towels, and soft toilet paper. And those miniature soaps and shampoos; for some reason those always tickled him, their Lilliputian neatness and the almost magical way they'd be replaced every day, even if he'd used only a tiny bit.

"Where do we go?" Lynn asked him.

"I don't know," he said. It was nearly dark out.

"English?" called a lilting voice behind them. Garrett spun around and faced the young woman who'd been trying to sell leather bags.

"American," he said. "We're looking for Jolly-Maker Chambers? M. Parni Ghazal?"

Her face lit up. "American. Oh, many questions!"

"M. Parni Ghazal," he repeated. "The import-export dealer."

"Parni Ghazal?"

"Yes," said Garrett, encouraged. "This is his daughter, Lynn. And she's here to visit him, and I'm her stepfather. Her mother couldn't make it, well, wouldn't, really—"

"No Parni Ghazal," the young woman said and shook her head.

Hoping for a mere language problem, Garrett dug out the piece of paper with Parni's address on it. "Jolly-Maker Chambers . . . Surudar," he said, reading aloud.

"Sar*un*dar," she said, correcting his pronunciation. But it was more than that; he looked at the wooden sign and again at the address and indeed they were spelled differently.

"Where is Surudar?"

She only shook her head and repeated, "Sarundar. No Parni Ghazal. Ranjini," she said, pointing to herself.

After some confused back-and-forth over the concept of "next train to Bombay," the woman said, "Today."

Garrett pointed to his watch and asked, "*When* today?"

Ranjini shook her long braid and emphasized with her fingers, "*Two* day."

Garrett glanced longingly toward the tracks, and this time noticed there was only one set, which trains from both directions somehow had to share.

☙

Lynn clung to Garrett's arm even though she was furious with him. How could he make such a mistake at the train station! Surudar, Sarundar—it was all the same to him since, after all, he was only pretending to be her father. And yet instead of throwing a fit, all she said was, "I'm sorry." She did not know what she was apologizing for, but a part of her felt responsible for his comfort on this trip.

"Come," said the tall Indian girl, waving them toward the woods. She paused by the banyan tree to pick up a long green appliance—some kind of weed trimmer. She fired up its clattering engine and pointed it like a walking stick toward a narrow path, which she widened as they followed her away from the village.

Lynn's suitcase bounced painfully against her hip. At last, they stopped at a mud-and-stone hut with two open holes for windows and a splintered wood front door. Inside, Ranjini lit a lamp, and a squadron of moths immediately darted through the open ports. The air was warm and thick with the smell of cooking and the last blue smoke from the weed trimmer, now leaning silently against a wall. In the room's center, a black pot rested precariously over a bed of embers. And in the farthest corner lay what looked like two or three animal skins; a river of ants flowed toward them.

Ranjini invited her visitors to remove their shoes and sit on the floor near the fire, which she proceeded to stoke. She set a morsel of food on the ground before a small brass figurine of a child on all fours. She then spooned the pot's remains into a clay bowl and passed it along for Garrett and Lynn to share. They took turns ripping pieces of soft bread and using it to shovel the lentil stew.

The spices made Lynn's tongue smart, and she felt a spark of guilty pleasure that they might be too strong for Garrett. Each spoonful pulsed on its way down her throat.

Ever since earliest childhood she had enjoyed eating with her fingers. There was something familiar about the aftertaste of this dish, too, and she soon recognized that it belonged to the food Nazar used to cook. Nazar was always preparing fragrant, spicy meals during the time she and Papa lived back home, and now this smoldering underflavor curled along the deepest passageways of Lynn's memory.

Ranjini watched quietly while the two of them ate.

"Wouldn't you like some?" asked Lynn, extending her bowl

toward the older girl, who, come to think of it, looked a little like Nazar, at least the way Lynn remembered her. "It's very good," she added.

"I am already eaten," said Ranjini and asked, "Marriage?"

"To each other you mean?" Garrett said.

Lynn shook her head vigorously, put her finger in her mouth, and feigned gagging, while Garrett tried once again to explain that she was his daughter.

"*Step*daughter," said Lynn.

"Mother in America?" Ranjini asked, and Lynn nodded soberly at the thought of her mother so far away.

"*Indian* mother in America?" Ranjini asked, reaching for Lynn's hair and holding a tress of it against her own braid.

"American mother," explained Garrett. "Indian father."

"Oh," said Ranjini, who dropped the hair and seemed less impressed.

Garrett offered to help wash the few dishes in a nearby stream Ranjini had mentioned. He turned to Lynn and asked her along, but she said her stomach hurt and she'd prefer to lie down.

"I'll be back in just a few minutes," he told her.

Lynn gave him a pained look. Ranjini collected the clay bowl, a wood plank, and a dirty knife and placed them inside the empty cooking pot, which Garrett carried as she led the way down a narrow path, widening it with the crackling weed trimmer. Her other arm raised a flaming rag torch, and in its glow, he studied the outline of her hip. The stream was farther than he'd imagined. As the hut disappeared, he felt a pang of remorse for leaving Lynn alone. A breeze, made syrupy from night blooms, rustled the trees around them. When it died down, the stream's gurgle emerged, and soon they stood at a small clearing.

Straddling the water, Ranjini took the bowl from the pot and washed it; Garrett, the plank. Torchlight licked at the curve of her cheek and cast crescent shadows under her breasts. The tip of her braid dangled close to the water. Smiling at Garrett, she quickly averted her eyes. Water trickled over his fingers, and then, a few inches downstream, over hers. The tree boughs were dotted with a strange luminescence and swayed in the breeze. Pulled by the current, Garrett's fingertips floated away from him and toward Ranjini and were about to graze her wrist. In the time left him for a single thought, all he could notice was the water's path across her knuckles, and the small alteration of its course, before he touched her.

The thrill of transgression felt like a pinprick against his chest. Ranjini moved her hand and was already pointing to the trees. "Serpents," she explained calmly.

It took him some time to realize the glowing dots he'd thought part of the leaves were in fact the eyes of snakes, dozens of them in each tree. Ranjini said they were not poisonous and treated their presence as a simple fact of life, but Garrett was disturbed by the prospect one might drop on him. On the way back, he carried the cooking pot on top of his head and was grateful Ranjini, still in the lead, couldn't see his cowardice.

Nearly to the hut, they heard over the weed trimmer's *thrum* a man hollering and a fist pounding on the wood door.

"You are stopping here," Ranjini ordered and ran the rest of the way back. Unwilling to wait in the dark under a canopy of snakes, Garrett tiptoed after her, his footsteps cushioned by a carpet of rotting leaves, and he soon could make out in the clearing before Ranjini's door a tall stoop-shouldered man, his face bright with anger.

Ranjini stood silhouetted in front of this man, her feet planted squarely, as he made some kind of plaintive argument. He extended his narrow fingers beseechingly, then pointed to the decrepit hut, and his voice cracked with distress. Ranjini said nothing, but when he took a step toward her, she brandished the garden appliance and gave it a long rev.

With that, he hung his head and spoke her name a few more times, then set off toward the railroad tracks and the village beyond. His tall form, slightly more stooped than before, soon became swallowed by the deep darkness, though his torch continued to flicker.

From inside the hut, Garrett heard a muffled sob, and he and Ranjini rushed to comfort Lynn, who lay doubled over.

"My stomach," she said. The hut smelled rancid, and Ranjini immediately began mopping a stained area of the floor.

"Do you want to go outside?" Garrett asked and took Lynn's hand, but she cringed.

"Do you know a doctor?" he asked Ranjini. "Doctor?"

"Next week," she said.

In despair, he asked, "Do you have something I can give her for this? Anything?"

Ranjini stepped forward and handed him the empty cooking pot.

In the distance there came a low-throated mechanical rumble. Garrett ran to the door in time to glimpse the first of a long blur of railway cars speeding toward Bombay. He turned to Ranjini and pointed to the train and then Lynn and himself, its rightful passengers.

"Ex-press," said Ranjini. She shrugged apologetically and crossed her arms in front of her. "Will not see you here."

"I could have tried," he said.

"No." Ranjini was adamant. "My brother was trying once. Train was not seeing him."

Lynn remembered eating lentils, she remembered Garrett leaving, and she had a sharp memory of the most awful yelling and pounding. And then a ripping pain in her belly and the burn of acid pushing up in her throat.

Now she lay on her side, holding herself. Her eyes were fiery and her lips dry and brittle. Her muscles all felt pulled.

"Every body sleep," Ranjini said, carrying her tiny statue into a corner of the room, where she tucked it under a scrap of cloth. She then lay down on the dirt floor and extinguished the lamp. Lynn remained in the middle of the room—Garrett seated beside her—and her eyes slowly drooped.

She woke up once in the middle of the night, her stomach twisted with nausea, and tried to crawl outside but wasn't strong enough. And when her chest heaved, Garrett slid the pot under her chin. She was ashamed to be so exposed before him; only her mother had ever seen her sick.

Her mother had been crying when she'd driven them to the

airport. And now? Maybe her mother loved her less for coming here. The fear of this squeezed Lynn's stomach, and there crashed inside her a wave of homesickness. Her vomit splashed against the metal pot.

Garrett stroked her hair. Occasionally, his fingers would catch, and he'd apologize in a quavering voice.

A fly alit on the corner of her eye.

In the morning, after Ranjini returned from the stream, she set a ceremonial drop of water before her figurine—the child Krishna, she explained—*avatara* of Vishnu. "See," she continued, pointing out the bulbous glob molded to his hand, "he is stealing butter. He is wanting what he cannot have. Yet he is loved still." Ranjini sighed and offered Garrett a drink of water.

As politely as possible, he struggled to tell her the water had to be purified first. "With fire," he said, making a mildly suggestive tickling motion with his upturned fingers. Ranjini began snapping twigs.

"Pretty girl," she said, nodding toward Lynn's sleeping form. "She is having your mouth."

"Oh, I don't think so." Lynn had her mother's mouth—slender and roseate with a beauty mark in the exact same spot.

Back home, nighttime had just begun. With luck and maybe some help from Valium, the *avatara* of Diazepam, May-Annlouise would soon be asleep in their bed, hugging his pillow against her stomach the way she would hold him when he was there. She looked especially lovely asleep, with her lips trustfully parted. In the two years they'd been married now, Garrett had never been separated from her overnight until this trip, and it bothered him that on this first outing he had brushed his hand against another woman's wrist. He checked his watch: nine hours ago he had touched Ranjini. In Baltimore time, he consoled himself, it hadn't even happened yet.

His thoughts drifted toward his wife's delicate, lacy laugh, the dimpled flesh on either side of her tailbone, her tendency, despite being tone-deaf and the whitest white girl he'd ever known, to sing along with Bessie Smith records. But even as he missed May-Annlouise and felt the grip of her hands across his chest, he couldn't help staring at Ranjini crouched before the fire pit. She blew gently to coax a flame, and he admired the taut arches of her feet as she balanced her weight. He wanted to tell her how beautiful she was but feared that even so small a flirtation might be sternly interpreted. Instead, Garrett explained again how he was not Lynn's natural father, and so his mouth couldn't possibly have any influence over hers.

Ranjini was not persuaded and pointed to his face, saying, "Smile. Smile."

He smiled for her, and she exhaled impatiently and moved closer to him. She smelled of marigolds, and he found himself taking a deep breath of her. "You are smiling," Ranjini insisted, pushing up the corners of his mouth with her thumb and forefinger. She then touched Lynn's brow. "She is seeing."

"Oh," he said, with a nod. "It's my smile that she sees."

"Yes," said Ranjini, breaking open a lush smile of her own.

Lynn awoke and saw the blurred figures of a couple kneading dough. She wondered where she was, even what age she was. In her mind's eye she saw her papa and Nazar in a long-ago kitchen, laughing, smudges of batter on their faces and on Nazar's blouse, a few words murmured between them in Urdu.

"Well, look who's up," Garrett said and traced a fingertip across Lynn's cheek. "How are you?"

"Thirsty." She gulped some water, and the dizziness she'd felt upon waking cleared. "How long have I been asleep?"

"About ten hours."

"Who was that man last night?" she asked.

Garrett explained that Ranjini's father wanted her to come home and marry some fellow from the next village.

"I dis-grace," offered Ranjini, "the old way."

Timidly Lynn looked herself over, concerned that she'd somehow soiled herself during the night. As subtly as possible, she sniffed under the arms of her *kameez*.

"Bathe?" Ranjini asked. She took some of the dough outside and slid it into a crumbling clay oven. Lynn looked at her stepfather apprehensively.

"Go ahead, if you like," said Garrett and volunteered to watch the bread.

Lynn followed Ranjini along a narrow path behind the hut. When they got to the stream, the older girl unwound herself, as though peeling the outer layers of an onion, and, bending naked before the water, scrubbed the plain white garment against a rock. As her hardworking shoulder blades waved amiably under her skin, Ranjini asked Lynn if she had any marriage plans.

"I'm only thirteen," Lynn said, defiantly, the high sun blazing against her brow.

Ranjini continued to talk about marriage—about the tradition of arranged marriage and how she despaired of persuading her father to allow a love marriage. "All love marriage in U.S.A. Yes?" Ranjini asked dreamily as she scrubbed. "Your mother, Garrett, love marriage?"

"I guess so," said Lynn. She'd never heard the term *love marriage* before. "This is her third."

"Three!" said Ranjini and frowned. After wringing her sari, she spread it across a bush—steam rising immediately from the wet cloth—and then pointed to Lynn's *salwar kameez*.

The thirteen-year-old squirmed out of her tunic and let Ranjini take it. Ranjini scrubbed, beat, and wrung, and when that was done, she took the billowy pants, the socks, and the bra. Lynn preferred to wash her own underpants. Once they were wet, they looked skimpy in her hands and about to disintegrate.

"Marriage age," Ranjini said. And Lynn realized with horror that Ranjini was referring to the grayish bloodstain on the cotton lining, just below the faded Smurfs print. After taking the underwear and setting it next to the other clothes, the older girl then pointed to Lynn's pendant. Ranjini smiled and began teasing that the locket contained a picture of Lynn's intended. "Let us see," she insisted.

"It's my papa," said Lynn. She felt superstitious about opening the locket without any clothes on.

"Ah," said the older girl, remembering. "Indian father. Hindu?"

"No, Muslim," said Lynn with caution, but Ranjini didn't seem to have any problem with this.

"Good man?"

Lynn nodded reflexively.

"Ask him his feelings of love marriage," insisted Ranjini.

Lynn had never given much thought to her own wedding, and now she wondered whether her papa would have any say in the matter.

Ranjini stepped into the stream and began to rub water up and down her legs, and Lynn found herself studying the older girl's body and imagining herself growing into it someday soon. She'd always wanted a big sister, someone to pave her way and, more important, someone to help her sort through the complications of her family.

The girls lay on a large rock in the sunshine, and Ranjini described her assigned bridegroom. He was old, like Garrett, and had some kind of "blemish" as well as a demanding mother, whom Ranjini would be required to wait on, and the only reason for this disturbing match seemed to be that Ranjini's parents couldn't provide enough dowry to attract a better husband from the limited pool of eligible men.

"You mean it's like a bribe to take you?" asked Lynn. It was all so calculated.

She thought sullenly of her mother and papa. Even in a love marriage, probably, one person loved more than the other. Assuming her papa had loved her mother—and hadn't he?—any love he gave her must have come at Nazar's expense, and the other way around, too. Whom had he "loved"? Lynn wondered. Who'd been "arranged"?

"Yes, bribe. Then more maybe," said Ranjini, sitting up now. "After they take you, they can ask more dowry, then more. If my father cannot give, then——" She made a swift slicing motion across her throat. "Sometimes"—and now she pretended to pound, as though with a hammer, smacking the side of her fist harder and harder against her palm. It took five or six attempts to get across the knotty idea of her own murder at the hands of her future in-laws. "Sometimes," she said, making ominous flames with her upturned fingertips, "they are burning you."

"You mean, all of a sudden, they——"

"Yes, exactly," said Ranjini. "All of the sudden they can decide this. And during, during, you are in wondering what will it be."

On Garrett's watch, the first batch of bread had turned to ashes, and at dinner, Ranjini teased him about his kitchen skills, implying that, but for his good fortune to be married, he would surely starve.

"What are you going to do?" Garrett asked her, tearing a piece from the second, edible batch of *naan* and clasping it around some lentils. Lynn, who wasn't up to eating, quietly sipped some tea and twirled a lock of her hair into ringlets. She seemed preoccupied; the lamplight flickered across her scowl.

"I must live," Ranjini pronounced, though Garrett assumed she meant *leave*. "To go city."

He regarded the small pile of barely dried skins, which had undergone only the most basic cleaning. He could feel Lynn's stare over the rim of her cup, and when he turned to face her, he perceived a subtle nod urging him toward some course of action.

"Ranjini," he said, pointing to the skins. He told her he'd been looking for a nice piece of leatherwork to bring home to his wife and asked if he could buy something of hers.

While Lynn bounced up and down on her haunches, Ranjini blushed and carefully selected her best bag. Its stitches were just wide enough to render the whole thing largely unusable. Against Ranjini's protests, he peeled off ten one-hundred-rupee notes—assuring her over and again that by American standards he was getting a bargain—when they were interrupted by a vigorous knock.

"Father!" she whispered, watching the bolt shake. To his pounding her father now added a series of loud imperatives. Ranjini shouted back with the shrill panic of a child and then suddenly, after looking just over Garrett's right shoulder, fell quiet except to murmur, "Uncle."

From the porthole behind Garrett spoke a new voice more reasonable than the father's but ringing with the same righteousness. The back of Garrett's neck prickled with warmth, and—realizing that the uncle was poking a lit torch through the window—he considered the morning's burnt *naan* and the hut's potential to become a large clay oven. While the two men outside conferred with one another, Ranjini slipped the money into a fold of her sari. Soon the knocking resumed until finally she opened the rotting old bolt. Her uncle and father strode into the hut.

His torch blazing, Ranjini's father didn't bother to look at the visitors, just fixed his clouded eyes on his daughter, show-

ering her with invective, especially one phrase, brief and gut-
tural. As he brought his arm back, poised to slap her face, his
brother whispered to him, and the raised hand wavered in
midair.

Charging from the far corner, Lynn lunged at him, crying
something about his daughter's sacrifice and clutching at his
dhoti as the two of them staggered against the door frame.
"How could you?" she shouted. Garrett had never seen his
stepdaughter so ferocious and wondered if she was still suffering from yesterday's fever. Ranjini's father dropped his torch,
which rolled onto the pile of skins and kindled plumes of thick
greasy smoke. With no time to put his hiking boots on his feet,
Garrett plunged a hand into each and batted at the flames. He
could feel the heat through the boot soles and on his face as he
breathed the foul smell of burning flesh. He reared up—a
hoofed centaur—and stomped wherever he saw fire and smoke
until he had beaten back the last fuming curls of heat.

Under everyone's watchful gaze, he slowly stood and freed
his hands from the boots, completing his return to human form.
He took a step toward the other men, raised his right palm in
the manner of taking an oath, and—in a voice just deep and
loud enough to convey the sense of, he hoped, benevolence and
credibility—asked for everyone to calm down. He explained
who he was and who Lynn was and how they got there.

"Please forgive us," said the uncle earnestly. He wore trim
sideburns and a pair of green beltless slacks. "Seeing only your
back, I inferred an altogether false impression. I thought you
were conscripting vulnerable girls for a city brothel. My older
brother, alas, cannot see well. American visitors," he repeated

now to Ranjini's father, who was still adjusting his dhoti. The older man squinted at Garrett's illuminated face and then at Lynn.

"Daughter?" he asked her skeptically.

"Stepdaughter," she said and smiled, flush and damp, at Garrett. Despite her quibble, she'd still managed to confer something special upon him with the warmth of that smile.

Ranjini's father walked over to Garrett, touched his shoulder, and said, "If you have daughter, you understand." He kept repeating "you understand," and Garrett believed the phrase was meant to cover a wide range of subjects, but especially Ranjini's engagement.

Garrett thought the older man didn't deserve a daughter, but kept his mouth shut.

Her uncle then invited the American visitors to return to the village and stay with his family. "Everyone come," he said softly, his arms spread open. "I don't know why you would subject yourself to these conditions. My home is not a palace, but you will be far more comfortable. You should not leave India with the impression that we provincials have no furniture. And I live near the village television," he said, appealing to Lynn.

"Everyone," repeated Ranjini's father, staring at his daughter.

"But we like it here," said Lynn, to Garrett's astonishment.

Emboldened by this show of solidarity, Ranjini stepped in front of Garrett and pointed her relatives to the door.

"Dear girl," the uncle continued in English for everyone to hear. "You must come home *some*time. And I do not appreciate you making off with my weed-trimming machine, which was a gift from your cousin's bride's family on the occasion of their wedding. You will ruin it in this jungle patch." Eyeing the burnt mess on the floor, he added, "And throw away those disgusting pelts before anyone sees you handling them! Have you no pride? You will undermine your marriage for sure."

Beaten down for the night, Ranjini's father made a final pronouncement to her in his own language before wishing the visitors a good night and leaving with his brother.

Ranjini bolted the door behind them and leaned against it. Her father had given her until tomorrow evening to regain her senses, or he would come back with enough relatives to forcibly escort her home. "They pressurize me," explained Ranjini sullenly. "Very angry, tomorrow."

"But you'll be in Bombay then," said Lynn, taking the young woman's hand and swinging it back and forth.

Ranjini cracked a sickly smile and continued to translate her father's parting threat. She spoke fast and less fluently than usual but repeated herself often enough so the following meaning emerged: somehow, if she refused to go through with the marriage, she could not expect to achieve grace in this lifetime and would certainly return to face an even worse marriage, and beyond that a worse marriage still, until she accepted her fate.

"How could that be?" wondered Lynn.

"Always my life on this earth," Ranjini said, looking past Lynn. "Never to end."

"You don't really believe him, do you?" Lynn asked.

"I am possible believing him. We wait, see." Ranjini then

toppled over, as though her legs had been pulled out from under her, and began raking her fingers through the dirt. Her back rose and fell with each sob.

Lynn fluttered around her, placing a hand on a shoulder, on a cheek, trying desperately to soothe, then cast Garrett a pleading look.

He was touched but alarmed that she seemed to credit him with knowing the right thing to do. Only a minute ago he'd earned her higher regard and already she was raising the bar.

"Say something," she demanded.

"What do you want me to say?" His heart pounding, he wished they were spending the night with Ranjini's uncle.

"Tell her what she should do."

"She's an adult," he argued. "She can make her own decisions."

"She's a couple years older than me. That's not adult." Lynn stared at him with such doleful urgency he sat on the ground in front of Ranjini and did his best to convince her that no worse husband waited for her in another life. That the gods would not maliciously bide their time, waiting to punish her for following her heart. Ranjini sat up and, as she regained control of her breathing, asked him to repeat his assurances over and over again. She made him promise he was telling her the truth.

"I promise," he said.

"Thank you," she said and grabbed his hands with both of her own, which distressed Garrett even more than her sobs. He believed he was telling the truth, or at least a more plausible truth than her father's manipulative threat, but whether it was the right thing to say, he had no idea. What would she do in

Bombay? It was a rough place. A girl with a baby at every red light! Did she know about that?

"Ranjini," he asked gently, "how will you support yourself?"

She tilted her head.

"For money," he said.

"Oh! Money!" She flashed the wad of rupees he had given her to show she understood. "Sell!" she said, nodding toward the junky pile of skins. "Rich!"

The girls laughed. Together they gamboled off to clean the dishes, and this time it was Garrett who was left alone in the hut feeling horribly queasy.

He plucked a cobweb of vein off his leather bag and put his boots inside to use as a pillow. Its gaminess stung his nostrils, and the bag was still damp with the gory fact of what it had been.

Ranjini and Lynn returned from the stream, and everyone retired to a separate corner of the hut. Garrett soon fell deeply into a night of strange dreams.

In one, May-Annlouise had flown to India and engaged the Bombay police to form a search party. "I trusted him," she told the sketch artist, whose rendering of Garrett featured a railroad spike sunk deep into each eye. Parni Ghazal ambled through another dream in his silk smoking jacket. Toward morning, Garrett dreamt that all the village patriarchs, led by Ranjini's father and uncle, marched to her hut, torches ablaze. When Ranjini opened the door, they streamed past her, until the hut was brimming; still more men stood outside. Ranjini looked all around her at the thick coil of men.

"Ranjini, listen, Ranjini," said her father, sitting on the floor and pulling his feet underneath him. The other men followed suit; some had to sit on the laps of their neighbors. "I have done you an injustice." His peers murmured their agreement and urged him, inexplicably in the style of a Baptist revival, to continue. "When you were born," he recalled with some hesitation, "I carried you down to the stream behind this very hut with plans to drown you because you were a girl, but I could not bring such karma on myself and refrained."

"Amen," said the congregation.

"Brought her to the river," said a man in the back corner, who was wearing a silk smoking jacket and whose face resembled the photo of Parni Ghazal from Lynn's locket. And then Garrett noticed that all of the men now wore silk smoking jackets and the face of Parni Ghazal, including Ranjini's father.

"Since then, your entire childhood has been one of forsaken happiness: only six years of formal schooling, cold leftover food, menial housekeeping, no sitar lessons. True, we hadn't money for a sitar, but even if we had, I would have granted your brothers lessons and not you. And now this whole dowry business. Why should you have to marry an old lecher with Tourette's syndrome just because I don't have enough consumer luxury items to spare?"

"Amen."

"He has Tourette's?" Ranjini asked.

Her father averted his eyes—Parni's eyes—in shame. "To live is to suffer," he intoned.

"I heard *that*," said the Parni in the back corner.

"But you have suffered more than I have, and that is unjust. All this will change, I promise you. My dear friend Sanjay has baked you some sweets. Where are those sweets, Sanjay? And can we extinguish a few torches? The temperature has risen twofold in here."

As some of the men obliged him, he shared a list of resolutions: he would take her fishing, schedule a regular father-daughter outing, even make leather goods with her, though it was beneath their caste. Eventually he would set her up with a little boutique in the city to sell them. As to marriage, he said, her happiness was his only concern. "You may marry or not as you desire. If your bridegroom's family is so greedy as to expect a large dowry, I will do whatever I can to provide it, even though it could mean my lifelong indentured servitude. So tell me, lovely Ranjini. Open your heart and tell me its true desire."

"Him." She didn't even have to think about it, merely turned and pointed an impeaching finger at Garrett. "I would like to make forbidden love to this man."

The congregation murmured its displeasure. Still more of the torches sputtered as they were extinguished, and in the remaining dim light the eyes of the fifty or so faces of Parni Ghazal glowed steadily at Garrett. . . .

He awoke rattled and vulnerable—his mind scrambling to piece together what was dreamt and what was real. Ranjini and Lynn sat a few yards away, looking at him and giggling in conspiracy. And he prayed, actually *prayed*, not to have talked in his sleep.

During their hurried breakfast of strong tea and leftover bread, it became clear Lynn had reinforced the young woman's decision and they would all three be taking the train to Bombay. This seemed more and more to Garrett like a terrible choice,

but the alternative was no better. Ranjini placed what few arti-
cles she owned, including the child Krishna, inside her cooking
pot and left the hut void of any trace of herself except the most
badly charred skins and the weed trimmer, which stood alone in
a corner.

They set off for the railroad tracks, pushing through the
early morning's clammy vapors. Still half-asleep, they spent a
quiet hour waiting before the train appeared.

It stopped just long enough for them to hop on. Miracu-
lously, this time there were two seats together, and Garrett offered them to Lynn and Ranjini, then stood over them both. As
the train picked up speed, Ranjini stared out the window, and
her eyes began to glisten.

Garrett asked if she felt okay, and she nodded. She was not
at all worried about Bombay, she insisted. But she continued to
harbor concerns about the hereafter. She asked Lynn point-
blank to state her position as a Muslim.

"Well," his stepdaughter said, "my papa is a Muslim. I'll
have to ask him when I see him."

Ranjini nodded warily at this answer and then looked to
Garrett for more. He personally held no vision of the afterlife
but tried to say something, anything that might make sense.
"It's a mystery," he tried. "We really don't know."

She gazed at him moistly, so he continued to babble about
theories and *interpretation* and *possibility*. By the third village
stop, her eyes were brimming. "How do you live?" she asked
him, lifting her cooking pot suitcase from the floor.

"Hey, Ranjini, wait," said Lynn, reaching for the young
woman's arm.

"I cannot be marrying again then again," she said.

"What about love?" Lynn tried to hold on, but Ranjini tore herself loose and scurried toward the train door. Now outside, she ran along the tracks in the direction from which they'd just traveled, the rising winds pushing her, swelling the folds of her sari like a sail.

Garrett took her empty seat and watched the horizon point beyond which she'd disappeared. With his fingers, he kneaded the leather bag she'd made, squeezing its suppleness, and pictured the burnt ones left behind. Against his stomach rested the purple belly pack—nylon, light, and impervious. He had failed to deliver Ranjini from some truly bleak prospects, and he sank now into dismay. Also, though, a tinge of relief; after all, if she came to Bombay, she might then want to return with them to Baltimore. He glimpsed a vision of May-Annlouise opening the door to find her most vivid nightmare repeating itself. *"Do you know,"* he heard the echo of his wife's voice, *"how much . . . trust you?"*

Glancing down the aisle, Garrett wondered if anyone was coming to collect their fare. He stank of smoke and tried to slide the window open, but it hardly budged. Outside, the train passed laborers hauling water, a white bird the height of a man, and an old shrine whose stones and mortar were being slowly pried apart by vines. The sky thickened with heat.

Neither Garrett nor Lynn spoke for hours. Eventually the girl fell asleep with her head on his shoulder and stayed that way until the train neared Bombay. She awoke with a start and looked around her, as if searching for someone or something. Flustered, she dabbed at the small sweat stain she'd left on Garrett's shirt and broke the long silence by remarking sadly, "She was so pretty. Don't you think?"

He nodded without looking at her. Outside, the sunshine vibrated in the air so visibly that the train appeared to tread water.

"What if," Lynn suddenly proposed, "she came to live with us?"

"You can't change someone's religious beliefs," said Garrett, trying to salvage a moral out of the past two days. "And besides, Immigration wouldn't let her stay without a family sponsor or an American husband. And I'm already married to your mother," he added inanely.

"You could be married to them both." She spoke with that rueful Indian lilt, as though merely noting a preordained event. "Papa was married to Mom and Nazar for a while. He had two wives."

"Well, I'm not Papa," he answered bluntly.

She turned away from him, toward the window, in which Garrett could now see his reflection, his mouth unbecomingly stern and his chin weak. He thought about his pillow-dream, his desire to chaperone in the first place, and he cringed at his own cynical vanity.

As their train eased into the terminal, Garrett and Lynn gathered their belongings and sat on the edge of their seats.

"OK, pick one," she ventured, in the sporting tone one might use when playing a card game. "Are you Mom's prize?" she asked. "Or her punishment, for her earlier marriages?"

He sighed. "Don't you think you're being a little hard on me?"

"I'm just asking. You can say prize."

"OK then. Prize."

"So you think you're better than him?"

"Than who?" he stalled. He did not enjoy the prospect of sinking even further in his stepdaughter's estimation.

"My father."

"No, I wouldn't say that. Of course not," he admitted finally, hoping to have given the right answer. She nodded, her face clenched in triumph.

"We wait," Lynn promised the window. "We see."

four

Parni's Present

With his daughter due at the apartment in just ten minutes, Muhammad "Parni" Ghazal felt his trousers scratching against his stubbly thighs. Leaving instructions with his wife, Nazar, Parni retired to the bathroom, where he removed his suit and tie and the rest of his clothes and climbed into the shower. He soaped himself vigorously, then picked up the gray metal safety razor on the tub's ledge and guided it along his right calf. He worked briskly, as though peeling a carrot. Luckily he had a hairless chest and back, which left only the tender cups of his underarms and the area of greatest privacy.

His ritual complete, he smoothed sandalwood lotion onto his chafed legs, then stood before one of the bathroom's many mirrors and admired the taut surfaces of his body. He was reminded of Michelangelo's *David,* and felt grateful to have sustained such youthfulness for so many years.

He glided back into his trousers and, resuited, took a last look in the mirror over the sink and said aloud, "What can she want from me?"

He hadn't seen his daughter, Leena, in ages, not since she was toddling. Every year he remembered her birthday with a card, and that, he liked to think, was sufficient. But now she'd come ten thousand miles—to "visit."

She was supposed to have arrived three days ago, but apparently she and her guardian had gone off on some little side excursion. *"Lost!"* she explained last night on the phone. *How does one become so lost?* Parni wondered, but did not wish to pry. He respected the privacy of others and valued such respect in return. This whole visit, he told himself, was an invasion of his privacy, and that calmed him a little—to feel he was a victim to his daughter. Just moments ago, she had phoned again, this time from the local train station, and insisted on taking a taxi over immediately, rather than wait for his driver to pick her up—such casualness!

Faintly now he could discern her high-pitched voice coming from the foyer. It sounded like the talking spider monkey in that animated short he'd recorded for her viewing enjoyment. Then he heard a man's gravelly baritone. The man must be Leena's new father. Parni caressed his face and wondered if it needed to be shaved again. It wouldn't take long, and he wanted to appear well groomed. He hated when people took no pride in their personal appearance and hygiene.

Nazar knocked gently on the door and said, "They're here."

"Yes, yes," Parni said curtly, trying not to move his mouth as the razor rounded his chin. Nazar chafed him. She catered to him in the most stifling manner, which, to be honest, reflected his expectations of her and how she'd been trained ever since they were both children, betrothed to each other. But there were times when Parni remembered Leena's mother, May-Annlouise—spirited, independent May-Annlouise—and the years they had been married, first alone, then with their child, and for a while with Nazar joining them, too. That was a happy, if complicated, time for Parni. He had everything he could have wanted: his American wife, his Indian wife, his mixed child—all gathered under one roof.

Life was unfair. It gave you happiness, then took it away. In that sense it was a lot like the government, always changing its rules. At first allowing the import of polyester rag, then raising the duty beyond the limits of affordability. It was a wonder how he stayed in business.

He rubbed some lotion on his face and felt reassured by the smoothness of his skin. In his mind's eye, he still saw Leena as three years old, though he knew she must have changed some over the decade.

When her papa entered the living room, Lynn was amazed how old he looked. His hair was half gray, and the deep shadows under his eyes made her wonder if he might be dying. Before he said a word, she ran to him and hugged him, greedily breathing in his cologne.

"Spider monkey!" he exclaimed and chuckled. "Just like a spider monkey! A little spider monkey."

She liked hearing him call her that and continued to cling to him, even after he tried to move forward to shake hands with Garrett.

"You must be Leena's new father."

"Leena?" Garrett asked, offering his hand.

"Forgive me," said her papa. "Of course she uses her American name."

"*Step*father," corrected Lynn.

"Forgive me again," he said. "I neglected the idiom. The reference is to a ladder, I take it? You certainly do not look trod upon!"

"Family trees, maybe?"

Lynn wished the two men would speak more naturally to each other. So intense was her desire for harmony, she almost suggested Garrett leave for a while. But already he was being offered a drink. She knew he would ask for a gin and tonic. Out of politeness, her papa made the same thing for himself. She wanted to learn her papa's true favorite drink.

Also she was curious to know: Did he blow his nose—like Garrett did—in front of other people? Did he pronounce the word *water* normally, like her mother, or with a long foghorn *a* like Garrett? Would he point out, during a sexy moment in the new Madonna video, that "regular people don't behave that way"?

The two men sat in leather armchairs in front of a large picture window overlooking the town. They tasted their gin and tonics very slowly as though each were afraid the other had slipped him poison.

"You have not brought much luggage for two people," her papa observed and was told Garrett's bags had been dropped at a small hotel on the way from the train station.

"Nonsense," said Papa. "You must stay here. There's plenty room. Two baths, two water closets. Air conditioning. Recessed lighting. All new construction."

Lynn was disappointed to hear things would become more crowded, more tangled.

"It's a beautiful apartment," said Garrett.

Nazar returned from the kitchen carrying a tray of cookies and tea, which she set in front of Lynn.

"Thank you, Nazar!" Lynn watched the woman's plump fingers fuss with the tea set and her bosom sway over it.

"Call me Mama," insisted Nazar, and Lynn said, "Thank you, Mama."

It gave her a warm quiver in her stomach to call Nazar that. And then she felt her forehead sweat as she recognized the betrayal to her real mother. She decided to keep her mouth full so she wouldn't be expected to talk, and quietly accepted cookie after cookie—wonderfully soft cookies with honey on top. But after five of them, she felt queasy and asked if she could be excused to take a bath.

"Come, this way," said Nazar.

Lynn was led to the most opulent bathroom she'd ever seen: it had a dark marble floor and golden fixtures that sparkled, and a huge tub—more the size of a kiddy pool. Nazar turned on the tap and sprinkled salts into the water. "You need a towel," she said, opening a large cupboard that must have held thirty. "Which is your favorite color?"

"Red," Lynn answered quickly.

"Red, what?" Nazar urged.

"Red, Mama?" said Lynn. Nazar smiled and rewarded the answer by handing over a towel. Finally, she left Lynn to herself.

Drowned out by the roar of the bath tap, Lynn knelt before the toilet and tried to throw up, but her body stubbornly held on to the cookies. Her knees began to ache, so she satisfied her impulse by spitting four times into the toilet bowl. Somewhat purged now, she undressed.

The insistent reflection of her face and body astonished her. She leaned toward the large mirror over the sink, supporting her weight with palms flattened against the marble countertop. Her tan skin and sleek dark hair and the curved, slightly larger, outline of her nostrils—features that had made her uncomfortable for the way they set her apart from her school friends back home—now seemed to her lovely and familiar.

She cast a wary eye toward her chest, which lately had put forth a lot of new growth. If given a vote, she'd prefer to end up small-breasted. It seemed less trouble, both practically and, she sensed, in some more general way. Folding her arms in front of her, she turned from the mirror and climbed into the tub. She closed her eyes and wondered where her papa planned to take her and if they might spend the next day together, the two of them.

After her bath, feeling relaxed and refreshed, she paused in the foyer to look at framed photos of him: standing at a lectern, accepting an award; holding a bale of yarn; leaning against a forklift. He had a confident smile, which creased deeply into his face, but sad eyes. No one posed next to him in any of the pictures.

She wandered into the living room, and was surprised to find Nazar reading alone on the love seat—her bare feet stroking each other.

"Where's everybody gone?" asked Lynn. Nazar sat up straight and closed her book.

"They went to the hotel to get Garrett's bags, dear. They should be back within the hour. Oh—Parni wanted you to watch this," she added, and pointed her remote control toward a tremendous television.

The VCR played a cartoon of a spider monkey and a boy building a tree house. Lynn couldn't understand what they were saying because it was in Hindi.

"Why did he want me to see this?" she asked.

"He thinks you're still a child. You don't care for this cartoon, do you?"

Lynn nodded eagerly, but her true feelings must have shown because Nazar said, "No, you don't. It's stupid." With that she zapped the television to a different channel and dropped the remote control into the pocket of her dress, as though returning a gun to its holster.

On TV, women in veils ran around a swimming pool. Lynn wondered what was taking her papa and Garrett so long. What could they be talking about? It seized her that they were ironing out some custody arrangement. How bizarre if Papa took custody of her, even for part of the year—her mom hadn't mentioned the possibility. But in India, where many marriages were still arranged, maybe her mom wouldn't even have a say in it. The more she thought about this, the more it made sense to her—what else could Garrett and her father have to talk about? Garrett might even be pushing for such a plan; it would explain his willingness to go with her on this trip. Maybe the two men were arguing over who had to take her. She chewed on the inside of her cheek and watched the veiled women twirl like windblown leaves.

Today began one of the many local festivals that Parni took little interest in, and rivers of people were flowing downtown for the artistic exhibitions and contests. His driver had to stop several blocks from the hotel, because Laxmi Nagar Road had been closed off. As he led Garrett, Parni walked spryly—avoiding the outstretched limbs of the lame and indigent—with a ballet dancer's grace. He had once dreamed of a career in dance. Of course, it was out of the question.

"We should have brought Lynn," Garrett called ahead.

"Yes, yes," Parni said, continuing to negotiate his way through the crowd. "Plenty of this for the next few days. She won't miss anything." Given his druthers, Parni would prefer to be at home in his study, reading Mir Taqi Mir, or Charles Dickens, or even Danielle Steel. But here was a truth: he wanted, whenever possible, to be well liked. With his daughter and her guardian here, relying on Parni for their entertainment, he would do his best not to disappoint them. He could do that much for them. If they wanted more, if they had an agenda, there could be conflict. And this was possible. Her mother, May-Annlouise, was a woman miffed. She had hated him mightily when she learned he was additionally married to Nazar, the revelation of which eventually drove him from America.

Marriage, marriage. He should never have been honest with May-Annlouise. It was the tragic mistake of his life, because she could not appreciate the delicacy of his circumstances, only the insult to her own ego. To her, his one marriage invalidated the other. Yet insult was farthest from his mind. He wanted to honor *both* women—as well as his status as a legal resident and his childhood obligation toward Nazar. Granted, polygamy, though sanctioned by scripture, clashed with modern standards. And it was no doubt hypocritical of him to invoke scripture on this point given, say, his fondness for a good gin and tonic. In the final analysis, he simply had been able to determine no other way. He wondered if May-Annlouise regretted throwing him out. She had gone crazy one morning when he called Lynn by her Indian nickname.

Reed music now puled from a bullhorn. Fortunately they were nearly to the hotel. Beggars were starting to notice them, and Parni gently shoved one aside. "Don't give them anything," Parni called back, "or we'll never arrive."

The strong sunshine turned the town into a large sauna. He started to perspire in his suit, even though it was a summer weight, and he began to envy Garrett his baggy white sport shirt. Garrett was a handsome man, though he seemed to have a lot of body hair. He'd heard that before Garrett, May-Annlouise had been married to a Nordic. Her life had not been easy. He still dreamt about her sometimes.

Most recently, just a week ago. In this dream, he reclined on a grassy hilltop with her and Nazar. The women, both naked, laughed gaily at a joke, a small joke at Parni's expense, but he welcomed the attention. Abruptly Nazar left, and May-Annlouise looked at him and asked, "Do you still want me?" "But I never stopped to want you," he replied, perhaps too quickly. Clearly something had offended. Suddenly she was clothed—in a bee-keeping outfit—and instead Parni lay exposed. She stood up, releasing from the ground a squadron of wasps, who swarmed around his tender abdomen and the area of greatest privacy.

No, that last dream was not auspicious. The idea that *wasp* might have a second, slightly more benign meaning was of little comfort to him.

They entered the hotel, and the din from outside registered itself in Parni's ear by its sudden absence. Some minutes later, they were able to locate Garrett's baggage, and by the time the two men had lugged it back to Parni's Ambassador, he was beginning to feel chafed.

"Where do you want to go?" he asked Garrett as soon as they'd settled into the backseat.

The American looked at him strangely. "How about home to Lynn?"

"She's all right with Nazar, you know," Parni said, hitching up his trousers. "She and Nazar are thick as the thieves. You mustn't worry." But Garrett appeared not at all interested in stopping at a restaurant first, so Parni reluctantly ordered his driver home.

"So," he said, once they were underway, "do you miss America? I miss America." He laughed when he realized the pun. "Miss America. A lot of pretty girls there," he added grimly. Garrett nodded in agreement, but Parni felt awkward and blithering, like a criminal who hasn't quite learned his alibi and is about to be arrested for rooftop sniping, or the sabotage of over-the-counter pharmaceuticals, or some other bizarre crime such as the sowing of his seed into May-Annlouise—he of another race, no less! He had occupied her area of greatest privacy and become a part of her, as she would later become a part of Garrett, this composed, white gentleman sitting next to him. One could almost say the two men were therefore related by sex. Yes, related by sex, though what man would care to recognize such a fact?

Soon his worried mind jumped to Leena and all she must be thinking about him, and he instructed his driver to make a right turn and stop in front of L. B. Rao. "I'll be back in a jiff," he said, leaving Garrett in the purring Ambassador.

L. B. Rao was a toy store of distinction. Parni often enjoyed shopping there for himself—he was a collector of unusual toys—and all the clerks knew him well. He stood in the center of the shop's two-story lobby, unsure what to do next.

"Good afternoon, Parni." It was L. B. Rao himself, on his feet but looking gaunt. He'd lost his hair, including eyebrows, doing battle with a long illness, which had also led to the removal of some tissue. It pained Parni to think about any of this.

"Sir," said Parni, salaaming. Mr. Rao was easily in his eighties. He was immeasurably kind to Parni and always let him try out any new acquisition at home for a week and return it if disappointed. Parni liked to pretend the fine knickknacks he bought were actually presents from L. B. Rao, whom he thought of as a grandfather. His own grandfathers were long dead. At least three of his relatives had died during Partition, and it pained Parni to think of this as well, yet he couldn't help but do so. It struck him, gazing into the chemo-ravaged eyes of L. B. Rao, that the pursuit of autonomy was always violent.

"Well, Parni," said the older man, "how do you enjoy the leopard?" Parni had bought the marionette—made of fine mahogany with brass joints—last week.

"Oh, he's beautiful, sir. I may buy the elephant to keep him company. But not today."

"What can we do for you today?" said L. B. Rao, leaning against a display cabinet filled with porcelain dolls.

Parni did not wish to mention Leena, because then Mr. Rao would insist on learning the entire story and there wasn't time. "I want something that will challenge my mind, something that will give me hours of uninterrupted amusement and that will make me forget about all my grievances with anything and anybody. And it should be expensive."

L. B. Rao excused himself and went into the back. He returned a minute later, holding the curtain aside for two young men, who carried an immense wooden box, which they set on the floor in front of Parni.

He stared at the cover appreciatively. "The Palace of Tranquility!" he whispered.

"It's cutaway," said Mr. Rao, referring to this model of the fabled palace. "One-ninetieth scale and including period furnishings. There comes with it a formidable book of instructions."

Parni eagerly counted out the money from his billfold while the two young employees lugged the box outside. It filled and then some the Ambassador's trunk, which had to be tied down with rope, and Garrett's bags transplanted to the front passenger seat.

L. B. Rao accompanied Parni to the car, something he never had done before, and the formality of this good-bye seemed uncomfortably final. "Parni," cautioned the older man in parting: "Don't glue anything until you decide to keep it."

"How beautiful!" Lynn said, gazing at all the miniature arches, domes, footstools, and kettle tubs—each neatly packed in brown paper.

There were so many pieces! It was as though her papa had filled the largest box he could find with hundreds of presents and given them to her all at once. Her fingers shook as she examined a tiny washbasin. It all must have cost so much money.

"It's *too* beautiful," she said, clasping her arms around her father's neck.

"What are those tears for?" he asked, pulling back and looking at her in astonishment.

"It's too nice of a gift," she said. "You should return it."

"Don't be silly. After we carried it all the way up here?" He sounded cross.

Lynn wiped her face with her shirtsleeve and said, "Thank you," to her papa and then she turned to Garrett and hugged him. "Thank you."

"Well, I like the hug," said Garrett, "but this is Parni's present."

"Thank you," she said again to her father, feeling unworthy of such a gift.

He flipped through a book of building plans and photos and explained to her that the Palace of Tranquility was an old fort inside which stood one of the most splendid estates in India and one of its most revered tombs.

"You mean this is a real place?" she asked.

"Yes, yes. An hour-or-so train ride from here."

"Can we go see it?"

"I suppose," he said, tearing open a brown wrapper and examining the pillar inside. He had a faraway look, and Lynn wondered if he'd forgotten about her.

"When?"

"I don't know," he murmured.

"Tomorrow?"

"I suppose," he said, opening another wrapper with terrific concentration.

"Are we going to build it right now?" she asked. "Or could we just talk for a while?"

He looked startled. "I was just seeing what's here."

Parni felt at a loss. His daughter wanted him to converse in that self-revealing style he found so unattractive. He had not talked like that since May-Annlouise. She had been the only one ever able to coax intimate conversation out of him and she did it with ruthless strategy. First she would confess something to him—the lonesomeness she'd suffered at her high school graduation, or the bizarre anger she'd held toward her parents for making the family live for three years in a trailer on the site where they were building their dream house. "My father even drafted the blueprints!" she had told him. "And it *was* a dream house, but children don't dream about real estate. At least, I didn't. I dreamed about sex." Then she would ask Parni questions, one after another. Complex, tricky questions, always with the words *how* or *why* in them. He would begin a sentence and find to his horror the prospect of disclosure gaping before him like a gorge suddenly opening in his path. Softly she would urge him to continue, and he would choose his words one at a time. No one had ever penetrated his chinks so well.

In his palm, he now hefted one of the bitty thrones and thought of the armchair he had once raised above his head, so high its legs scraped across the living-room ceiling of the apartment he shared with May-Annlouise and the unborn child of whose existence he'd just been informed. That evening, he'd been wearing a satiny shirt with horses galloping across his breast; he could still smell the cologne he'd worn back then, an admittedly juvenile scent—sweet and loud, and applied so strongly as to scream for attention. On the record player spun the new album Parni had bought. He was teaching himself to disco dance and had wanted to go to a club that night, when May-Annlouise brought up the fact of her pregnancy. It was the revelation of this child that altered the course of his life, that, in fact, prompted him to introduce to the scene Nazar, who had been begging him to let her conceive before he was ready. When exactly he made this foolish decision, he was not quite sure, but the train of his logic ran along these lines: the baby would placate both women and allow him to consolidate his affairs. Even this mediocre plan would not occur to him for several days, and still gripped in the panic of May-Annlouise's tidings, he smashed the chair. It cracked so loudly when it struck the floor that she screamed in fright. He then doubled over, clutching his stomach; there seemed to be splinters sticking inside him. Slumped on the floor, he pulled his ankles close to him. The chair legs had made dark streaks against the ceiling.

Parni now put the miniature back in its paper wrapping. He looked at the large crate skeptically, aware of all the pieces inside and doubtful he and Lynn would be able to build it in the short time she'd be visiting.

Lynn had never seen such a long line of people as stood to get into the Palace of Tranquility. The festival marking the end of "foreign entanglements," her papa explained sourly, put all the locals in a historical mood. Lynn wondered if her papa considered her "foreign."

He'd been reluctant to bring her here, but she'd insisted. And when Garrett said he'd stay behind and take Nazar to lunch, Nazar seemed so happy! Papa didn't like that idea either, but Nazar took a deep breath and said, "Too bad! We're going out to lunch!"

Even more than Papa, Nazar seemed to have grown old in the last ten years. A sorrow, like gravity, pulled her toward the ground. Lynn thought it might be due to Nazar's not having any children of her own. She felt bad for Nazar and tried to call her Mama whenever possible.

But Lynn relished having her father to herself for the afternoon. As their line inched forward, they passed the fort walls, made from blocks of sandstone each as tall as Lynn herself and together jutting fifty feet into the sky, completely obscuring her view of the palace within. Whoever had lived here, she concluded, had certainly been well protected.

Heat rose off the cobblestone walkway up through her sneakers, making her feet sweat. A girl her own age, wearing a stained sari, walked up to them and tied a bracelet of loosely strung flower petals around Lynn's wrist. Introducing herself as Reena, the girl explained in very good English that the flowers were a gift and she didn't want any money.

"Good," said Papa, turning away from her.

"What is your name? Where are you from?" she asked.

Lynn responded bashfully.

"That is a pretty name," said the other girl. "Lynn, I am going to tell you something. My little sister needs powdered milk. A can of powdered milk. They are selling this right over here—"

"What do you think?" shouted Papa. "That we are tourists?"

"She says she is U.S." Reena took a step back.

"Yes, yes, but *I* am not U.S.! I am not U.S.!" He then launched a tirade in Urdu—spoken forcefully enough to drive Reena far down the line.

"But her sister—" Lynn whimpered.

"There is no sister."

"How do you know?"

"I know it," he said wearily. "That girl is laughing at us right now."

"But she seemed truly poor."

"Of course she's poor," her father snapped.

After rounding the corner, they entered a large gate and beheld the palace, a glorious assemblage of cusped archways, bulbous domes, and ornate pillars. By this point, her papa had relaxed a bit and begun speaking eloquently on the fine workmanship they passed: vines of jade inlaid against marble, and complex geometric patterns that displayed the designers' hunger for orderly beauty.

Her hand in his, they moved along with the thick crowd past a tapestry of Muhammad Kahn, the provincial sultan who'd presided over the palace's "golden age," according to a plaque. Muhammad Kahn was also an avid writer of poetry, other plaques went on to say, and his literary *mehfils* were attended by a large and erudite community.

"He was a nobleman of tremendous cultivation," Papa told her. "Have you read any of his verse?"

Lynn confessed she'd never even heard of the man, and this caused Papa to pinch his brow. His scowl only deepened as they passed later plaques detailing how the sultan's line died out with his great-grandson Ibrahim and how the palace eventually came under control of the British civil service.

She and her father toured dozens of rooms, most of them empty, and he became more and more critical of the government's negligence. "That *jali* screen is chipped," he muttered and found much else in disrepair.

In one especially small room, they waited their turn to look at a canopy bed with velvety covers. Lynn was so tired from standing and walking. Her calves hurt again—they had been hurting a lot this year. She wanted to lie down, and might have if there hadn't been so many people in the room.

Her father glared at the bed. "British flotsam—this piece doesn't belong," he said. "The curator is sloppy."

Lynn had worries of her own. How could anyone consider such a huge palace home? She wanted to know where the children slept—if their rooms were in the main wing, or whether children had ever been allowed to live here at all. The marble floor was so hard and slick that they would always be falling down and bruising themselves.

Her papa led her deeper into the complex of buildings and courtyards, until, at its very heart, they came to a small round chamber with a domed ceiling—the tomb of Muhammad Kahn and his wife. Roped off in this room's center rested two slabs of marble, each about the size of a twin bed, one black and the other white and both inscribed with Arabic letters.

Lynn stood pressed against the constraining rope. Because of her position under the dome, every cough and sniffle reverberated. Her thoughts turned inward to when she'd been very very young, taking Suzuki piano, and her first recital. Her mother and Papa and Nazar were all in the audience, the three of them sitting in the front row, resembling a white piano key followed by two dark ones: Lynn couldn't stop thinking of them as C, C#, and D#. She was so conscious of wanting to devote equal attention to each of these notes that she forgot her piece in the middle of playing. Her teacher called out the next phrase, but Lynn placed her fingers on the wrong keys; discord lingered in the still recital hall. On the verge of tears, she gave up and had to leave the stage. Now, ten years and ten thousand miles away, the melody returned to her and she began humming earnestly: C-E-G-E-D-D#-E . . . it went. She wanted to tell her papa she loved him, but noticed he was frowning again.

"What's that?" he asked her.

"The Worm Comes Out When It Rains."

He recast his gaze toward the inscribed marble slabs and remained silent for a long time. Finally, she couldn't hold herself any longer and had to know, "What does it say?"

Startled from his reverie, he read to her in a scratchy whisper. "*This present life is no other than a pastime and a disport.*" Lynn could hear him with perfect clarity, as intimately as if his mouth rested against her ear. "*But truly the future mansion is life indeed.*"

"Is that one of Muhammad Kahn's poems?" she asked him, eager to know. "Is he talking about the afterlife?"

"No. And yes." He regarded her sadly. "I don't suppose your mother has promoted your Islamic education." She shook her head.

He directed them to the small gift-and-book shop near the exit of the palace complex. There Lynn bought two postcards of the tomb, one to send home and one to keep. Her papa was thumbing through Qur'ans, in search of a good translation for her. After she'd paid for her purchase, Lynn stood in the shop's doorway, rubbing her sore calves and waiting for him. The muscles above her ankles felt twisted and stretched to the point where they might rip.

There was an armchair in front of the shop, and although it seemed very old, there was no rope protecting it, and Lynn thought it might even be for sale. It seemed to match some of the miniature chairs in the model. Delicate vines curled along the armrests and feet.

She inched her way toward the chair, knowing she should probably ask her father's permission first, but afraid the answer would be no, and she desperately wanted to sit down for a minute. The fabric felt plush against her hand like moss on a dry rock. She turned and gingerly lowered herself onto the seat, gripping the leafy armrests. The chair seemed sturdy enough to support her; still, she immediately felt guilty and decided she'd better get up. Just as she started raising herself, her papa pushed through the crowd, shoving people out of his way to get to her.

"You mustn't sit there," he said and grabbed her arm.

Parni tried to separate Leena from the old chair before some great damage was done. So bold, this American girl, he thought.

"Please don't sit there," he said, trying his best to sound gentle, hoping to mask his distress. When he reached for Leena's arm to help her up, she flinched—not all the way out of his grasp, but enough so that he could feel the tug of her arm against his fingertips.

In confusion, he muttered a few scolding words about respect for the emblems of one's heritage, though his heart was burdened by some other, lingering sadness, as he thought of the chair he himself had so badly misused years before.

"My legs hurt," she explained, rubbing the back of her left

calf through the fabric of her pants. "Sometimes they hurt so bad they feel like they're going to break."

They were long slender legs, he noticed; perhaps she should be taking ballet. He wondered if she liked the ballet. Perhaps she had never even seen one. He did not know, it pained him to admit. He did not know.

How much he had to learn!

How much he had to teach her!

He noticed his own calves aching with a tenderness he had never felt before but would feel again, he suspected, more often with each passing year.

"What would help?" he asked her.

"Some milk," she whispered.

He guided her back into the old green chair and told her he'd return at once. Hurrying along a restless hallway, he hopped over nicks and cracks in the marble floor. Where in this crumbling mausoleum was there a glass of milk for his baby girl?

five

Changeling

They dressed up for the fertility clinic. May-Annlouise wore a red silk sheath, and Garrett wore his charcoal suit. As they sat in the waiting room, her hem brushed her calf and she was ashamed to realize she looked sexy. *How inappropriate,* she thought, and noticed the other woman in the room, lumpy under a Yale sweatshirt, with dark circles under her eyes. She scared May-Annlouise. *Will I look like that before this is all over?* she wondered. *Will I suffer like that?*

She turned her attention to the stark oak coffee table in mission style, and the primitive washing board and single-blade plow hanging on one wall, which gave the waiting room a frontier feel. Doctor visits disturbed her. Whenever she thought of doctors, she thought of cool dry hands taking her measure. But

Dr. Maia Bang strode into the waiting room exuding something—*different.* She was very short, with Picasso-like features:
a large nose—double-humped like a camel—splotchy skin, red
shaggy hair, and, strangely, one brown eye and one blue. Most
of all, May-Annlouise noticed the doctor's damp handshake—
her palm even felt gritty, as though she'd not washed it in a
while. For some perverse reason, this charmed May-Annlouise,
who felt she was holding the creative hand of an artist.

Dr. Bang led the way into her office, sat on the edge of her
desk, one loafer tucked behind the other, and invited May-
Annlouise and Garrett to use the two armchairs.

"Thank you," said Garrett, "Dr. . . . am I pronouncing it
right: *Bang?*"

"Yup." Her smile was a little crooked. "It's Norwegian."

"My second husband was Norwegian," said May-Annlouise
and immediately regretted introducing herself that way—it
could not possibly make for a sterling first impression, and, in
fact, the doctor seemed to raise one of her shaggy eyebrows.

"Do either of you have any children already?" she asked.

"I have two," admitted May-Annlouise, handing over the
file from her gynecologist. "One from each of my, um, my
previous marriages." *Oh, brother, she thinks I'm a slut,* May-
Annlouise feared, *or worse, she thinks I'm greedy.*

Dr. Bang made a notation on her clipboard and took a moment to browse through the file. She went on to ask them about
their efforts so far to have a baby and their expectations now.
May-Annlouise had simple, perhaps naive expectations: Dr.
Bang would help them conceive, and then their family would

be complete. Somehow she could not acknowledge this out-right. As she searched for a more circumspect answer, the doctor had this to say:

"First of all, I'm going to try to talk you out of the idea. IVF costs a fortune. It's a hormonal roller coaster. The whole procedure can really rock your world. And there's no guarantee of success—far from it."

May-Annlouise wondered what her chances for success might be. She thought of the lumpy Yalie in the waiting area and found arising in herself an ugly, competitive impulse to contrast her own prospects against this other woman's.

Garrett was pinching the crease of his slacks. "Why are you being so negative?" he asked the doctor. "Don't you want couples to do this? I mean, isn't it food on your table?"

May-Annlouise frowned at her husband; he took her hand and squeezed it, seeking alliance, and gazed at her as though they alone occupied the room. May-Annlouise, whose previous two husbands usually ignored her, always found Garrett's attentions disarming.

"I have enough food, Mr. Hughes," the doctor was saying. "I think it's important for you to know what you're getting into."

She handed them a packet of paperwork to take home and study. "If you do decide to forge ahead, I hope you'll consider signing the release form that allows us to use any extra eggs, should that contingency come up."

"Extra?" asked Garrett.

"We're occasionally able to match them with women who can't afford to hire their own donors, for example. It's always best to address these issues in advance."

"I, um," stammered May-Annlouise; something about the idea made her queasy. "I'll think about it," she promised.

During the car ride home, Garrett made some joke about Dr. Bang's parents living in a petri dish.

"You don't like her because you think she's ugly," said May-Annlouise and conceded, "She is sort of—"

"What?"

"I keep thinking of a Norwegian troll. What an awful thing to say."

"Didn't she seem somehow unhygienic? What if one of her eyelashes lands in our embryo? The baby could come out covered with red fur."

"Well, if we want to make a baby together, just you and me," said May-Annlouise, "what's a little red fur?"

"But that's what I mean—it's not just you and me. And isn't there some old myth about trolls swapping their own babies for human babies? Why would they do that?"

May-Annlouise shrugged. "Better schools?"

They returned home to Crosslinks Village, the tidy northern-suburb community where they'd bought a house last year. It always surprised her, the tremendous comfort she took in watching the striped railroad-style arm at the entrance gate rise to let them in.

They had both taken the day off work, and the children weren't due home from school for another two hours. Hungry for some purely recreational sex for a change, May-Annlouise indicated this to her husband by pressing him against the towel rack in the master bathroom. "You're mine," she whispered in his ear and began to undress him.

To make up for her previous marriages, May-Annlouise tended to dominate in this one. Garrett was three years younger, had never been married before, and was the most accommodating of all her husbands. True, she sometimes felt lonely being the one to make so many decisions about the children, about money, about sex. Not all of the decisions all of the time, certainly, but most of them most of the time; Garrett was that accommodating. She considered her first husband, Parni, and how she wouldn't mind a dose of his callous manhandling right now. But you couldn't get just a dose of it; you had to sign on for the whole demeaning package. More and more it occurred to her lately, this seemed the choice all married people made: one either took charge or was taken charge of. As she humped Garrett standing up, she turned her head for a moment and watched her mirrored ass clench with each push as though she were stapling him to the wall. "You're *mine*," she promised him fiercely now.

That evening, retreating to the backyard gazebo, her refuge and favorite part of the house, she read about the hormones she would be given—culled from the urine of other women, and designed to make her ovaries "blister" with extra eggs. Could it be that what helped one woman become life-bearing could be found, cultured, and conveyed from the urine of another? Who were these other women? Were they poor? She pictured an assembly line of third-world inmates, hooked up to catheters, each woman squeezing out her last drops for pennies.

May-Annlouise pressed one arm against her stomach as she read painful descriptions of needles boring through her vaginal wall or abdomen.

"What's that?" Lynn asked, appearing from nowhere. The girl wrapped a warm brown arm around May-Annlouise, and together they looked at a photo of scarred fallopian tissue. May-Annlouise closed the booklet when she saw her daughter's teenaged face tighten at the idea that such intimate territory could somehow be marred.

"Is that what's wrong with you?" the girl asked.

"Um, possibly."

May-Annlouise felt her daughter lean slightly away. A stab of shame; her children's questions could pierce her like nothing else. Certainly, years ago, when Lynn had asked where her father and Nazar had suddenly gone, that had been the hardest. "The other side of the world, honey," was the best May-Annlouise could muster at the time.

"So," she said now, changing the subject, "what should I make for your school picnic?"

Lynn shrugged. "You don't have to. You've got bigger problems."

"Of course I'm going to make something," insisted May-Annlouise. "I just haven't decided what."

Dr. Bang emerged from her office with one arm around a young woman: dark and bony with bloodshot eyes. The doctor spoke to her half in Spanish, half in English. When they got to the front door, Dr. Bang sent her off with a final stroke of the shoulder and said, "You've got my home number if you need me."

In the examining room now, the doctor asked May-Annlouise to sit on the freshly papered tabletop and had her pull up her hem. Garrett took a seat in the room's far corner. Dr. Bang opened a drawer of glass ampules; they clinked together—the sound of a toast.

May-Annlouise had always been sensitive to any kind of drug. The wine in fondue was enough to intoxicate her. A cup of coffee could make her eyelids flutter, which is why she drank only apricot herbal tea, even in the morning. She told Dr. Bang all of this, and the doctor replied that they would carefully monitor her response. May-Annlouise wanted to be reassured, and she thought of the young woman to whom the doctor had spoken in such dulcet Spanish. "Who was she?" May-Annlouise blurted out. "Who was that pretty girl who just left?"

"A client," murmured the doctor, while filling a syringe, as though she were a large mosquito.

"She's so young," said May-Annlouise. "And how can she afford you?" The question had just come out; she hadn't meant for it to sound arrogant or racist.

"Well, now, don't you fret about that," the doctor said, not unkindly, as she swabbed May-Annlouise's thigh with cool alcohol-soaked cotton.

"And you gave her your home phone number?" May-Annlouise marveled out loud, unable to stop puzzling over this extraordinary doctor.

"I'll give it to you as well, so you won't feel left out." Dr. Bang smiled. "By the way, have you thought any more about signing our release?"

Oh, damn. Just as May-Annlouise was starting to relax. "You know—about that. I have to say I'm kind of uncomfortable—casting myself to the winds. I'm sorry."

"All right then." Dr. Bang approached with the needle. "Perhaps you'd prefer to close your eyes?"

After the initial prick, May-Annlouise felt a tingle spread along her leg as though her body thirsted for whatever it had just been given.

"Thank you," she said for some reason.

"You're welcome," said the doctor and winked her one blue eye.

That night, after she tucked Lynn into bed, May-Annlouise noticed on the girl's dresser a letter written on skin-fine airmail stock and flagged with brilliant stamps. It quivered in the window breeze.

May-Annlouise glimpsed the return address, penned in cryptic Arabic letters that looked like enlarged microbes. Why hadn't Lynn mentioned that her father was writing to her, beyond his yearly card? Had she and Parni developed a steady correspondence? *What sort of things was he telling her?*

Suppressing an unruly desire to read the letter, May-Annlouise backed out of the room.

In bed, the burning in her leg prevented her from sleeping on her favored side. She had bad dreams and woke up at dawn with a strange licorice taste in her mouth, a black and bitter taste that scared her until she swallowed most of it away. All her limbs ached; someone apparently had borrowed her body during the night for a game of beach volleyball, or at least some rigorous gardening.

When Garrett's alarm clock woke him at seven, he stopped

it with a groping hand and curled against her, tracing a finger-tip along the damp cave behind her knee until she twitched away from him. He offered to stay home, but May-Annlouise, wanting the day to herself, urged him to go to work. He kissed her neck, rolled out of bed, and shuffled toward the bathroom in his pajamas. She told him to leave her some hot water. That's when he stopped and looked at her queerly.

"You just called me Parni," he said.

She blinked.

"You just called me Parni," he repeated.

"I'm sorry, dearest," she said, pulling the sheet up to her mouth. "I'm still asleep. Don't pay any attention to me."

After he left with the children, May-Annlouise crept out of bed until she was standing under the warm pulse of the shower. Having taken the day off work, she gave little thought to time. Then, somewhat awake and feeling unusually warm, she padded naked into the kitchen to make something for the school picnic. The cupboards offered few choices, and she kept searching until she found a sack of onions. Three pounds of onions, as yet unopened and already they were starting to develop little green toes.

She broke the papery skins with her fingernails and denuded each onion over the sink, pulling out onion within onion, a universe of onions. She had some vague goal in mind, not so much a recipe as a taste that her hands were working toward. Her eyes stung bitterly, but she didn't stop until the entire three pounds lay in pieces before her on the counter.

Tossing the onions into a black skillet over a high flame, she then drizzled some olive oil. Finally, she reached for a bottle of *samsa* pepper puree, years old and originally brought into the country and into her kitchen by Nazar. Yellow resin had sealed the cork stopper tight, and May-Annlouise twisted with her entire body before the bottle opened. She dropped an ample dollop of the dark red paste into the skillet, where it began to spatter like a string of firecrackers. Sparks of oil leapt out and stung here and there: just over her navel—on the outer curve of her left breast. She didn't bother to step back, but merely noticed each twinge as it traveled the length of her nervous system.

She remembered a festive moment from years before: Lynn's first-birthday dinner. May-Annlouise and Nazar were united in their zeal to prepare a wonderful meal of celebration. Side by side they cooked, May-Annlouise melting cubes of dark chocolate and Nazar simmering something—was it onions?—in *samsa* pepper, producing an aroma very much like this one. Flour dusted the black hairs along Nazar's arms. Hip grazed against hip as the two women moved around the small kitchen. Nazar searching for a wooden spoon and May-Annlouise showing her where to find it.

They were even having a friendly conversation about Parni, about his foibles, of which there were many. And then Nazar had to spoil the day by belaboring her *claim* on him, stressing how she'd been married to him since age nineteen and how he'd returned to India for her in order to honor his *commitment*—even though he'd wed May-Annlouise in the meantime.

"One of the riddles to Parni," Nazar babbled on, " is that he cannot let go of anything he has acquired." She took May-

Annlouise's chocolate-splattered hands and tried to look directly at her. "Such a trait inevitably affects the human beings around him."

Just because her husband was a bigamist didn't mean May-Annlouise had to stand there in her own kitchen and discuss this. "Well, I know how it's affected me," she said, refusing to meet the older woman's gaze, then pulled away and turned toward the sink, where she ran her hands under the tap to wash away the chocolate. . . .

Now, May-Annlouise ladled her still-smoldering creation into a glass bowl and sealed it under cellophane. She slid her body into a cotton skirt and a light blouse, and after setting the VCR to record *All My Children*, she drove past the golf course and beyond the gate of Crosslinks Village toward the picnic, stopping on the way for another injection. Supposedly she could have given herself these shots, but she felt more secure having Dr. Bang do it.

May-Annlouise arrived at the city park behind her children's school at noon, cradling her big bowl of onions. Warm for autumn, the day was almost hot. She walked past the park fountain—two women hoisting cracked urns through which water spilled ceaselessly. A blue jay stood drinking from the fountain's lip and then screamed.

Already kids were gathering around the long tables that had been decorated with crepe paper and pumpkins. A few fathers meandered across the grass, but mothers were everywhere: arranging the plates of sandwiches and cookies, pouring lemonade into small paper cups, and making change for the students' play money. Apparently, the Brandon Academy was using the school picnic to provide lessons in consumer awareness and personal finance.

A profoundly pregnant woman, wearing an outsized rugby shirt, took May-Annlouise's dish from her and uncovered it. "This smells heavenly," said the woman and set it next to a stack of sandwiches marked PB&J—$3. "What's it called?" she asked, marker poised. May-Annlouise stared at the woman's striped stomach and the name tag clinging between her breasts—SANDY—and tried to remember what Nazar had called similar dishes, but could only think to say, "Onions." Sandy smiled and wrote on the note card, ETHNIC SURPRISE—$5.

Looking at the array of cupcakes, crackers, and individually wrapped slices of American cheese, May-Annlouise knew her Ethnic Surprise would likely go untouched, and she wondered why she'd brought such an unsuitable dish. As she walked away from the table, however, she saw Sandy spoon a large serving for herself. She smiled at May-Annlouise, and soon there seemed to be a fold of pregnant women around that end of the table, all devouring her onions. "Cajun," said one of them brightly.

Empty-handed without her glass bowl, May-Annlouise walked with her arms crossed in front of her. She paused under the shade of an oak to scan the crowd for Turpin. The boy soon walked up to her, flipping through a wad of bills.

"We're doing a unit on hostile takeovers," he said, flashing her a fake twenty. "I got a perfect score."

She told him to put his play money away. "Do you have any new friends this year you'd like me to meet?" she asked.

"No," he said. "Come on, Mom. Let's have lunch. I'm buying."

"Where's your sister?"

The boy shrugged. In the sunshine, his hair glowed, impregnably white. This hair, passed down from his Nordic father, always amazed her—how unlikely for such a creature to have once slithered out of her body.

He led her to a table where kids were jockeying for prime spots, holding up little fistfuls of dollars and calling out orders as at a commodities exchange. A tiny blond girl asked one of the mothers to sell her two peanut butter and jelly sandwiches for five dollars and then promptly resold one of them to her friend for $2.75. May-Annlouise cringed. She tried to recall: were all the school events this obnoxious?

Turpin wormed his way back through the crowd. He'd "scored" the last tuna sandwiches and a can of Jolt soda that some mother was insane enough to have brought. May-Annlouise's face pulsed with warmth, and sweat began to drip down the bridge of her nose. The fountain beckoned her. Several of the pregnant women had taken off their shoes and were sitting by the edge, dangling their swollen feet in the clear water. May-Annlouise eyed them enviously, glancing at her own delicate ankles.

A hand touched her shoulder and she flinched. It was her daughter. "You made onions."

"How did you know?" asked May-Annlouise and brushed a crumb off the girl's olive-brown cheek. Lynn resembled her even less than Turpin did, except for a downward cast to the eyes and a beauty mark over the corner of her mouth. May-Annlouise had one in the exact same place, and she used to take comfort—when Lynn had been little—touching each beauty mark in turn, reassuring herself of their sameness.

"Nazar used to make onions." She was wearing the Indian-flag sweatshirt her father had sent for her last birthday. Extra-large, at her request, it billowed over her figure, hiding the curves that seemed to embarrass her.

How on earth did she remember those onions? "You were just a baby."

"So what? I remember everything." The girl stubbed her sneakers against the grass.

May-Annlouise stepped forward to hug her, but a chime rang, summoning the students back to class. Turpin handed his mother the remains of his Jolt and asked if she'd take it home for him.

"You must have me confused with your maid, young man," she said and grazed a wisp of his white hair with her lips before he escaped her reach. She turned back toward Lynn to try that hug again, but her daughter had disappeared.

May-Annlouise collected her glass bowl and waited until the other mothers left before venturing near the fountain. She waded into the shallow water, which lapped teasingly against her shins. Sunshine glittered painfully bright. She was dizzy from the heat, and the coolness around her ankles only made her feel more so, as though her feet were no longer connected to her but belonged to someone else.

Her husband had defrosted a casserole, which she now chewed with determination, trying to satisfy some faraway craving. She ate ravenously, making up for the lack of flavor with quantity.

Turpin shoved away his plate and patted his stomach. "I got full at the picnic."

"You should finish what you've taken," his sister argued. "There are starving children in India."

"That's ridiculous," complained Turpin.

"No it's not. I've seen them."

"I mean," Turpin argued, "they're irrelevant."

"You're irrelevant."

"They're irrelevant to this particular plate of food, you irrelevant smellephant."

"Hey there, you two," said May-Annlouise, not sure where to begin. How did she usually handle this sort of situation? Some admonition seemed called for, but she heard a babel of voices in her ear, some siding with Turpin and others with Lynn. "Stop it!" she shouted.

Both her children recoiled in unison.

Later that evening, May-Annlouise checked on them after they'd gone to sleep. She closed the book her daughter had been reading—careful to mark the girl's place with an emery board—before noticing its title. The Qur'an, she read with a spasm of heartburn, "Selected Suras."

Outside, leaves rustled in the wind, and May-Annlouise found an afghan in the trunk at the foot of the bed and lightly spread it across her daughter. She then turned off the bedside light with her right hand and stole the letter with her left.

Next to Garrett's sleeping body, she unfolded the feather-light pages. They trembled against her shaking knees, and she had to close her eyes a moment and breathe deeply before she could steady herself enough to read. The letter talked about a palace, or a model of some palace, that Parni was building in Lynn's honor. "I have finally installed the last of the furnishings! We are awaiting a visit from you for a proper ribbon ceremony. You'll be seventeen soon," he went on. In their city, Parni and Nazar knew some nice boys from good families; perhaps an introduction could be made, possibly even an engagement, if that was not too presumptuous. "Nazar has been nagging me: 'Even if I am not a real mother,' she says, 'I am eager to become a grandmother!'"

An arranged marriage? May-Annlouise shuddered. *In India? Or is he hatching a new scheme to return stateside?*

At the bottom of the page curled a few Arabic squiggles. May-Annlouise puzzled over these, held them under the dim lamplight, looked at them sideways and upside down, and eventually found herself reading into their curves and angles a slicing pain. She stared at the very last characters—until they blurred before her eyes—and she whispered: *treasured . . . daughter.*

How could that be? May-Annlouise hastily refolded the shaking pages. Parni hadn't even *wanted* Lynn when May-Annlouise had first told him she was pregnant. The entire basis of her memory of him rested on that simple fact. It shook her to think her ex-husband could have changed so much. How had he come to write such a tender line? How had she come to understand it?

In the middle of the night, she dialed Dr. Bang's home number. Someone picked up on the ninth ring, and a deep, clotted voice coughed its way toward human sound. May-Annlouise finally recognized the doctor, and insisted the injections were not going to work out.

"You need patience," murmured the sleepy voice at the far end of the line. "What you're going through isn't unusual."

"It *is* unusual."

A raspy sigh. "Only to you. But there've been other women before you on this path. And other women will follow. Think about them."

"I don't *want* to think about them," she whispered into the phone.

"If you still feel that way in the morning," said the fading voice, "call me back."

The women before and after her? What did they have to do with anything? Much more pressing, it seemed to her: Who were the women stretched languorously through her body? Who the hell were they? She felt them settle into her joints and between her organs. When they turned in their sleep, they woke her up. She didn't want to think about them. She wanted nothing to do with them. How on earth was she supposed to get rid of them?

May-Annlouise smelled *samsa* pepper.

Nazar used to dump it on everything; she even reeked of it herself, her skin, her sweat. A burnt flower, that's what it smelled like. On the evening that Parni had returned from one of his many business trips abroad—returned this time with Nazar in tow—he pleaded with May-Annlouise to let the stranger stay. He described the direst of slums from which she'd supposedly come, though this theme seemed conveniently embellished.

"In your land of plenty, you cannot even conceive of such poverty, my love," he told her, on his knees, as if proposing.

"*Our* land of plenty," she reminded him.

He raved about what a fine cook Nazar was, and in this way made the new woman seem to be some sort of live-in help. Nazar waited in the hallway, clutching a frayed carpetbag and a large bottle of Chanel, a peace offering for May-Annlouise, picked out and paid for by Parni. Of course it would become apparent soon enough that Nazar was really Parni's wife; May-Annlouise intuited this from the start. She wasn't stupid.

This is who May-Annlouise was at the time: she was twenty-one years old. She was an orphan with no family to fall back on. She had a six-month-old baby girl to care for. She was living on four hours of sleep a night. Her back hurt. She earned a small salary as a travel agent, and yet she was expected to believe that she was, relative to Nazar, rich and powerful. And maybe so! The idea was sadly exciting. Nazar moved into the spare room.

In the beginning, if Parni was sleeping with her, he was discreet enough to do it when May-Annlouise was out of the apartment. After a few months, however, he took to alternating nights between the two women. May-Annlouise was surprised to learn that she just didn't care that much. Most of her energy went to the baby, and this left her exhausted. It was almost a blessing, having another body for her husband to grope. And Nazar was in fact a wonderful cook and cleaned as though her life depended on it. Once in a while, May-Annlouise even left the baby at home with her.

On top of all this, Nazar turned out to be the most amazing seamstress. She made shirts and slacks for Parni and soon all manner of clothes for Lynn—a brown corduroy jumper and gingham culottes and, without a thought to practicality, a fancy *salwar kameez* that Lynn was so taken with she would wear it around the apartment. "We'll save thousands," Parni crowed when he bought the used sewing machine for Nazar.

This flurry of production seemed magical and suspect to May-Annlouise, who would leave for work in the morning noticing a bolt of fabric on the dining room table and come home in the evening to find the material transformed into blouses, pants, and vests. As a Christmas present, Nazar made silk pajamas for everyone. Parni's were rust-colored with white piping and an elaborate *P* embroidered on the breast pocket. She gave to May-Annlouise a lime-green pair with purple piping and the monogram *M-A*. No one had ever made for her anything so luxurious; the silk lay blissfully soft against her nipples. She felt strange accepting such an intimate gift from her adversary, but really the pajamas were quite lovely.

Lynn, of course, adored hers. She was growing so fast Nazar would make a larger but otherwise identical pair every few months. Constantly fussing over the child with a measuring tape, Nazar seemed hot to be a mother. May-Annlouise overheard her pulling out all kinds of reasons to convince Parni:

Lynn needed a playmate; May-Annlouise wouldn't have to take leave from her job to have another baby; waiting would just make things harder—"my eggs," she complained, "are becoming old and useless."

May-Annlouise wasn't sure where she stood on this issue. Maybe with a kid of her own Nazar wouldn't hover over Lynn so much.

One winter morning, May-Annlouise walked past Nazar's bedroom, saw the fuchsia sheen of Lynn's pajamas, and watched from the hallway as Nazar tickled the girl's stomach while Parni smiled indulgently. They were all three in bed, a riot of giggles, squirming silk, and pillows. Outside, flurries began to fall, but the bedroom was warm and filled with the milky sweetness of recent sleep. Nazar cooed: "Who loves little Leena?" and Lynn laughed back, "Mama Nazar." Nazar stroked a long fingernail across Lynn's pink-soled foot, and the girl writhed with delight. "Who loves little Leena?" Nazar persisted. "Mama Nazar, Mama Nazar."

And then she touched it; *Mama Nazar* touched the beauty mark above Lynn's lip, and May-Annlouise felt her breakfast push against the top of her stomach. The air she breathed seemed to have no oxygen, and the brightly colored pajamas made her think of a car wreck.

"Come on, Lynn," she said from the doorway. "It's time for preschool."

"Oh, let her stay home with me," Nazar asked, smoothing the girl's collar.

"Not today." May-Annlouise gripped her daughter's wrist

and pulled her across the hallway into the girl's own room and removed the tiny pajama top so quickly that a button popped off. Lynn began to cry.

"You're upsetting the child with all this angriness," Nazar called out.

May-Annlouise didn't answer as she rifled Lynn's dresser for some tights. "Come on, sweetie, let's get these on." She then covered the girl in a purple dress that Nazar had made. Thinking better of it, she yanked off the purple and found an older plaid one, bought months before at Hutzler's and so snug that Lynn bulged against the fabric like a stuffed animal. She had stopped crying by now and stiffly allowed her mother to finish dressing her.

Even though the snow was starting to stick, May-Annlouise drove furiously, the car fishtailing at every turn. Lynn sat quietly strapped in beside her. The girl's eyebrows, thick and wild, pulled toward a knot of puzzled displeasure that her mother was to see again and again after dropping her off that morning at Tumble Tots.

May-Annlouise had been willing to withstand a lot so that Lynn might grow up knowing her father, but no more. She couldn't anymore. And Parni had done well enough for himself these past couple years, so nobody would starve. . . .

Instead of going to work, she drove straight back home. Parni and Nazar were getting dressed. The bedroom now smelled of sex—sex and *samsa* pepper—and Parni looked surprised to see her.

"You're back," he noticed.

"I'm back," said May-Annlouise.

"What was that all about?" he asked.

"Get out," said May-Annlouise. "Get the hell out of my home. Get the hell out of my country, or I'll put you in jail."

Nazar stood silently in the corner of her bedroom holding a blouse in front of her naked chest. She began to murmur something like, "unfair, dear."

"Quiet!" said May-Annlouise. "Not another word, or I'm calling Immigration." She glanced malignantly at the Princess phone on the bedside table.

She would not let them wait to say good-bye to Lynn. She would not let them write the girl an explanatory note. She would not allow anything that would keep them in the apartment a minute longer than was absolutely necessary. She rounded up all the clothes that Nazar had sewn over the past two years, including the silk pajamas, crammed then into plastic garbage bags, and tossed everything into the hallway.

On his way out, Parni paused near the front door and said, "I'll come by for the sewing machine."

"It won't be here," said May-Annlouise and watched the two of them walk toward the elevator.

In her sleep, she must have swung and hit Garrett full force in the thigh. He sprang awake and yelped. "What are you doing?"

She had been closing the door. In real life she had shut it quietly, but in her dream she was slamming it. Parni stood by the elevator, as he had been years ago. She couldn't remember how far exactly Nazar had gotten down the hall; in any case, just now in the dream the older woman lagged behind and looked back over her shoulder. The elevator bell rang. The two women locked eyes. May-Annlouise expected to see simple hatred in Nazar's rich brown stare. But there was something else that May-Annlouise couldn't make out; it threatened her even more than hatred, so she slammed the door and leaned against it.

"What's going on with you?" Garrett asked her.

There was a lot going on with her. Dizzy much of the time, she had more energy than her old body knew what to do with, stretching the borders of her skin, buzzing against her eyes, and yanking—like some overeager dog on a leash—her own breath behind her. Bright lights now gave her headaches, and the slightest sound kept her awake. There was a blue jay in the backyard that screamed all the time as it raided the other birds' nests and devoured their eggs.

"Don't know," she said, certain he would not understand.

He kissed her temple. "Maybe we should drop the baby project," he said, moving on to her ear. "I don't trust those shots you're getting. They're a hormonal roller coaster."

"No," she said, pulling away. "It's not a project." She almost called him Parni again. Parni who had argued against having a baby with Nazar. His reluctance would only have grown since being banished to his homeland: India was still a poor country, and their child could have lived in the land of plenty. He would dwell on that loss, distracting him from the greater loss of not having another child—until it was too late. And then what would he and Nazar do? Nobody tried to raise fertility in a poor country, May-Annlouise bet, and even if there were fertility clinics and Parni was prospering, could they really afford it? What stranger's egg would pass muster?

"I just hate to see you like this," Garrett said, pulling her back from her reverie. "I want to help, but I feel so—so far away from wherever it is you are."

"Yes." She cupped his chin. "We'll ask the doctor to give you a shot so you won't feel left out."

"All right," he said. "I deserved that. Just tell me what I can *do*. Arrange an evening alone for us maybe? Just you and me? A special Wife's Day!" He traced a finger along the ticklish grooves of her palm. "Your favorite restaurant. Your favorite everything."

"We don't—" She kissed him and took back her palm, unsure what she might even want of him at that moment—convinced, in any case, that he couldn't provide it. "I don't know what my favorite is anymore," she said. There were more important decisions to be made.

During the next days, May-Annlouise became increasingly light-headed; she had to grab the edges of furniture in order to move around the house. Periodically, she would picture Nazar gazing at her. *Even if I am not a real mother, I am eager to become a grandmother!* Why did Nazar always have to drag Lynn into her plans?

The ground seemed to shift under May-Annlouise's feet. She no longer could drive herself to the doctor's office and took a cab instead. Her skin began to smell of *samsa* pepper, she was using so much of it in everything she ate.

"We want to ask you something," said May-Annlouise, as Dr. Bang jabbed her with a needle. The doctor focused both eyes on the plunger.

"If I sign the release, can I choose who gets some of my 'extra' eggs? Can they be frozen, these eggs? Shipped to a medical colleague abroad?" *Transplanted to a woman on the other side of the world?* "In theory," May-Annlouise asked, "is it possible?"

Dr. Bang laughed at this flurry of questions. "Every day," she said, "new things become possible. Must it be one of your own eggs?"

May-Annlouise pictured the pink arch of Lynn's foot, the beauty mark above her lip.

Yes.

❧

The harvest could be performed at Dr. Bang's office, in the procedure room. May-Annlouise presented her arm for the intravenous drip that was apt to put her "on Mars," as the doctor explained, "depending on how high I set it."

Dr. Bang swiveled on a squeaky stool and adjusted the angle of her ultrasound monitor. She asked if May-Annlouise preferred to watch what was going on or have her view obstructed.

"Watch," said May-Annlouise. Her husband, standing nearby, squeezed her hand.

With an assistant hovering at her side, Dr. Bang got to work. Behind her pale blue mask and under a pale blue bonnet, she looked even stranger than usual. Her eyes blinked steadily as she concentrated on May-Annlouise.

"Goodness, you've got great skin," the doctor said, touching the inside of May-Annlouise's thigh. "Like a woman in her twenties."

"Skin," said May-Annlouise. Someone squeezed her hand. She felt hot, her ovaries twin fireballs.

"Okay, here we go." Dr. Bang blinked rapidly.

On the monitor, May-Annlouise watched a satellite view of the Ganges. She wondered how many eggs she was producing today, and where exactly they would go once they'd left her body, and what, or who, they would become. She wondered how Parni and Nazar would respond to the letter she'd sent them. She wondered, for a brief moment, if she had made a terrible mistake in signing the release.

"Let me know if anything hurts," said Dr. Bang. As she continued to move inside May-Annlouise, the doctor's bonnet bobbed like the crest of a blue jay. May-Annlouise gasped, and her hand darted to her stomach.

"Did I hurt you?" the doctor asked, lowering her mask. She asked the question again, her lips moving in another language, her eyes, both a deep brown now, Nazar's. "Did I hurt you, dear?"

The paper gown over May-Annlouise clung to her sweat. She studied the eyes, forced herself to linger on them, and she came to understand what she had once seen in them by the elevator. It wasn't hate, and it wasn't envy, it was just aloneness.

"I know you didn't mean to," she told the eyes and lowered her own and hoped, for everyone's sake, that the harvest would be good.

six

Several Answers

It was an accident: Turpin opened the bathroom door at the very moment his older half sister emerged from her bath. Before she could cover herself, he found himself gawking at her breasts, rivulets of water still streaming across and between them toward the sodden patch of kelplike hair below.

"You're so lame!" she railed, towel now clutched to her throat.

"Sorry," mumbled Turpin, bumping his elbow against the doorjamb on his way out. Retreating to his room, he hunched over his math homework and stared at a parabolic curve, trying not to think about his sister. Her body had changed *a lot* since the last time he'd accidentally walked in on her. It wasn't just rounder and hairier; it seemed swept up in some sort of biological rapids.

He heard a click behind his head, turned to see his sister, clothed now, pointing her camera at him. She took another picture.

"Quit it," he said, raising his hands in front of his face.

"Why?" she asked, continuing to take pictures, using her camera's rapid film advancer. "Does this bother you?"

He wouldn't mind, really, if she were doing it to be nice.

"I said I was sorry," he told her. "I'll do your math homework."

"You're the reason Mom and Garrett have been trying so long to have a test-tube baby," she said, clicking off a dozen more frames. "They want to clone you. Except leave out the defective parts."

The finished roll began to rewind with a mechanical whir, and Turpin lowered his hands. "Come on, they can't do that."

"Nowadays they can do anything," she said, popping the film canister out and tossing it onto his desk.

That night, Turpin dreamed about in vitro fertilization. He pictured rows of test tubes—each containing an embryo with his own face—and his mother and stepfather consulting charts to determine which tubes they'd promote to the next level. In a way, it was kind of a compliment; he was good in school, for instance, and maybe they were trying to propagate that. On the other hand, maybe there were so many defective parts to get rid of, the final product might hardly resemble him.

Blurry-eyed from the night's restless sleep, he joined his

family for breakfast. His mother set up four small glasses in a neat row and filled them with orange juice, topping them off so she could dispose of the carton.

Turpin said he wasn't feeling well. "Maybe I should stay home today."

"Do you have a temperature?" His mother grazed her lips against his brow. "You seem normal. Are you sure you want to stay home?"

Turpin didn't know how she could possibly tell his temperature that way. "I guess I'll go to school."

"Are you sure? You can stay if you want."

Everyone had taken an orange juice; there was only one glass left. He wondered if lip prints left a usable DNA sample.

"Drink your juice," said his mother, "especially if you're not feeling well."

"But you said I was fine," he protested.

His half sister made a rectangle with her fingers and looked at him through it—pressed an invisible shutter.

"I'm sure you *are* fine." His mother cocked her head and sighed. "Fine, fine, fine."

Turpin definitely wasn't "fine." Too worked up for school that morning, he decided to play hooky at the mall, home to one of his favorite hangouts: an amazing gadget store called Life-Tools, which sold neon jogging belts, calorie-counting pet treadmills, dimmer switches controlled by the loudness of your voice.

"Do you have cloning kits?" he asked the salesgirl.

She said, "Not yet, but someday for sure." The lightest peach fuzz clung above her smile.

Turpin browsed anxiously, in search of something he couldn't quite picture. When suddenly, he saw his father.

His genetic father.

Once larger than life, with his thick hedge of beard and white teeth straight as blocks of limestone, Turpin's father had succumbed to a bizarre disease six years ago. Now, here stood a life-size cardboard cutout of a man who looked just like him, jogging along in a blue sweat suit, as part of a display for a gadget called PulseWatch. Some kind of wrist monitor that kept continuous track of a person's vital functions and allowed one to record encouraging aphorisms, like YOU CAN DO IT! and NO PAIN, NO GAIN!

The jogger smiled confidently at his PulseWatch, as if it were a treasured amulet, and the promise of technology whispered to Turpin. He reached for the demonstrator watch and strapped it to his wrist and listened to the heartening metronome of his existence. BEEP, BEEP, BEEP. . . .

IS THIS THING ON? BEEP, BEEP.

TELL DETECTIVE FERRAGAMO HE'LL FIND THE BANGALORE EMERALD UNDER . . . ARRGHHHH . . . BEEP, BEEP, BEEP. . . .

Browsers before him had crowded the watch's voice chip with odd messages. Turpin decided to add one of his own: MY MOTHER, he confided, WANTS TO CLONE ME. When played back, his message didn't quite convey the darkening sense of threat he felt, but the PulseWatch itself was definitely cool.

It cost $49.95—more money than Turpin carried. The mere thought of shoplifting quickened the beep from his wrist, impressing him all the more. He'd never stolen anything in his life. As a capitalist, he believed in everyone's right to keep an honestly earned dollar. But entranced by the PulseWatch and its ability to reveal his own life-beat, the verifiable quantum of his well-being, he felt the need to take action. He struggled to uncouple the demonstrator watch from its display.

"If only you'd owned one of these," Turpin said morosely to the cardboard likeness of his father, then plunged his beeping wrist into the hole-riddled pocket of his imitation hospital scrub pants. "Nowadays, they can do anything."

He pretended to drift aimlessly toward the dust ionizers in the next aisle. Then toward the exit.

At the door, he set off an alarm, the piercing whoop of an ambulance siren.

Turpin ran. Ran so swiftly, the tips of his sneakers yelped against the mall's hard waxed floor. Outside, sunshine gleamed through the leaves, at their peak of color; some had already fallen and now sputtered beneath his feet. A security guard sprinted toward him, then suddenly two, then four—a terrifying mitosis.

Vibrant with adrenaline, Turpin found himself beeping next to an idling car. The car beeped as well, to inform its driver— bent over the open trunk, arranging the awkward box of a new microwave oven—that his door was ajar. The two beeps beeped in harmony. Turpin ducked behind the steering wheel, then quickly oriented himself to the transmission, the emergency brake, the accelerator. He took a deep breath of new-car smell and floored it.

The thirteen-year-old had never driven before.

Clutching the steering wheel, he struggled to maintain a straight course. He drifted. He overcorrected. Sped and braked. Rumbled across potholes. The trunk lid flapping in his rearview mirror was no help at all.

And yet: he was a quick study. After a couple minutes, he was controlling the large machine with remarkable adequacy. He would drive himself far from the mall, head toward some obscure suburban pocket. Then park and escape. It was a plan. The power steering became an extension of his will.

FOUR SCORE AND SEVEN YEARS AGO, OUR FOREFATHERS— WHAT'S NEXT?

Turpin cruised past the Brandon Academy, the elite private school that had promoted him a year and a half ahead of his classmates (and would have promoted him even further except he lacked "sufficient emotional foundation," as his record put it). If he didn't show up soon, he would miss a quiz on the stock market and the reasons why the 1929 crash could never happen again, just one of them being new computer controls that automatically suspended trading in the event of a rapid decline.

The car was amazingly quiet. Turpin could barely hear the traffic around him. It felt like gliding through town in his own impenetrable pod.

MY MOTHER WANTS TO CLONE ME. BEEP, BEEP.

He didn't quite believe it—that his mother could clone him—but the more he thought about it, the whole in vitro thing seemed suspicious. In fact, his mother behaved in lots of suspicious ways, especially since his father's death. Nagging

Turpin to take vitamins, for instance. And then other times, like this morning, she'd insist, almost willfully, that he was fine. And what about his father's death itself? She'd actually let him spend his final weeks at home, even though she had just recently married Turpin's stepfather. She was a complex woman!

YOU ENSNARED MY WALTER WITH YOUR VOODOO, YOLANDA, AND NOW IT'S PAYBACK, GIRL. . . .

Though he'd been merely seven at the time, Turpin had kept vigil at his father's deathbed, handing him the big tattered atlas, even turning the pages for him. Yet the man died during a rare moment when Turpin had gone to the kitchen for an orange.

Turpin couldn't help but think about that moment from time to time and, paused at a red light, he thought about it now. He remembered tiptoeing toward his mother, who was speaking into the phone at length and who seemed to be leaving a detailed message on a machine—probably for one of the many doctors she'd consulted about his father's illness. He remembered her softly inquiring about "pain management." Then as Turpin passed her, she cupped his chin and looked him over. She began to describe him into the phone, his height and weight, his appetites and allergies, the frequency of his toilet visits. Her eyes a camera, she created a portrait of his physical body for the doctor, while Turpin stood still, frustrated but also enjoying the attention. His sleeping habits, his lactose intolerance—his mother seemed calmer with each detail, as though transmitting this information was somehow helpful to her and she was getting some burden off her chest. After a few more moments of this, she hung up, tousled his hair, and began to hum while she made dinner.

Feeling suddenly ignored and lonesome, Turpin got his orange and returned to the master bedroom only to find his father dead.

It wasn't Turpin's fault! His father had been urging him to eat more fruit. In fact, his last words to Turpin were *my fruit,* the exact meaning of which he'd been left to consider ever since.

A minivan—its crumpled rear devoured by rust—cut into his lane, and Turpin swerved, his right front hubcap scraping against concrete.

YOU ENSNARED MY WALTER WITH YOUR VOODOO, YOLANDA, AND NOW IT'S PAYBACK, GIRL. . . .

TELL DETECTIVE FERRAGAMO HE'LL FIND THE BANGALORE EMERALD UNDER . . . ARRGHHHH . . . BEEP, BEEP.

His pulse racing, Turpin spied what appeared to be a sleepy cul-de-sac, and he turned from the main artery, a little too narrowly as it happened, because the car's side panel kissed the corner of a parked station wagon, making a sound like the final twist of an inflated balloon animal. His wrists trembled as he inched the car further into the cul-de-sac.

FOUR SCORE AND SEVEN YEARS AGO, OUR FOREFATHERS— WHAT'S NEXT?

Trying now to angle into an open parking space along this stubbornly circular street, Turpin's foot slipped off the brake and onto the accelerator. The engine growled, and the car shot forward, hopping the curb and slamming now into a very solid utility pole.

As his chest and head hurtled toward the steering column, he saw stars—hundreds of them, suspended throughout the great void. *I'm going to die,* thought Turpin, the sounds of his watch now jumbled: TELL . . . MOTHER . . . WHAT'S NEXT? BEEP. FIND . . . REPLACE . . . FOREFATHERS . . . BEEP. VOODOO . . . VOODOO . . . TESTING . . . BEEP? ARRGHHHH . . . BEEEEEEEEP. He envisioned not his own life but his father's last moments, seen from a great height, as though Turpin were watching from the ceiling. Lying in bed, his father opened his eyes and glanced brightly around the room—looking for his son, who was in the kitchen getting an orange. On the man's right cheek blossomed a strange Texas-shaped rash, and his breath, shallow as it was, smelled of mildew and berries. His once-beefy hand groped across the unslept-on pillow beside him until he reached a dark thread, which he plucked carefully between thumb and forefinger and which Turpin recognized as an auburn strand of his own mother's hair. His father began to wrap it around his wrist, tried to tie a knot, his hands contorted from the effort. "Not yet," he implored the pillow. His last breath.

Now—Turpin's forehead having covered two-thirds the distance to the steering wheel and closing in rapidly—an air bag exploded with the sulfuric flash, pop, and fanfare of a vintage photograph. The bag rose to meet him, and its pressure felt like an imprint, an open palm penetrating beyond his face.

He heard his father's voice, not frail or rambling, as it had been toward the very end, but robust and keen. "We are given a moment to speak," the voice said. "That's nice."

What was this?

The man's voice seemed to emanate from within Turpin's own aching skull.

"Dad," he wondered, "where are you?"

"I have been assigned some interesting placements." Part of him, his father described, was a catfish at the bottom of Lake Titicaca. "Just the other day, while passing through the Ozarks, I recognized myself in a bowl of pipe tobacco." And, in Turpin's own neighborhood, Crosslinks Village, his father was serving as a patch of moss in the little park, by the slatted footbridge that spanned the creek.

"You're moss?" Turpin tried to picture it. "Dad, you were a famous explorer."

"Moss is important, son." He still spoke with his Norwegian accent. "It prevents erosion. Though I'll admit to you I was puzzled at first by some of these smaller assignments. They contradict reincarnation as I'd conceived of it, in which one whole being returns as another. But that version, of course, was an invention of human ego. Instead I am called upon to manifest on an as-needed basis."

"Oh," said Turpin, peering into the deep night sky in the hope he might glimpse something of his father.

"Son," the man said. "I behold your suffering, even from a great distance, and it moves me. Thus, I was allowed to occupy the airbag in this luxury import so you might have an opportunity to ask a few questions of me and perhaps ease whatever is troubling you."

"I thought you came through the watch," said Turpin.

"I was going to, but then I chose the bag."

Turpin cautiously considered what he might ask. "How many questions do I get?"

"Let us say 'several.' We won't count that one."

Turpin couldn't yet bring himself to raise his most burning subject, so he began with a smaller question, though one that still kept him up nights:

"Who does my mother love more, you or my stepdad?"

His father sighed—a gentle breath that caressed the underside of Turpin's scalp—and answered, "There was a chemical bond between your mother and me that a person is lucky to experience once in a lifetime. I do not wish to seem conceited on the matter."

For some reason, the pleasure from this answer buoyed Turpin like sea salt, and then, suddenly guilty, he made sure to check: "She does love him, right?"

"Yes, indeed. He's very sincere. Also, he tries his best not to hurt her, and she appreciates the novelty of that. He is open to her ideas regarding the bedroom. The vein along his forehead reminds her of the first boy she ever kissed. And by and large he likes to stay close to home. In general, he's very different from her first two husbands."

"You hurt her?" Turpin deduced.

"Once or twice. Out of carelessness."

Embarrassed, Turpin entertained a queasy curiosity about his mother's bedroom ideas but didn't want to spend a question on them. He decided he'd better brave his main concern.

"Is my mother having me cloned? Without the bad parts?"

His father laughed gustily. "No, no. That sort of procedure won't be available for many years; at least ten, I'd guess, long after you've reached legal age."

"So the test-tube baby has nothing to do with me?"

"Only so far as your mother's desire for another child might be heightened, let us say, by her fear of losing you someday to my illness."

Turpin swallowed dryly. His throat continued to tighten, and his next words came out higher—childlike and a little whiny. "But she told me I wouldn't get it. The doctors said."

"I see." His father paused. "Well, perhaps her fear was subconscious. I don't wish to contradict your mother."

"*Am* I going to get your disease?" Turpin asked meekly.

He waited through the most complete silence he'd ever had to endure. A pure and terrible silence. The silence of the void. Turpin began to fear he'd lost contact with his father. Until, finally, the man answered:

"Son, I simply do not know." He cleared his throat. "But if you do, it shouldn't affect you for many years, and just as likely, you will die of something else first. Possibly even something from your mother's side of the family. I'm sorry if I've divulged more information than you needed."

Suddenly angry, Turpin demanded: "Why didn't you go to the hospital when you were dying?"

"Because there was no cure."

"But you didn't even *try*." Outrage flared inside Turpin as he thought of his father's rapid decline and refusal of treatment, the absurd, feeble end of an otherwise Herculean life.

"Listen," the man said, annoyed, "I have nothing against medical science when it is appropriate. In fact, my brother, your dearly departed Uncle Lokke, has returned to this world as Zoloft, one of the pending antidepressants. Good old, cheerful Lokke. But in my circumstance, there was nothing anybody anywhere could do. And so I chose to spend my last days with you, my son."

These words, perhaps meant to sound reassuring, fell like a death sentence on Turpin. The starry sky around him now glistened as grown men in brimmed hats leapt from windows, streams of ticker tape unfurling behind them. Loose oranges fell like hail.

He now thought about his mother and how, although she pretended otherwise, deep down she'd allowed for the possibility of his death and, worse, had devised a contingency plan. The very idea rubbed against Turpin like a large soft eraser. "My life!" he shouted. "Ruined!"

"Now, now, shhh," soothed his father. "Nothing's ruined, except the bumper of this Lexus. Try to accommodate uncertainty. It veils all that we know—to refuse its mystery leads only to madness and misery. Last question, son, so make it count."

Turpin shuddered at the urgency of a final question. Perhaps he should ask if he might delay the illness by exercising more, or taking things easy. By avoiding sick people or those who'd traveled abroad. By bathing more often or by forgoing hot water. By eating high-fiber foods. And the stock market—would computerized controls *really* prevent a crash like the one in '29? And if a person, hypothetically, had a passing bedroom idea involving his half sister, just in a dream really, that didn't mean anything terrible, did it? Then, too, the meaning of *my fruit* gnawed at him, and he wondered if it was worth his final question.

"Dad," he began, "is there any chance you could come back? I mean as my father?" he blurted. "Maybe for just a while? You could give me driving lessons."

"No, son. I wish I could. It means the world to me that you asked."

His father then made a request of his own: that one fair day, perhaps in the spring when the breeze was warm and the daffodils in bloom, Turpin bring his mother to the park, by the slatted footbridge that spanned the creek. "Suggest to her it might feel nice to walk through the moss in her bare feet. Don't tell her it's me. I have to go now. Stay in the car and wait for help, son. You've made enough decisions for one day."

The air bag promptly deflated—an empty skin. Turpin wiped his cheek and shook his head and wondered what had just happened. *How many questions do I get?* he recalled himself asking and cringed; even in his near-death hallucinations he still behaved like someone without "sufficient emotional foundation."

The wristwatch was silent, its face cracked, yet Turpin clearly lived and breathed. He opened his door, tapped one foot on the pavement, gauging whether he was on ground solid enough to make a run for it. But finally he decided to heed the voice of his father, or at least the idea of the voice of his father, and wait for the police to arrive. He would try to accommodate uncertainty.

Turpin was sentenced to a month's house arrest, except for school hours. The only tangible consequence of his misadventure, besides having to reimburse his mother over time for the damaged car, was the county-issue wristband, which generated a beep that Turpin would play over the phone for a computer that called him at random times of the day.

He'd gotten off easy.

If he screwed up his house arrest, he could face detention at the Charles Hickey School, which handled some very rough dudes.

"In some countries," his stepfather teased him one night at the dinner table, "they'd cut off your hands—"

Turpin looked at his hands.

"—and you wouldn't be able to pass me my fruit."

"My fruit?" Turpin blinked. Was this some kind of awful joke?

His sister pushed her plate aside and said, *"'The man who steals and the woman who steals, cut off their hands as a punishment for what they have earned, an exemplary punishment from Allah.'"*

His parents looked at her then at each other with puzzlement. She'd been acting a little weird ever since photography camp.

His stepfather cleared his throat. "The fruit," he repeated, "could you please pass the bowl?"

"You should have some fruit, too, Turpin," his mother urged.

What exactly did she *mean?*

A week later, as Turpin rounded the front walk on his return from school, he heard the phone ringing. He reached into the pocket of his hole-riddled scrub pants for his key and discovered with distress he must have lost it. He circled the house, checking each entrance, but they were all locked. The patio's sliding glass door gave an eighth of an inch before freezing in its tracks.

His mom was usually home by now. Was she trying to undermine him? She had, after all, foreseen the possibility of his death. She had allowed for it—the unallowable—and a part of her had moved beyond it. She proved unforgivably resilient.

The phone began to ring again. He pressed his cheek to the patio door. "I'm home!" he yelled, his voice bouncing off the glass and back into his own face. "I'm home!"

His mother's car pulled into the driveway, crackling the leaves that lay everywhere. Turpin ran around to the garage, where he found her hefting two large grocery bags.

"Oh, sweetie, hi," she said, keys dangling from her pinky like worms flopping in a beak. "Can you take one of these?"

"Mom," he panted. "Let me in. My phone thing."

She thrust one of the bags at him, and in exchange seemed to take on some of his panic. Worrying her key into the kitchen-door lock, she struggled with the knob and dropped her grocery bag, which split apart as it hit the ground. She kicked a can of corn nibblets off her shoe and threw open the door, allowing Turpin to enter.

He answered the phone, punched his four-digit code into the side of his wristband, and held up its affirming beep for the computer's approval. The phone acknowledged him, his physical proximity anyhow. Although the wristband was sure an impressive piece of hardware, Turpin had lost some of his enthusiasm for gadgetry.

He watched his mother through the kitchen doorway as she knelt and reached for scattered boxes and cans. He imagined himself someday gone and her left without him. Maybe she was thinking the same thing, because she was weeping, murmuring about the stolen car, Turpin's episodic hooky, the seeming rash that had emerged, Texas-shaped, on his face but that resolved quickly into a benign cluster of zits.

"How do you expect me to cope with all this?" she said, reaching for a grapefruit the size of an infant's head. "If anything bad should happen to you—"

He felt sorry for her, even as he jealously plucked the grapefruit from her grasp, but he just couldn't help himself: "It has to, someday," he said. Then added, mercilessly, "and you won't be able to replace me."

She looked up at him with a woeful gaze, her lustrous hair framing her face. There was something achingly beautiful about the sight of his mother weeping.

He helped her to her feet and then gathered the rest of the groceries, wondering how best to make up with her for that last wounding remark. He suggested a walk.

"Turpin, they could call at any time."

"Just a little walk," he said. "Over to the creek and back. By the footbridge." He was in a mood to tempt fate; tempting fate seemed related to the accommodation of uncertainty, in a black-sheep way.

"Turpin, it's too risky."

He found himself milking a tremendous guilty pleasure from her worry. "They probably won't call again so soon. Come on, Mom. We never go for a walk. I'm going anyway, see?"

He set out down the driveway, and she quickly caught up to him, voicing her ongoing concern. The more she made known her anxiety, the more invigorated Turpin felt. They entered the little park, and the creek came into view and, not far upstream, the slatted footbridge.

Though the day was unseasonably warm, she huddled against his arm, a little too close for Turpin's teenage comfort, but he didn't complain. And as they walked, he wondered how he might, without calling to mind anybody's bedroom ideas, persuade his mother to walk barefoot over the approaching moss.

seven

The Omelet King

Veiled she was, no: shrouded, this stepdaughter of his, and almost to the top of the stairs when she tripped forward into his arms, laughing.

"I knew you'd be there," she said, wellspring of faith, patting his jaw.

"Be careful with that." He meant her wedding dress, a red tentlike affair with matching face curtain. Garrett wished she'd at least take off the veil before she hurt herself, but Lynn was determined to work on her purdah skills. To everyone's amazement, she had devoutly adopted her natural father's religion and then—the real shocker—insisted he arrange a marriage for her.

She didn't want to date or even to flirt with any of the boys she was meeting in college. To her mother's anguish, Lynn thoroughly rejected the idea of an American-style courtship and marriage and, implicit in those, the risk of an American-style divorce. As a result, her natural father and his wife had flown in from India last night, along with Lynn's future in-laws and husband-to-be, a twenty-two-year-old mechanical engineer named Hafiz whom she'd never met. They were supposed to have arrived the day before, but their original flight had been canceled, and so they were due at the house any minute.

"Can you see at all through that thing?" Garrett wondered.

"Oh sure," she said. "A little." She smelled of sandalwood and cool clean skin, breath sweet as parsley, and Garrett felt downright mournful about losing her to holy matrimony on this stunning fall day.

He saw Lynn to her bedroom and waited in the doorway until she was safely seated inside. And then, against his better judgment, he decided to check on the other child, Turpin. Smoke seeped from under the boy's door, which was plastered with rebellious bumper stickers, and instead of knocking, Garrett pushed his way in to find his stepson sitting amid a hot blue haze.

"I thought I told you not to smoke in this house," said Garrett, wishing suddenly that he'd left the door closed, but he was committed now to this bust. Turpin didn't even bother to launch a comeback. There was something strange about his tux; he'd cut a fist-sized hole over each knee. Garrett's mouth hung open, and he pointed to the boy's exposed legs. "Have you been doping up?"

"Doping up?"

The smoke seemed to be from legitimate pipe tobacco, a rich blend that Turpin claimed his real father used to smoke. "You're on something," Garrett insisted nonetheless, "I know it."

"I'm high on marriage, dude."

"Turpin," said Garrett, slumping against the doorjamb. He wished he were giving away Turpin's hand today. "Why must you always be so selfish?"

The boy looked at him mutely, unable or unwilling to register the question. "You don't know anything," he countered.

Garrett's wife, May-Annlouise, always said he had to love the boy before the boy would love him. It was that simple and that hard. Garrett believed that for a while he'd been on the *verge* of loving Turpin—then the boy hit puberty and began making everybody's life difficult. Stealing that car a year ago hadn't helped his case any either. And now Garrett was left questioning the strict covenant of parenthood—the one about unconditional love: maybe there was some loophole since, after all, he was a mere stepparent.

He glanced at his watch. "The omelet guy isn't here yet," he muttered. It was less distressing to worry about the caterer, Guillaume *Voila!* the Omelet King, wizard, famous for his inspired combinations—braised morels with shallots and crème fraîche, for instance—who'd promised he would even whip up a few Mughal dishes for the occasion. Where on earth was he? And could he really be as good as everybody said he was?

Guillaume *Voila!* the Omelet King ran an aged yellow light, his tires squealing from the sharp turn. His assistant Paolo yelled from the passenger's seat for him to be careful.

"We're late!" barked Guillaume. In his ten years since be-coming an American caterer—at the advice of the Madonna herself, whose appearance he had witnessed in an omelet he was mixing while still an orphan in Dijon—he had never been late. But just this morning, as he'd been dicing a little egg salad for himself, she'd come to him again, this time in tears. Weep-ing for him, he assumed, because he was going to die.

After waiting impatiently for the gate of this ticky-tacky suburban community to open, Guillaume found the correct two-story white frame house, parked in its driveway, and sprinted around back to the kitchen door. He stopped before knocking, though, because he heard the raised voices of a man and woman from inside.

"If that son of yours ruins this day—" said the man's voice.

"Of *mine?*" The woman sounded tearful. "I thought you wanted him to be your son, too."

"I do, I do. It's just—why can't he be a little more like his sister?"

"I don't know, Garrett," she said. "Why can't you be more like me?"

Guillaume paused, had to catch his breath. In the long si-lence that followed, he was again a child on the "*jour des visi-teurs,*" when occasionally one of his more cherubic playmates would catch the eye of some desperate couple from Paris, and the family constellation of the orphanage would shift once again, though Guillaume himself would never be plucked from it because he was not purebred French.

Standing behind him, Paolo whispered, "truffles in paradise," an old catering joke. Guillaume returned to the van for a moment to compose himself.

From a crack in his sister's bedroom doorway, Turpin watched her pray and was alarmed to notice sweat on his hands and a slight stir in a hidden place beneath his ribs. As she bowed before her dresser, eyes closed, her hair covered by a fabric remnant, his sister *aroused* him. Well, technically she was his half sister, so maybe this freed the other half of Turpin to find her attractive?

What a waste that she'd promised herself to a stranger. Someone with no knowledge or appreciation of her. Someone who couldn't begin to guess what was written in her diary, or which stuffed animal had slept each night of the past ten years between her knees. (It was the green koala, Mr. Hans Binky Andersen, recently renamed Shah Jahan.)

To calm himself, he touched the Percodan in his pocket. Normally by this time of day he'd already be into a nice mellow, but he'd waited because he needed a straight head to confront her.

He cleared his throat. Startled, she lowered her veil and turned her obscured face toward him and said, "Oh, it's you. But we've talked and talked."

It was scary how she sometimes anticipated his thoughts, and he wondered if, under the veil, her other senses had become heightened. He felt the air tickle his knees; he'd cut the holes as a protest, and she probably couldn't even see them clearly. How inept of him.

He took a step into her room and said, "You're going to ruin your life."

"*I'm* going to ruin *my* life? Look who's talking, Mr. Pharmacist."

So he'd developed a soft spot for analgesics; they were a better opiate than evangelism, weren't they?

"And what about Mom?" she continued. "Garrett's her third husband. Picky picky picky! Not to mention just a little bit ego-centered, don't you think? *'Those that deny Our revelations We will burn in fire. No sooner will their skins be consumed than We shall give them other skins, so that they may truly taste the scourge.'*"

"What are you saying? That Mom's going to hell?"

"Marry, divorce, remarry, divorce, remarry. . . . Doesn't that sound hellish enough? Why not spare myself? And my kids!" she cried, turning away from him. "The way I see it, I'm doing God's will. *'It is not for true believers to take their choice in their affairs if God and His apostle decree otherwise.'*"

She said *God* and *His apostle* with such fulfillment Turpin felt a singe of jealousy. He was not prepared to argue theology; there seemed no way that his beliefs—slender and half-formed—could compete with hers. "Why do you parrot that book all the time?" he asked.

"Oh, Turpin." His sister sighed, lifting her veil and looking at him sadly. She gentled him out of the room with a cool afterthought of a kiss. "Don't be an infidel."

The willowy dill he was chopping reminded Guillaume of the soft underarm hairs of his fiancée, the lovely Sarah Hsu, an amorous investment banker of Jewish and Chinese descent whom he'd met on a gourmet barge tour of the Loire Valley. Guillaume believed he'd been born with an image of love etched on his heart, and that he had met over the years various people who matched this image to some degree or other—an alarming number of women and men, in fact—but on meeting Sarah, he recognized her so completely, so instantly, it was as though he had loved her his entire life. And now that he and his beloved wished to marry and have a family, he'd undergone a blood test, which, to his horror, he failed.

One ray of hope remained: the lab had performed only the preliminary ELISA test and would now try something called the Western Blot. Even the test name seemed ominous, suggesting the ruin of civilization. The results were to be rushed to his doctor later in the day, and in his anxiety, Guillaume had instructed that a call be placed to him immediately at this wedding. He hadn't breathed a word of his fear to anyone yet, not even his fiancée.

Now, as he chopped dill weed beside Paolo, Guillaume thought about having to call each of the men and women of his past to tell them that his love perhaps meant their death. He thought of his schooling at the orphanage *lycée* and the fall of man from the garden, how it had been for the sin of sexual pleasure, as the nuns found it convenient to imply, and he was now filled with shame. He disputed his entire life, ruled as it had been by appetites.

"Ah, *Dieu!*" Guillaume nicked himself, and a drop of blood peeked out from his finger. His pulse vibrated across the droplet before its surface broke and the blood trickled toward his palm. He considered what to do. With his good hand he picked up the chopping board—the sprig of dill on it as well as the knife—and carefully slid it all into the garbage can.

"What are you doing?" said Paolo. "That's a $200 knife."

"It's a terrible knife," Guillaume muttered.

"Just rinse it off," said Paolo.

"Leave it be!" hissed Guillaume.

In the bathroom, he washed away the blood with scalding water and fumbled with a box of bandages, using his unspoiled hand. When he closed the medicine cabinet, he saw his fiancée's face in the mirror. How would he tell his beloved Sarah? He would come home from today's wedding and shrug off his yolk-stained jacket and walk toward her slowly. Because she'd have been puttering around the apartment, she'd be wearing her glasses, a very expensive pair that had been purchased, he suspected, with the idea of glamour, but on her they had the delightfully unintended effect of turning her into a convent schoolgirl. He would slide them gently off her face, easing Sarah into her myopic trust of him, and he'd carry her into their bedroom and undress her and enfold her in his arms and tell her she should have herself tested, and that now they would not be able to have the children, the many, many children, they'd wanted.

May-Annlouise brushed her daughter's sleek dark hair, letting it cascade over the wall of the wedding dress, savoring these last few moments before telling the girl that her birth father, Parni, and his wife were waiting downstairs—and that they'd brought a surprise with them: a baby.

"Mom," said Lynn, breaking the silence. "You don't think I'm making a mistake, do you?"

May-Annlouise stopped her brushing in midstroke. It wasn't like Lynn to voice insecurity; at least, not like her in this recent Islamic-fundamentalist period, and the question, so wide open in its plea for reassurance, seemed to May-Annlouise like some sort of trap. "Of *course* you're making a mistake!" she wanted to say, had tried to say in a thousand different ways. But she held back, because the Lynn of today had her own very firm ideas and would only resent her.

"You're doing what's best for you," said May-Annlouise, adding this fine print: "You'd know if you weren't." She couldn't get enough of her daughter's hair. It felt so luxurious, and May-Annlouise realized she might be brushing it for the last time.

A few minutes later, in response to the burst of crying from downstairs, Lynn asked, "What's that?"

"A baby," admitted May-Annlouise.

"Duh."

Unable to stall any longer, May-Annlouise revealed: "Your father and Nazar are downstairs already."

Lynn jumped out of her chair and looked at May-Annlouise in frank disbelief. "They have a baby? I didn't think they could have a baby."

"Well, amazingly they did," said May-Annlouise and, understanding that more was required of her, added, "They went to a fertility doctor." Her daughter had surely gleaned a thing or two about fertility doctors from May-Annlouise's own fruitless experience. Well, not completely fruitless, after all, because she'd ended up donating some of her surplus eggs to Parni and Nazar.

May-Annlouise was unsure how the girl might take this last part of the story. When she'd originally sent the eggs abroad, May-Annlouise believed she was doing the right thing, even a virtuous thing. But now she wondered. Perhaps the infant would supplant Lynn in her birth father's heart. Perhaps Lynn would be jealous.

The girl circled the room slowly, like a prowling cat. "You just found out a few minutes ago? Why didn't they tell anyone?"

"They were superstitious about it," said May-Annlouise, half-truthfully. Parni in particular had been afraid to provoke fate by gloating over their scientifically contrived miracle. Feeling unable to avoid her daughter's other question any longer, May-Annlouise added, "I knew before. They made me promise not to tell."

Her heart sank. She had just now confessed that she couldn't keep a secret or a promise, and even worse, she was starting to wonder: what if she'd helped Parni and Nazar have a child of their own just so they wouldn't steal Lynn's affections?

"So why did they let you in on it?" the girl asked, pointing a henna-stained finger. Her eyebrows knotted in that look of puzzled displeasure May-Annlouise had seen so many times over the years. A look that said: *I don't know exactly what you've done, but when I find out, I'll never forgive you.*

May-Annlouise had painted herself into a corner, though in all likelihood Lynn would have figured everything out after seeing the baby, who, in a way, was Lynn repeated. They shared, just above the mouth, a beauty spot each girl clearly had inherited from May-Annlouise. Seeing the baby moments ago herself had given May-Annlouise a chill of pleasure and sadness. Sadness because she remembered all the years of Lynn's life gone by, and she wished she could have them again. She knew so much more now than she had when Lynn was born, could be so much better a mother.

Slowly, May-Annlouise divulged that this baby was actually Lynn's full sister. "When you go look at her, see your infant self. Her future is so open . . . What joys would you wish for her?"

The rest of this message remained implicit, unspoken: *How can you marry that boy unless you've chosen him? How can you choose not to choose? Don't be afraid to choose!* Instead, May-Annlouise begged Lynn not to say anything about the eggs. The girl nodded, still wearing her enigmatic scowl and said finally, "You're amazing." May-Annlouise blushed and shook her head.

"I mean it, Mom, you surprise me. *'It is God who splits the seed and the fruit-stone. Such is the bounty of God.'* But you helped." She continued to stare at her mother appraisingly and concluded, "That was a saintly act." Her daughter kissed her on the corner of the mouth, at such an angle that their two beauty marks were almost in alignment. She then turned to go see her visitors—her birth father, his wife, and their test-tube baby—and disappeared.

If May-Annlouise were any kind of saint, she'd have been willing to risk her daughter's love to ensure her daughter's happiness. She would have tried to prevent the wedding, yes? To be a saint, May-Annlouise suspected, was to suffer an intense loneliness in one's daily life that she knew she was not cut out for.

His cheek still smarting from the taunt of his sister's kiss, Turpin retreated to his room and downed the Percodan that had been burning a hole in his pocket, plus another from his sock drawer.

As the warm, cottony fog spread along his limbs, he looked out his window and saw the Omelet King's van in the driveway. Suddenly he wanted to help in some way. This impulse was unlike him, but his family had worn him out with their disapproval. He needed to set himself a task that would buy some acceptance. Desperate now to help, Turpin lurched down the stairs and outdoors. He stood before the white van and briefly considered its painted slogan—YOU'VE GOT TO BREAK A FEW EGGS—before looking inside. With disappointment, he noted that the equipment had already been unloaded.

The refrigerator compartment, however, a huge vault with glass double doors, held more eggs than he'd ever seen—a stack three feet high. There was something formidable about them, and a little scary, like a late-show science experiment. He had to touch one.

Cautiously he opened the refrigerator doors and stood before the chilly hoard of eggs, running his fingers across their skinny oval tips. He supposed he should carry some into the kitchen but couldn't bring himself to do so. Instead he lingered, remembering the day he first met his stepfather. It had been sometime near Easter, the precise equinox, in fact, and Garrett had delighted the family by standing an egg on its end and leaving it somehow to balance on its own. For months afterward, Turpin would sneak into the kitchen and try vainly to repeat that magic, his resentment growing along with the conviction that Garrett had somehow tricked him. Tricked everybody, only no one else could see it.

Instead, they all focused their distrust on Turpin, especially since the car episode, and he knew that one more foul-up would put him on an eternal shit list. He probably shouldn't be standing in this van, he decided, probably should just return to his room for a nap, congratulate the happy couple sometime in the evening, and call it a day. He could live with his sister's bad marriage, couldn't he? There was only so much one person could do to help another. And God knows Turpin was unable to control this situation.

Wasn't he?

He thrust his head downward. *Crunch!*

The shells stuck to him, dripping their jelly. He gagged from the splattered yolk and slammed his head down again and again, bursting still more of the fragile orbs, and again, until the entire top tier was broken and bleeding. Pounding his fists, he found he could crack the second tier, which was protected by only a thin nest of cardboard. When the second tier was smashed, he climbed atop the entire stack and lay down as though in his bed, and with his fists and forearms and knees and feet he flailed, sobbing. Slowly the layers beneath him flattened, and even though he was clearly sinking, sinking, sinking, he felt lighter.

It was Garrett, just back from a last-minute ice cube run, who found him. He pulled on the sleeve of Turpin's tuxedo until the boy slid out of the refrigerator case on a river of slime. A thousand scratches on his face and hands, Turpin staggered to his feet.

"Dad," he said, blinking rapidly.

"I don't believe this. Not even from you!" Garrett sputtered. "This mess!"

The van looked like it had been targeted by vegan vigilantes. And never had Garrett seen a tuxedo more violated. All his worst fears about his stepson were inflamed.

"Dad," Turpin said again, brushing a flake of shell from his cheek. "Try to understand. I had to do it."

"You had to ruin your sister's wedding?"

"Yes," he said and climbed out of the van. "It's for her own good."

Stepping outside too, Garrett looked back at the vandalized vault. "My God! They should have thrown you in jail!" he said. "You're a menace!"

Coiled on top of the wheel well lay a long braid of jumbo garlic, which Garrett reached for and hefted now like a limp baseball bat. Aiming more or less at his stepson's slippery head, he only vaguely registered the look on Turpin's face: brow pursed, mouth buoyant. In the days and months ahead when he was to remember this look, Garrett would read into it a glowing pilot light of resolve, conviction even, and would regret what he was about to do. But just now, he couldn't help himself; seeing only a teenager's mocking smirk, Garrett stepped into his swing, shifting his weight forward, whipping the garlic around, when something snagged the braid from behind until it broke apart, feathery bulbs scattering like startled doves.

He turned to find the French caterer holding on to the braid's tail.

"No hitting," Guillaume explained. Turpin took advantage of this reprieve to run for the house.

"But look!" pleaded Garrett, pointing toward the refrigerator case. "What a disaster!"

How could he love the boy first? This unlovable boy. It would be wrong to love him. It would be like loving evil. "That boy is," he said, trying it out loud, "evil."

Guillaume climbed into the van to survey the damage. He pressed his thumb and forefinger against the band of his toque. "This will be a bitch to clean," he conceded. "I applaud your commitment to hire disadvantaged youth, but I could have referred you to more reliable help."

Garrett hung his head. If only it were so simple. "No, no. He's my stepson. His father," he added soberly, "died when he was seven."

"Then how can you call him evil?" the caterer asked, his eyes squinting in what may very well have been reproach. He hopped out of the van. "I've seen many bad boys. He is not. A bad boy would not be crying."

Garrett didn't remember seeing Turpin cry. But maybe so, maybe so, though why that mattered Garrett remained uncertain. He became very still and tried to hear what was going on inside the house. He'd have felt surer of himself if his wife were also yelling at Turpin. He strained to pick up any little thing, a slammed door, a shout, but could hear only the crackle of tabla drums as the DJ tested her sound system.

"Go to him," said Guillaume, his eyes moist slits.

"Hey, it's OK," Garrett told him, setting down the mace of garlic and putting a consoling hand on the caterer's shoulder. "We'll get everything fixed and cleaned. We'll replace all the eggs."

"Go make up with him."

Garrett sighed. "I'm not that generous. I don't have it in me."

"First you do it," said the caterer, "and then you have it in you. Like eating."

As Garrett peeled lingering bits of garlic from his hands like old, dry skin, there came a shout from above: "I'll make you understand!"

It was Turpin's voice, far away and weepy. He was standing on the roof, cupping his hands around his mouth and shouting something about God.

"What did he just say?" Garrett asked Guillaume.

"He says God demands a sacrifice." All color seemed to have left the caterer's face.

"Do you need some water, Mr. *Voila!?*"

He shook his head feebly. "I am expecting a phone call," he murmured and walked toward the kitchen entrance.

Garrett looked at the rooftop. "Turpin, why are you up there?"

"I'll prove it!" the boy's voice echoed back. "I'll prove it to you!"

Garrett worried over the combination of *prove, God,* and *sacrifice*—it reminded him of crusades and suicidal philosophers. He had no idea why the boy was up on the roof but figured someone needed to get him down before the afternoon became irreparable. "Hang on a second, Turp, I can barely hear you."

Garrett jogged toward the house—not the full sprint that would signal to Turpin, and himself, that he was afraid. Once upstairs, he climbed the spring-loaded ladder to the attic, then followed the slime trail across dusty floorboards to a porthole window, its circumference coated with egg, already drying in the breeze. Reaching an arm up to the shingles, he tried to squeeze through enough to step on the window's ledge. After many contortions, he managed to drag himself up onto the roof. How would they ever get back down?

He could see, on the pitch's far side, the top of Turpin's head. His hair, his hair . . . Garrett remembered that long-ago day at the courthouse when Turpin led them all on a merry chase up to the roof. He had never explained why. Was this some kind of brain-chemistry compulsion of his? How the sun that day had played through the boy's hair, so white and fine. But now . . . Garrett regarded his stepson's hair now: a clot of bent spikes and splotchy color, like an abused paintbrush.

After scraping his way up the thirty-degree slant, his shoe soles slippery from albumen, Garrett sat for a moment on the roof's spine. Lynn's future in-laws had arrived and were congregating in the backyard with Parni, Nazar, and their baby. Everyone looked up at the roof.

"Mr. Garrett!" Parni waved. "Come meet your new relations!"

"Mr. Hyder, Mrs. Hyder!" Garrett called out to the future in-laws. "Hafiz! Welcome to Baltimore! Hi, Nazar! Parni, I hope May-Annlouise is getting you a gin and tonic!" Immediately, he regretted mentioning Parni's favorite cocktail in front of the in-laws, who might very well not drink.

Parni clasped his hands in front of him. "What brings you up to the roof?"

"Just fixing something! Down in a minute!"

Turpin stood at the edge, near the gutter, and stared across the backyard, then slowly turned toward Garrett. "Do you know God's will?"

"Could we maybe discuss this after the wedding?"

"No."

Garrett sighed. "Since when did you start caring about God?"

"Just 'cause I never talk about it with you doesn't mean I don't care."

Garrett could not refute the logic of this; still it stunned him to think of this disheveled punk contemplating a higher power. Himself, Garrett did not know whether to believe in God but had tried to lead his life *as if* God existed. This, he realized, was not the same as believing.

"Your sister seems to know a thing or two about God. Have you spoken to her?"

"That's the whole point. My sister's got it all wrong," said Turpin, moving a bent clump of hair out of his eyes. "She's so wrong, she's going to marry some guy she doesn't love."

"Hey, keep your voice down. I'm sure Hafiz is a very nice guy. Probably." He waved tepidly to the wedding party below. "What are you proving by standing on the roof?"

"No," Turpin said slowly, as though talking to a child, "by jumping *off* the roof. It's . . . it's God's will. He wants me to stop the wedding."

"How do you know this?"

"Be . . . because," he stammered as though improvising. "If He didn't want me to jump, He'd have made you man enough to stop me."

You little shit, thought Garrett. Who in today's world went around measuring manhood? And where did Turpin get off saying what was enough? The very idea of having been judged incensed Garrett, let alone that he'd come up short. Still, he grudgingly admitted, the boy earned a few points for caring about his sister. Garrett wondered if he'd been completely fair to his stepson, and also: how much manhood did this situation require exactly?

"Turpin," he said, inching his way down the slant, angling his weight toward true vertical. "I want us to be—better. I know there's more I could have done. Can we at least talk about it?" He offered a handshake and meant what he said.

"Too late!" yelled Turpin, slapping away Garrett's hand. The boy's knees buckled and he sent one foot into the gutter in search of his balance, his arms twirling like propellers, and he was looking right at his stepfather as if to tell him: *I'm having second thoughts.* In the brief moment during which all this passed, Garrett took a step forward and reached toward the boy and now grabbed his wrist.

No matter what else was to happen, Garrett had reached, and Turpin had seen it. *This counts for something,* Garrett told himself and would continue telling himself over a long convalescence. *This has to count for something.*

The phone rang, and Guillaume pounced on it before anyone else in the house could pick up. He prayed his test was negative and wondered what he would give up to have his wish and if this included the love of his precious fiancée or perhaps even the very existence of God.

"Yes?" he asked the phone.

"Guillaume Lehalleur, please," the faraway voice of his physician demanded.

Guillaume did not want to live in a world without Sarah or a world without God, but better to keep Sarah, better to live blissfully in a world of no meaning than in a meaningful world of pain.

"Yes?" He stretched the tangled phone cord toward the kitchen sink. He feared he might need to throw up.

"Guillaume, you're a very lucky man," said his doctor. "A very lucky man. But Guillaume," he said, pausing, "as usual, your cholesterol is sky high."

Guillaume swallowed. As he looked out the kitchen window,

he glimpsed the blur of two bodies falling to earth, and his inner eye observed the man gripping the boy, the strange boy, whose lips curled in an almost beatific smile.

Guillaume thanked the doctor and would have thanked the Virgin for pardoning his promiscuity, except he was beginning to suspect that his understanding of certain religious matters had been clouded and that, for example, Adam and Eve had been banished from the garden not so much for their sexual pleasure, after all, but for the arrogance of believing they'd make good parents.

He rested the phone in its cradle, picked it up again. He wanted to call Sarah, just to hear her breathe. He thought about his cholesterol, and the cholesterol of all the people he had served over the years, and decided to send Paolo to the market for artichokes instead of eggs.

I will become the Artichoke King, thought Guillaume, his blood pounding in his hands, his chest. He was alive on this earth. Alive. And because he would be blessed with many, many children, surely his greatest sins lay ahead.

eight

Virtue

A couple of weeks after her mother's suicide, twenty-four-year-old Adriane Gelki determined to give her virginity to her boss, Garrett Hughes, and she went about preparing for this the same way, ten years earlier, she had found God: she read up on it. She read Kinsey, Hite, and even Sade. She studied the illustrated *Kama Sutra*. She visited newsstands and brought home copies of *Big Muff*, *Biker Lover*, and *Cherries Jubilee* and immersed herself in back issues of an erotic journal called *Nippleodeon*. She was intent not merely on pleasuring her boss—who had suffered a terrible ordeal—but felt the need to *revive* him.

Hobbling on crutches, he returned to City Hall from his sick leave on a cold November Thursday; he kept to his office and was bent over some files when Adriane peeked in on him that afternoon. Half his face was still bruised the color of Tropical Swirl sherbet.

"Come happy hour," Adriane proposed, "I'm buying you a drink." And then she added, even though he was older than she was, "young man." He gave her a look of such childlike gratitude she thought about making a move on him right then.

The Spanish restaurant on the next corner had great tapas for happy hour, and today the steam trays offered herb-battered calamari, fried goat cheese in marinara sauce, and creamed crabmeat in pastry shells—all tempting, all bad for her. "Restraint," Adriane had read somewhere, was "the highest expression of power," but this evening she was going for something altogether different: *Fuck it,* she thought, and assembled a generous plate for each of them.

His crutches leaning against the bar, Garrett picked at his food and barely touched his martini.

"Would talking about it help?" Adriane asked. She already knew the brunt of it: His fourteen-year-old stepson had fallen off the roof at home, and Garrett, reaching to save him, had also fallen—and landed on top. The boy was still in the hospital and, in the future, would almost certainly need to use a wheelchair.

"The sound his bones made—" Garrett shuddered. The flesh around his mouth, usually a bit lax, remained taut.

"How's your wife handling this?" she asked.

"Things were strained before the accident. Now she'll barely talk to me."

"How unfair," said Adriane, hoping to have summoned the right inflection.

"She didn't want me coming here to talk with you either."

"Perhaps you should have been a little discreet," she murmured. There had always existed a mild flirtatiousness between Adriane and her boss; it pleased her to think his wife noticed and minded.

"What's there to be discreet about?" he said obtusely.

Adriane decided not to press the point. "Does she blame you for what happened?"

"Hell," he said, "*I* blame me."

"How unfair," she said again.

"She doesn't have to be fair. Her son can't walk."

"Does she want to lose her husband, too?"

This was meant to sound supportive, but he glanced away, offended maybe at the suggestion that he could leave his wife. Adriane put a hand on his cast, over the red heart his stepdaughter had drawn. He looked so haggard, Adriane wanted to bathe him in her whirlpool, press hot towels to his face, massage him back to life.

"So," she said—a new tack—"who do you like on Sunday?"

He eyed her curiously. "Sunday?"

"Football." Adriane had always watched NFL football with her father on Sundays until she was fourteen. She'd taken it up again recently.

"I never watch it."

"Wow. Good for you, I suppose." She touched the salt and pepper shakers together and nodded toward his martini. "Bottoms up."

He'd ridden the bus to work since his cast prevented him from driving, and Adriane offered to take him home. She pulled her car in front of the restaurant, so he wouldn't have to crutch very far, and leapt out to open the door for him.

"I have a detour in mind," she said once they were under-way, her breath shamefully visible in the cold. He gave her a skeptical look when they stopped in front of her Mount Vernon apartment, a stately down-at-the-heels building. Her family had moved in when Adriane was three. Later, after her father died, it was just Adriane and her mother. And recently, Adriane alone. She led her boss into the dingy elevator, then along the narrow carpeted hallway to her door.

"You're not planning to kiss me, are you?" he asked, as she jiggled her key in the lock. He sounded disoriented—like someone sliding in and out of a dream.

"I might be planning something like that."

"So that's why you urged discretion." He sighed deeply and then admitted, "Maybe just a kiss. I could use a kiss."

"Then you shall have your kiss."

"Just a kiss couldn't hurt," he mumbled, following her past the scuffed Steinway that took up half her living room. "How'd they ever get that into your apartment?" he asked.

"It was my mother's." She eyed the urn resting on the piano lid near the music rack. "I'll never be able to move."

"I'm sorry I couldn't come to her memorial service."

"You were in traction," she observed.

She led him toward her childhood bedroom, the only room in the apartment that felt completely hers, and they paused now before the beaded curtain that had served as her door since she was three. She parted an opening for Garrett, who faltered a moment, then entered ever so gingerly, as though submerging himself in a brisk lake.

Adriane had changed the sheets that morning, bought lilies for the bedside table the day before. Folding her coat, she laid it on a green leather ottoman and did the same with his; she then sat him on the edge of her bed and neatly slid the crutches underneath.

She loosened his tie and clasped her hands around the back of his neck and pressed her index fingers along the knotted muscles that ran toward the base of his skull. Moving her hands around to his face, she caressed his furrowed forehead, his temples and cheekbones, and was surprised to feel the oiliness of tears. She kissed one of them and went on to brush her lips across the entire surface of his bruised face.

Over the past few days, she couldn't stop hearing in her head that balmy Marvin Gaye tune "Sexual Healing." She hummed it now as she lit a candle, turned off the light, and began to ease Garrett out of his trousers, which snagged over the rough hump of his cast. His legs were leaden in her hands, so unaware did he seem of her actions, but she worked gently and persistently. From her bedside drawer, she produced a condom. She placed it over his penis and, using her mouth, rolled it along the first timid inch of him—translating a skill she'd perfected on zucchini. She glanced up and saw him looking at her with wide-eyed distress.

"Is this such a good idea?" he whispered, as though he'd only now considered his nakedness.

She nodded emphatically and imagined herself the Florence Nightingale of Oral Comfort.

"It might be hard to take back," he said.

"Why would you want to do that?" she asked, vaguely insulted.

"Don't you ever wish you could take things back?"

"No." She glimpsed the plaid flannel pajamas her mother had given her peeking slyly from beneath the pillow, mocking her with their primness.

"Excuse me," she said, and carried the pajamas into the bathroom. They belonged to another era of her life, the Age of Sexual Denial, and had no place in this, the Age of Conscientious Seduction. (Certainly she would never have considered seduction, conscientious or otherwise, while her mother was alive to comment on it.) She tossed the pajamas into the metal wastebasket, splashed them with nail polish remover, and set them on fire.

Flames exploded from the trash can—as though Adriane had opened the door to a small blast furnace—singeing the delicate hairs along her wrist. She gasped and turned on the exhaust fan. By now the blaze had settled into a regular rhythm as it consumed the flannel. They're not even flame retardant, she noted with a dour sense of self-preservation. As she undressed, she glanced at herself moodily in the unflattering light her mother was able to cast even from beyond the grave.

"I smell something burning," Garrett called out.

"No. Nothing," she shouted and then chimed stupidly, "secret girl thing."

Back in the bedroom now, she straddled him, eager to awaken his passion. His face relaxed, and his hands came to life, caressing her stomach, tracing a finger around her navel, though she couldn't help notice he was nowhere near erect. Adriane was unprepared for this; her heartbeat squirmed inside a fist of failure. All of her technical reading deserted her, and she could think only to grind herself against his pelvis, which elicited from him a moan that made her shiver, it echoed with so much sorrow.

"Come on," she coaxed. "Up and in me." She nipped at his earlobes and squeezed her legs against his flanks, as though he were a stubborn trail horse. After a few more unsuccessful minutes, she dismounted.

"A regrettable performance," he told the ceiling.

"Oh, now. Don't be absurd." She made herself laugh breezily to emphasize how absurd he was being. Silently, she vowed to arouse him more completely some other time, for his own good.

At least, she thought as she drove him home, his face looked peaceful and younger, released from some of the grief that had recently held him. She'd pulled him back toward life, at a time when his wife was unwilling or unable to. Adriane felt mildly proud of herself.

They shook hands good-night.

Later, before going to sleep, she said her nightly prayers. She had not been raised religious. But ten years ago, after her father's death, Adriane retreated into an urgent spiritual quest. She read everything she could find—the Upanishads, the Qur'an, Bible comics—and cobbled together a theology from the Eightfold Path, the Ten Commandments, the Sermon on the Mount, and other acknowledgments of virtue, temperance, and righteousness. She began to attend a nearby Unitarian church. And she spent long hours imagining God.

Early on, she pictured a compassionate cloud. And then the Milky Way or sometimes a flock of geese, a pear blossom. Once, the Autobahn appeared to her in a dream. Intellectually, she resisted patriarchal images, yet her favorite and most compelling idea of God was an old man's ear, disembodied and hurtling through the cosmos. Cradled along the warm curved rim lay Adriane, her body comfortably supported by a slope of pink flesh, her head resting on a pillow of the softest silver ear hair. She had only to whisper, or even just to think, for her most personal self to be heard throughout the universe.

Dear Gentle Listener, she began now. *Please apologize to Moses for me the next time You see him, but I hope You Yourself will be open-minded about tonight. Garrett is a decent man. I'm sure he'd never want to hurt his wife, but he needs this, he needs me, and I for one will not stand idly by when I can do some small measure of good in this world, though I guess my technique needs polish. As You know, I've been saving myself for a worthy occasion, not to mention a little maneuvering room. That someone like Garrett should need me so soon after my mother's passing, well, it's a clear sign, and I thank You for not beating around the bush. Truly, I feel on the verge of unleashing a great force, and I want to use it wisely. Well, anyway, my picks for Sunday: Vikings, Bengals, 'Skins, and Raiders. Whatever You can do.*

At work the next afternoon, a messenger delivered flowers to her desk: a small arrangement of geraniums growing out of a ceramic pot with the words *home and hearth* painted on it and no card. Passing secretaries eyed the gift with indiscriminate envy, but the arrangement looked funereal to Adriane, who'd seen enough such flowers at her mother's recent memorial service.

Several times Garrett walked by her desk and smiled at her. He glanced at the flowers and pretended to have no connection to them, which she found sweetly coy. And that inapt planter: such an oversight; how male, how like her father.

She thought to order her boss a dozen red roses—but chickened out. Too pushy a declaration of feeling it seemed; plus she didn't wish to show up his more modest arrangement.

The next Thursday, Adriane took Garrett straight to her apartment after work. He paused as she parted the beaded curtain for him, and his forehead creased. "That sound," he said.

She undressed the both of them, and then, curious to try the missionary position that seemed the bread and butter of most people's sex lives, she pulled him on top of her, wanting to feel his weight. But as he lay on her, his forehead creased even more deeply, and his eyes clouded over. She asked if his leg was uncomfortable. And when he didn't answer, she remembered he had landed on top of his stepson.

"That's the sound," he said, "of his bones crunching. That curtain." He rolled off her, hobbled to the curtain, and parted it, let the beads fall against each other, parted them again. "He could have died, just in that split second. I was sure he had," he said, his back to her. "You'd think life and death would be separated by a big solid door. Oak. But they're not." He blew on the beads and made them rustle. "This is all that separates life and death."

"Life's on this side," she beckoned.

He turned and stood before her, naked except for his cast. "I was angry with him. Shortly before we fell."

"So what?"

"What if I didn't reach fast enough?"

"It was an accident. There was nothing you could do."

"He's not showing any progress."

"You're not to blame."

"What if I am?"

"An accident. Stop letting your wife beat you up about it."

"She's not beating me," he said. "It's more like she's been beaten. I try to touch her and she flinches. She has no reason to be afraid of me."

"Of course not."

Using his bound foot, he spread open his underpants on the floor, then stepped into both leg holes before reaching forward to pull the briefs up. "I love her," he said and sat next to Adriane on the bed.

"Uh-huh." She watched him struggle with his pants now and tried to think of something to delay his leaving. "Why?" she asked.

"You want to know why I love her?"

"Sure," she said, trying not to feel jealous. "What the hell."

"Well," he began, "I know I first started to love her when I saw how she was with her kids. I remember thinking, *there's someone who really knows how to love*."

"Lots of people know how to love," said Adriane, though she didn't truly believe that. She wondered what sort of loving glow she herself might radiate toward children and was not encouraged. Children, her mother had taught her long ago, were whom you blamed for your own unhappiness.

"You've been to our house," he said. "Did you notice the gazebo in the backyard?"

"Not really."

"May-Annlouise wanted that house because of the gazebo."

"You can buy them at any Hechinger's," she said, for the sake of argument.

"I know. But she liked this one because the bench had a knothole and she looked through it and saw a cat's-eye marble in the grass underneath. Left behind by the previous family. Green, luminous cat's-eye. She said it was watching us, and that it meant we belonged there. And she truly believes that—maybe not that the marble is really watching, but—"

"But *what?*"

"Well—that something as small as a marble in the grass can make you feel at home." His voice drifted off, and Adriane bet he was still thinking about how much he loved his wife for raving about that stupid marble. Why couldn't people keep their mysticism to themselves? Adriane, after all, didn't blab about her Gentle Listener, who provided the only sense of belonging she felt in the world. Certainly she'd lived in this dreary apartment almost all her life without it feeling like home.

"Then she sat on my lap in that gazebo and began to kiss me, very gently, but passionately. I mean, we'd been married for years already, you know? These very charming, lovely kisses that must have gone on for a quarter hour—"

"Geez, in front of the marble and everything?"

"The real estate agent was right there in the kitchen," he said ingenuously.

She sighed and studied his smooth chin. "You've been a good boy all your life, I'm guessing."

Again that look of gratitude from him.

"You know," she went on, "I've been a good girl."

"I'm sure you have," he said and buckled his belt.

She wanted just then to make him beg for her and whatever depravity she might cook up. It frightened her, the bitterness of this urge, and after dropping him home, she approached the subject in her bedtime prayers.

OK, she began, *I admit I wasn't expecting him to still love her, though he probably just said that out of guilt. I mean, if he loves her, why would he spend Thursday evenings with me? Right? Am I right? Maybe I was a little out of line to get jealous back there, but as long as my heart's mission is virtuous, I don't think it matters that he's married or that he might not be free to love me any time in the foreseeable future.*

By the way, my bookie says I'm breaking his balls, but if he's reaching for more than his vig, then he deserves to get them squeezed. No one likes a greedy middleman. Amen.

That Friday morning, a new pot of geraniums was delivered to her desk, this one with a little kitchen scene painted on the side and still no card, which was getting irritating. Last week's somewhat faded flowers (she probably should have watered them) stared at her like a gathering of wizened faces; the fresh ones watched her too, with more cheer and hope. It bothered her to share such a fetish, this need to feel watched over, with May-Annlouise. Still, Adriane very much wanted to think of the flowers as Garrett's affectionate way of keeping an eye on her, of turning his Cosmic Marble, so to speak, toward her. A half hour later, he walked by and remarked, "You seem to have a very tenacious admirer."

"I inspire tenacious admiration."

"Ah." He smiled coyly and returned to his office.

Something was not right about this exchange, and she brooded about it all morning.

At lunchtime, she could stand it no longer and looked into his office. He was sitting in a beam of sunlight so strong it seemed to illuminate every bruise and wrinkle on his face. The sight released in her an overflow of yearning. He was a good twelve years older; perhaps this explained why she'd dedicated her attentions to him: because he was fatherly? Well, other girls had gone down that road. Did this make her heart's mission any less virtuous? Adriane didn't see why it should. "By the way," she whispered, "thanks for all the flowers."

"They're not from me." Again that uncertain smile. "I was going to ask what other gentlemen friends you had."

Backing out of the room, she managed a sickly grin and shrugged her shoulders.

She placed a call to the florist and learned both arrangements were charged to the credit card of Garrett's wife.

Adriane knew a mind-fuck when she saw one and was not

about to let this go unanswered. She ordered an identical arrangement to be sent immediately to May-Annlouise at her workplace.

Why did Garrett feel compelled to tell his wife whenever he was spending time with Adriane? And how many details had May-Annlouise dragged out of him? Adriane was livid. She believed there ought to be a commandment against people like May-Annlouise Hughes.

"And on the note?" asked the florist.

Adriane hated notes, but hated the absence of notes even more.

"Leave me alone," she snapped. "I mean, it should say, 'Leave me alone.'"

❧

On the past few Sundays, Adriane had been indulging her desire to watch pro football, an infatuation long forbidden by her mother. That was surely part of the attraction, and maybe the sport also provided Adriane a harmless, even pleasant diversion from her mother's death, and why shouldn't it?

Around eleven A.M., after phoning her bookie and placing her bets, Adriane faced the interminable wait before kickoff. It was an awkward length of time, too brief to attend church, but long enough for the walls of her apartment to start closing in on her.

She approached the large piano crowding her living room and decided it might look better against the far corner. Heaving herself against its dark bulk, she managed to roll it a foot to the left. Last week she'd moved it two feet to the right. This had been her only recent contact with the piano, reduced to serving as a pedestal for her mother's ashes. Adriane just couldn't bring herself to sit down and play it. The instrument seemed cursed. Music, after all, had been her mother's foremost language, the only way she could express herself with any beauty or grace, and in the end it had failed her.

Someone was knocking on Adriane's door. She saw beyond her peephole a wide-angle distortion of May-Annlouise. Christ! Didn't she get the flowers? Couldn't she read? Adriane recoiled at the thought of suffering the older woman's pious outrage— recoiled even as she hurriedly unlocked the deadbolt and flung open the door. The two of them stood on either side of the threshold, each waiting for the other to speak first.

Finally, Adriane invited her visitor inside. As a pretense at politeness, she even offered hot chocolate. Surprisingly, May-Annlouise said she would have some and followed Adriane into the kitchen.

"Put your coat anywhere," said the reluctant hostess.

May-Annlouise leaned against the kitchen wall, her arms folded in front of her. Her face was puffy and red, and her eyes quivered. She looked even worse than Garrett had a couple of weeks earlier.

Neither woman spoke.

When Adriane handed her the steaming mug of chocolate, May-Annlouise took a sip, spilled a little on her sweater, sipped some more. "Garrett has always thought highly of you," she said at last.

Adriane suspected a disarming ploy. "That's nice," she said coolly, trying to quell her desire to hear what high things he'd thought about her. "He's the only person in the entire city government whose opinion I respect."

"There must be a few others."

"Not really," Adriane said. "I dislike most people."

The two of them tried to stare each other down. At last May-Annlouise asked, "What are you doing with my husband?"

"I wouldn't be doing anything with him," Adriane blurted, "if he was happy at home."

May-Annlouise squinted at her. "Right." And then, her face seemed slowly to break up, like the ancient continents drifting apart, seas pouring into the spaces between. There was no sound coming out of her mouth—a quivering hole, and at the bottom of it was loss, pure and hopeless.

Adriane leaned away, frightened. "Hey, please don't cry. That's not fair. Come on, please?" she whispered. May-Annlouise continued to stare in agony. "Are you getting some counseling?" Adriane asked. "Do you have a pastor or someone you can talk to?" Only a choked silence from May-Annlouise.

"This is beyond me," Adriane said. She took back the mug, carried it to the sink, and washed it thoroughly. The hot water over her wrists reminded her of the one resource at her disposal, the whirlpool in her bathroom, her single lunatic luxury that, in the end it seemed, had saved her life a couple of times. "Come on," she said, leading May-Annlouise by the hand.

Adriane turned on the bath taps, added bubbles, and found a fresh towel, then fired up the gurgling machinery—a dinky portable model that rested on the side of the tub like an outboard motor, but still it could sometimes work magic. She turned to May-Annlouise. "You'll be all right?"

Perceiving a slight nod, Adriane beat a retreat to the living room. She thought about calling Garrett to have him come over and take care of this, but didn't want to cause a scene. It was bad enough May-Annlouise knew he'd been here; there was no point in telling him about his wife's visit. Why destroy whatever sense of refuge the apartment held for him?

Adriane turned on the TV and tried to distract herself by thinking about the day's upcoming games. She had bet $200 each on the Falcons, Lions, Cardinals, and Patriots to beat the point spread. If she won, she would let it ride on the Raiders in the late game. In this fashion, she'd managed to rake in nearly three thousand easy dollars in less than a month.

Her father would have been proud of her. He used to watch football on Sundays and made her join him, claiming she was his good luck charm. Actually, she coveted Sundays, when she had him, more or less, to herself. Late in the morning, as her mother washed the breakfast dishes, he would mix a pitcher of Manhattans, pour one into a chilled glass and take it into the bathroom, where he sat on the edge of the tub, puffed an imported cigarette, and let his daughter shave him. Using an antique brush, she would gently apply a cream that smelled of meadow grass. And then with the utmost care, she held the bone-handled straight razor, also an antique, to the edge of his sideburns and slowly erased the shadows that had grown across his face during the night. Adriane had always found him painfully glamorous.

Around noon, her father would choose his teams for the day and then place calls to several bookmakers. Throughout the games, he'd continue to smoke cigarettes and drink Manhattans and shelter Adriane under his free arm, while on the television sweaty muscular men flung themselves against one another, grunting and thrusting, and rutting through the mud—to her and her father's great pleasure.

This was back when the Colts still played in Baltimore, before they skipped town in the middle of the night. It was fun having a home team to root for—though her father often bet against them. Over time, he ran up such huge gambling debts and had crossed his creditors enough that certain underworld elements took him down.

Specifically, they brought him to the Quality Inn on York Road and shot his beautiful face off. Despite the absence of a note, his death was made to look like suicide—a theory Adriane discounted because her father could never abide leaving her. The police didn't bother with any real investigation, undoubtedly because the people her father had angered were very, very powerful.

Her mother certainly believed his death a suicide and chose to punish Adriane through a prevailing silence. Even the lone compliment she could savor from those years—a reference to her "alluring" eyes—seemed tainted by accusation and innuendo. Honestly, there was nothing untoward about her relationship with her father; he just didn't love her mother as much—a simple if difficult fact that Adriane couldn't change even if she'd wanted to, which she didn't.

Anxious now for something to do, she mixed a pitcher of Manhattans and poured two drinks. She knocked on the bathroom door but, getting no response, barged in anyway. Still clothed, May-Annlouise sat on the edge of the tub, which was near to overflowing. Adriane sat down next to her, handed the woman a Manhattan, and felt mildly pleased with herself. Here she was, ministering to her lover's wife, comforting the poor thing, helping. "Bottoms up?"

May-Annlouise nodded drowsily, her face blank, a stray lock of hair dangling in front of her eyes.

This is what grief does to you, Adriane decided. She'd seen it in Garrett and now his wife. *It cripples you.* She felt grateful that the buoying presence of God had cushioned the grief in her own life.

"What do you want from me?" May-Annlouise asked.

"I'm just trying to be of service here," said Adriane, shutting off the water and the whirlpool. That dangling lock of hair was really starting to bug her, so she reached over and tried to fix it when out of nowhere, a hand slapped her across the face, causing her to drop her cocktail.

"You have no shame!" May-Annlouise was shouting all of a sudden. "You're—a *home-wrecker.*"

Adriane looked down at the floor, saw her maraschino cherry lying by the toilet. "You probably shouldn't drive," she mumbled, trying to regain control of the situation.

"Don't tell me what *I* shouldn't do." May-Annlouise stood abruptly, stepped around broken glass. "Just stop messing around with my husband."

"Nothing's been consummated." Adriane was able to muster some belligerence around this factual accuracy.

"I should hope not! Whatever you're doing, knock it off!" May-Annlouise stormed out of the bathroom.

"I'll do what I think is best!" Adriane called after her. Then felt compelled to add: "You know, some poor kid lost that cat's-eye marble."

But May-Annlouise was already gone, having left the front door contemptuously ajar, and Adriane found herself talking to an empty apartment.

She curled up on the sofa and steeled herself to endure the remaining half hour before kickoff. Pulling an afghan up around her chin, she beseeched her Gentle Listener: *The woman was suffering, and I was helping her*—You *saw*—*and, and ... Please don't be mad.*

Thanks again for that field goal last Monday night. You didn't have to do that. Adriane suddenly clutched a pillow and wept. *You're way too good to me.*

The next Thursday was Thanksgiving.

Adriane found an open sports bar and camped out for the day's special football games, nursing a yard of ale and winning both her bets by a wide margin. She stayed for dinner and, against her better judgment, ordered the Holiday Plate: pressed turkey and a stuffing that stuck in her throat. She needed another yard of ale just to wash it down.

How easily she had grown to think of Thursday evenings as her time with Garrett; it was a small pattern they'd established, for no particular reason, but she felt its interruption. Making things worse, he'd taken the week off work.

In the back corner of the bar, two young men wearing Hopkins lacrosse shirts waved Adriane over to play darts with them. She smiled politely and shook her head. "I have terrible aim," she called out. They seemed like children to her.

The following Monday, Garrett suggested happy hour at the Spanish restaurant, where they helped themselves to tapas. Adriane put only a little on her plate, but Garrett hobbled back to their booth carrying a small mountain of food. "Good news," he said, as he sat down. "There's some feeling in his fingertips. It may be nothing, his doctor says, but it may be something, too."

A pang of empathy squirmed into her throat as she thought about the boy, not an especially pleasant kid from what she'd heard. Still, there are some things that should never happen to anybody, and she wanted to feel for him, for his struggle, but what she said instead was: "Did you like your wife in bed, back in the days when she let you touch her?"

He pushed his plate aside and reached for Adriane's hand across the table. "I wanted to talk to you about her." He was choosing his words slowly. "There's been a thaw," he went on, "some kind of truce between us. We've been talking, kissing again."

"She's a good kisser, I hear. She just doesn't sound very stable. I mean, you bought a house because she found a marble in it? I wouldn't trust a woman like that."

"We had a long fight—about you, among other matters. And it was, um, it was good for us." He smiled sheepishly at the small irony. "It cleared the air about a lot of things."

Adriane stared at him. She was a "matter," one among many.

With his free hand he picked up an unlit candle and looked underneath it. "I'm concerned that I've been using you."

"You're using *me*?" Adriane coughed out a laugh. "Believe me, I know what it's like to be used, and this isn't it." Even though that was just a comeback, she wondered now if it might be true.

"Maybe," he said, "but if we were to continue, in light of—"

"Did you know the Steelers are going to beat the spread on Sunday?"

"The spread?"

"If you want me to place a bet for you, let me know. It'll be the easiest money you ever made."

He let go of her hand to reach for his wallet, and she stood up suddenly and blurted, "Don't give me any money—I'm not a whore!"

Heads turned along the bar.

Garrett cringed and whispered, "When do I give you money?"

"I'll be giving *you* the money," she said, eager to dispense with the transaction and get out of there. "So how much are you in for?"

"I don't know," he said, that boyish look again. "How much are people usually in for?"

"I'm not asking you to pledge to the United Way here," she said, gazing down at him. "Minimum bet's fifty dollars."

He seemed puzzled at the conversation's turn, and she felt a trill of pleasure over her ability to manipulate him.

"How much are *you* betting?" he asked.

"Oh, you dear man." She put on her jacket. "You wouldn't be able to sleep tonight."

☙

On Sunday, the first snowflakes of the season began their descent, but at Three Rivers Stadium in Pittsburgh the sun shone brightly, and it was the weather at the game that lately seemed to Adriane the real weather of her afternoon. That morning as planned, she'd placed her season winnings on the Steelers minus 14½ points. The Steelers were two-touchdown favorites, but, as of last week, Adriane's bookie had begun making her give up an extra half point because of her track record. Now, less than an hour before kickoff, she called him a second time to throw the rest of her savings into the pot.

"Look, Amber," he said (they never used real names on the phone; she didn't even *know* his last name). "I can't take that."

"I don't believe you."

"Swear on my mother's grave. I've got too much weight on the Steelers already."

"You son of a bitch, you can take me." She was never rude to her bookie, but she was frantic to place this bet. He simply had to bend to her will. "I'm good for it," she insisted. "Or, if you prefer, just shoot my face off."

"Christ. You yuppies and your gangster fantasies. It doesn't work that way."

"I know how it works," she said. "Either take my bet or start listening to your phone for strange clicks." Adriane was getting way ahead of herself. "You ever have a problem with me, mister, you know where to find me."

He exhaled slowly into the phone. "I was just trying to look out for you," he said finally. "I like you, kid."

"I'm not aiming for likable anymore. Just take my action." Satisfied to have prevailed, she hung up. Her hands trembled. She wondered if part of her was trying to provoke violence against herself. Out of some urge to reunite with her father. A crazy idea. Her mother had entertained such thoughts when she'd checked into the same fateful room at the Quality Inn on York Road and swallowed a bucket of pills. No ambiguity surrounding *that* death. In her baleful cursive, her mother had left a final note, voicing her ambition to "rejoin my beloved husband." Adriane read it as a gratuitous, parting mind-fuck. Not to mention a sucker's bet. Everyone knew—you didn't have to be religious to know—that suicides and the victims of gangland-style executions did not share the same afterlife. Her parents weren't even buried together; Mom's ashes sat over there on the piano, which was a whole other story Adriane didn't even want to think about.

She settled in front of the TV with a large bowl of popcorn, and her fingers continued to shake as she brought the first kernels to her mouth. What realm of the afterlife would she herself one day inhabit? She made a mental note to read Dante as soon as football season was over. Whatever points she would likely lose over the adultery, she was hoping to recoup and then some for her role as sexual healer. It sort of depended on who did the judging; she was still getting a feel for it.

By the time the third quarter began—her team up by seven—she considered the implications of her bet. If she won, she'd have amassed enough to take a year off and do almost anything she wanted. She began to wonder what that might be.

Halfway into the final quarter, she heard a knock at her door, and to her amazement, on the other side stood May-Annlouise. The circles and bags under her eyes had faded, and she showed some teeth this time—an actual smile. She looked good, quite attractive, in fact, and Adriane found herself opening the door a little wider.

"I just wanted to stop by and, well, apologize isn't really the right word," May-Annlouise said, stepping inside. "I mean, I'm still upset about you and my husband, but I behaved badly when I was here, and I'm not happy with that."

"Oh," said Adriane. She couldn't recall the last time anyone had apologized to her. What was she supposed to do in this situation? She wanted to be gracious, but she had a game to get back to.

"You like football?" she asked. "Too bad you didn't come by earlier. I could have gotten you in on a sure thing. The Steelers are a lock."

"Gambling's not my poison," said May-Annlouise, taking a seat.

"It makes it a lot more interesting to watch."

May-Annlouise politely shook her head. "Anyway, I need to relieve Garrett soon at the hospital. There's a little bit of feeling, he must have told you, in my son's fingertips."

"Your husband's in for a hundred."

"Oh, is he?" said May-Annlouise, cocking her head. "Then I'm already in for fifty. I guess I can stay for a few minutes. Which ones are the Steelers?"

"Yellow and black. They have the best secondary in the conference this year."

Adriane took a moment here and there to explain the game. Since childhood she had known it was all so stupidly simple. May-Annlouise had the basics down in a minute, and when Pittsburgh scored on a deep post, she even let loose a little cheer.

Well, Adriane thought proudly to her Gentle Listener, *a new convert to the sport.*

"Things are better between Garrett and me now," said May-Annlouise.

Adriane held a finger to her lips. "Wait till a commercial." Despite Pittsburgh's last touchdown, she was growing a little nervous, that extra half point she'd given up starting to haunt her.

May-Annlouise said she really should be going.

Adriane gripped her armrest and scowled. "I've got a lot riding on this one," she said, her jaw tight. "You could call this a life-changing game. Can't you stay a little longer?"

May-Annlouise thought about it and excused herself to call Garrett and tell him she was running late.

"Don't mention you're here," Adriane said over her shoulder.

"Of course I will. We may have our problems, but dishonesty isn't one of them."

"Yeah," Adriane muttered, "you guys are a regular Ozzie and Harriet."

In the kitchen, there was a short, hurried phone conversation, during which May-Annlouise didn't specify where she was calling from. Adriane took this as another small victory and flashed her most winning smile when May-Annlouise returned.

"Things are better between Garrett and me," she began again, in the middle of a Pittsburgh screen pass. "I was so out of my head for a time there. I'm still crying every day, but at least I can *see* him again, I can let him help me. We can help each other—"

"Sure," said Adriane, boosting the TV volume.

"You know," continued May-Annlouise, "I'm still sorting out how I feel about his infidelity. Maybe it'll upset me more later. But right now, it seems like you've done us a favor. In an odd way. Maybe even helped our marriage. We were just talking about that the other night."

"You mean I've, like, pollinated you two?" Adriane glared at her.

"No." May-Annlouise laughed. "More like woke us up. Alerted us that something valuable needs rescuing—"

"Look!" shouted Adriane. "Don't put this on *me!* If you two are pathetic enough to stay together, do I deserve the blame for that? Do I have that kind of power? You don't even love him," she found herself adding. "You don't know how to love."

"Adriane, don't be absurd." May-Annlouise smiled, but the tilt of her head expressed a pained curiosity. "Have you been telling him that?"

Adriane ignored her. On the TV, Pittsburgh leisurely pushed forward. With less than two minutes remaining, the

Steelers were content to grind down the clock with running plays straight up the middle. *Come on, score. Don't hang me out to dry here. Do something.*

And then, as though her Gentle Listener had stepped in, a neat hole opened in Cleveland's line and the Pittsburgh running back—some cocksure rookie who was always mouthing off for the press—dodged his way toward the end zone. Two defenders converged and, just as he crossed the touchdown plane and won Adriane's bet for her (all that money! all that freedom! hers!), dove at him from opposite sides, colliding against his rib cage.

A splintering crunch came from the TV, the sound of a beaded curtain parting.

Adriane let her breath out, had some trouble taking in another. *Was that really necessary?* she thought, as the kid lay motionless.

What fans remained cheered for the extra score. And there were patches of celebration on the Pittsburgh bench. Other players craned to see what was going on with the injured kid, not a popular team member, but some things should never happen to anybody. Adriane muted the television, dropped the remote.

I cursed him, she thought; the idea seemed as preposterous as it did certain. She uttered the word out loud: *cursed.*

"What's the matter?" May-Annlouise asked, staring at her. "Didn't we just score?"

The team doctor jogged onto the field; Adriane remained motionless on the couch. *Get him up, won't You?* she thought. *Hello?*

"How much," May-Annlouise asked, alarm creeping into her voice, "did you lose?"

The weight of grief pressed Adriane against her sofa, and she continued to hear, behind a prevailing silence, the parting of that beaded curtain, the one separating life from death. She peered across to the other side. In some distant realm of possibility, her mother and father—together after all—embraced, gently yet passionately. Making tenderest love. Just as Adriane might have wished for them, if only she were a better human being.

nine

Yoga Is a Personal Journey

Ziv Mitzna left the photocopy shop with a hundred leaflets denouncing his brother. Then drove west along Reisterstown Road, pulled into a strip mall, and parked in the shadow of its trash bin. Across the lot: his former business, BALTIMORE YOGA WORKS. Ziv stared at its sign with injured disdain.

Walking toward him came a small boy with a squeegee and a bucket of water, even in this cold. The boy pointed to Ziv's dirty windshield. "Twenty-five cents for the front. Fifty for all of 'em."

"Okay," said Ziv. "That's a fair price."

The boy got to work, starting with the front.

Ziv stepped out of his car and asked, "What's your name?"

"Jerome." The boy looked about eight. A small crescent scar clung to one cheek.

"Jerome, how would you like to earn ten dollars for very little work?"

The boy shrugged as he continued clearing the windshield. "Maybe."

"Jerome, you see these?" asked Ziv, handing over one of his leaflets, which featured an unflattering photo of his brother performing the Lion's Pose, eyes rolled back into his head and tongue protruding, fierce and ugly. It read:

AMIT MITZNA HAS CHOSEN THE PATH OF WRONG ACTION.
PLEASE DO NOT BUY YOGA FROM THIS MAN.
GO-YOGA, 4 BLOCKS EAST. FIRST TIME FREE W/COUPON BELOW.

The boy nodded and handed back the page. Began cleaning the passenger's side.

"I want you to place one of these on each windshield, also when new cars come, till about five-thirty, let's say, and I would like you to start with that silver car over there."

"The Toyota?"

"The Alfa Romeo. The little sports car. He married well." Ziv pointed out the license plate, which said BREEV. "If the guy who owns that car confronts you, please tell him, 'The family of humankind bears witness to your deceit and is ashamed of you.'"

The boy nodded.

"Let me hear you say it."

After dipping his squeegee into the bucket, Jerome soaped the back window. "The family of humankind. Bears witness. To your deceit and is ashamed."

"Of you."

"Of you."

"Good. He'll yell, but I have never known him to be violent. Now, Jerome, you seem like a businessman of your word," said Ziv, withdrawing his wallet. "I'm going to pay you in advance. Cash transaction. No withholding." He handed over a $10 bill, which the boy folded and stashed in his jeans before finishing the last of the windows.

"Good job," Ziv said and paid the fifty cents he'd already agreed to. "Thank you."

Jerome took the leaflets and headed toward the silver Alfa.

Feeling chilly, Ziv climbed back into his own car and started the engine. He waited till the first leaflet had been delivered before driving off to work.

May-Annlouise drew her navel spineward as she exhaled, then felt an adrenal jolt as Ziv, the instructor, placed a hand on each of her hips and fine-tuned their angle. She heard a drop of her own sweat ping against the mat below. The teacher liked to keep his studio warm; he claimed it loosened the muscles.

"You want to do it *good enough?*" he asked the class rhetorically. "There is no *good enough*." He prowled across the wood floor in his bare feet, wearing nothing but a pair of bicycle shorts. "Only *what is*. Only *the breath*. Whatever you came in here with tonight," he went on, "set this aside. Center your mind on the immediate presence of your body. Let's move into Cobra now. . . ."

May-Annlouise tried to center her mind, but she continued

to feel embarrassed by his last correction, the pressure of his fingertips on her hips.

"He picks on me," she complained during the ride back.

"No, sugar," said Dorothy, her friend and boss. "He tweaks everyone's poses. And you're still new," she added, reaching for her turn signal. "Maybe he's flirting."

"Flirting?" May-Annlouise squinted from an approaching headlight. "Don't be ridiculous. Nobody's flirting."

Dorothy pulled into the parking lot of the Fiske Travel Agency. "So. How's married life? Everything squares in that department?"

"Garrett and me? We're all right."

Shutting off the car, her boss looked at her and said, "You know I like having you come to class with me. But it *is* two nights a week. Anything at home you're—avoiding?" The engine ticked cooler in the winter air.

"I'm just really getting into it. I was thinking about adding a third night."

Her boss arched a penciled eyebrow. "Is Garrett healed enough to come with?"

May-Annlouise laughed and shook her head. "He wouldn't be caught dead doing yoga," she said, climbing out of the warm car.

"Okay. Wouldn't want to force anybody," said Dorothy. "See you in the a.m."

As she drove home, May-Annlouise noticed she'd already lost most of her good mood from yoga, her yoga high, as the instructor liked to call it.

She found her husband and son in the den, watching a sit-com. Garrett's leg, nearly as meaty as before the accident, lay propped on a pillow. Turpin sat bolt upright, his head still immobilized in its halo: a harsh metal contraption that would remain screwed to his precious head till the end of the month. Ten weeks had passed since the two of them had fallen off the roof—the boy having gone up there to make a scene, and Garrett following to talk him down. Trying to comprehend it much beyond that gave May-Annlouise a migraine. Turpin laughed now at a joke from the TV, his mirth lurching out of his confined torso. It killed her to see him laugh like that. She longed for the day when he could slouch again, with determination and with every part of his body.

"How was class?" asked her husband.

"Good," she said, despite her mixed feelings. Then found herself adding, "Maybe you should come next week. You look ready for some physical therapy."

He grimaced.

"I'd like to go," offered Turpin, shifting his eyes toward her. "I'm almost ready for physical therapy."

"Well, you'll have your own special ones first. You don't play around with a fractured neck."

"You don't play around with a broken leg either," argued her son.

"That doesn't begin to compare. Besides, he's all better now," she said, turning toward her husband. "Aren't you?"

"I guess," he allowed.

Later in bed, after turning out the lights, she brought it up again. "You could stand to develop greater mindfulness," she said. "It's a beginners' class."

"The one you're taking with Dorothy?"

"You go at your own pace. Ziv is very, um, patient. He—"

"Your boss thinks I'm a bastard."

"She does not." May-Annlouise propped her head on her elbow to get a better look at him in the darkness.

"Come on. You must have told her about. . . ." His voice trailed off.

"About what?"

He swallowed. "You know."

May-Annlouise felt surprised he'd bring that up. Wasn't it the prerogative of the aggrieved spouse, to decide when and where to discuss such matters? And with whom? She did usually tell Dorothy Fiske everything, but in fact May-Annlouise had kept her husband's affair to herself because she already knew she was going to forgive him and didn't want to poison the well. Too angry to reassure him just now, she rolled onto her other side.

After a long silence, he said, "Ziv is an Indian name?"

"I doubt it. He's from Tel Aviv."

"Hmm," Garrett murmured.

An Israeli yoga teacher wasn't authentic enough for him? she wondered.

"Yoga's a lot cheaper than couples counseling," she pointed out. She wanted him to come with her to class, she decided; suddenly it seemed the least he could do.

"Are you saying we need couples counseling?" he asked.

She stared at the ceiling and sighed. "I'm not sure."

She *was* going to forgive him, believed she already had, almost. He was sorry, genuinely and deeply—May-Annlouise knew this. But as she lay awake, she kept picturing him and that assistant of his, dawdling at the bar near their office, confiding. Hand stroking hand, she pictured, and felt a rasp beneath her ribs.

The next day was Friday, and Ziv came home after his new evening class and listened to the answering machine. His brother had left hourly phone messages, growing more and more irate. "*You* no longer wanted to be business partners, Ziv. Not me. *You!* If you compromise my reputation, the consequences on you will be terrible."

Fingers trembling, Ziv took a deep breath and visualized his hand becoming steady, but when that didn't work, he poured himself a nonalcoholic beer.

He sat on the kitchen stool and replayed that last message, which had been left around four-thirty and was intended to be the last word of the day, as Amit had recently renounced using the telephone on Shabbat, though he did still drive his wife to shul, claiming it was too far to make her walk. His brother's selective interest in Jewish law seemed pointed, like a weapon, toward Ziv, the less righteous.

". . . Not me. *You!*"

Ziv drained his beer and checked the clock, which said nine-thirty. He picked up the phone and began to dial Amit's number. But the idea of leaving a long message while his brother and Debra listened in judgment without so much as taking a step toward answering made Ziv hang up in frustration.

In happier times, they would all be sharing Shabbat dinner together. Used to be, Ziv would squish himself into the back of the Alfa Romeo and go with them to Friday night services. He'd stay overnight and through Shabbat, which they would celebrate as a family. But all that had ended with the last election.

Ziv suddenly wanted another nonalcoholic beer, although he was loath to ingest the carbs. Dazedly, he walked to his refrigerator and stood before the closed door a long time before pulling its handle. Cursed election. He stared into his near-barren fridge, waiting for something inside to create a preference for itself, then hefted a jar of kosher pickles and immediately put them back. Amit and his Likudnik politics. A deadlock was the best Ziv could have hoped.

Ineligible for absentee ballots, which were reserved for state employees serving abroad, it would have been stupid for them both to fly back to Israel only to cancel out each other's vote, so: the pledge to abstain. By the time Ziv figured out, however, that his brother did not have a "bad, bad summer cold," as the willful Debra had insisted, covering for him, lying for him, it was already election morning and would have been impossible for Ziv to get a flight that arrived before the polls closed. That his candidate won made little difference; his brother's betrayal carved the beating heart out of Ziv.

He had no idea how to get over it. If it weren't for the classes he taught at least four times a day and which were as much for his own refuge and peace of mind as for his students', Ziv—well, he didn't know what. He missed his brother and his brother's wife, who was like a sister to Ziv and was a very good bookkeeper-receptionist as well. If only he could find a girl-friend like her, but women like Debra were rare. There was one who came to his class twice a week who bore some resemblance, her auburn hair and delicate feet. She wore a wedding ring, but that could be just a ruse to protect her from unwanted attentions. He'd once asked her name and it was May-Something—strange and hard to remember, so he tended instead to think of her as the "other Debra." Though probably she was nothing like the real Debra beneath the surface—sanguine, resolute Debra whom he still admired, despite that she would lie to him and betray him in solidarity with Amit, though even that last part, her loyalty, seemed admirable. The other Debra probably wasn't even Jewish.

Logy with carbs and melancholy, Ziv climbed into bed. When he awoke the next morning, the thought of crossing his brother's path at temple felt like a large hand pressing his face against the pillow. Maybe he should look for a more liberal congregation; to him, going had never really been about religion anyway, but about family. He decided to sleep longer. After he awoke again at noon, he ate a light breakfast of muesli with soymilk, then tried to finish last week's crossword puzzle. A new one would be coming tomorrow, and he didn't like to let them pile up. He had just penciled in *areola* when he was distracted by a car honk.

He looked out the window and saw Amit getting out of the silver Alfa; he was wearing his thick wool topcoat over his good suit. His pulse racing, Ziv opened the door in his pajamas and steeled himself for conflict.

"Are you ill?" demanded his brother, through the storm door.

Ziv considered his response, then said, "I have a bad summer cold."

"Don't start." Amit yanked open the glass door, letting in a gust of winter along with himself. "You missed shul. And again this morning. I thought you were ill."

"I'm fine," said Ziv, in secret grateful for his brother's concern.

"Put your clothes on. Let's get a drink."

Ziv glanced at the shiny little car and murmured, "You drove here on a Saturday."

"I won't tell if you won't," said Amit in a gentle tone of voice that Ziv had not heard in a long time.

He pulled on some clothes and his peacoat, a pair of ski mittens and a knit cap. Then the brothers climbed into the Alfa and sped away in silence. Amit liked to use all the gears as much as possible, downshifting on every curve; he had worn through two clutches already in as many years. When they arrived, Amit held the front door open for Ziv and said, "You're having the usual, I assume."

Ziv folded their coats and lay them on the next stool, while his brother ordered.

"One wheat grass and carrot," Amit told the portly teen behind the cash register, "and one wheat grass with celery and bee pollen."

The whir of blenders always relaxed Ziv.

"So I spoke with your new business associate," Amit shouted over the noise. "The little *schvartzer* in the parking lot—"

Ziv winced at his brother's language. "Jerome."

The teen rang up their total and Amit beckoned to Ziv. "Get out my wallet would you and pay the man," he said, parting his suit jacket to expose his hind pocket.

"I've got it," said Ziv, reaching for his own wallet.

"Don't be silly. I invited you."

Ziv reluctantly dipped into his brother's pants and withdrew the wallet, pulled out a ten and handed it to the perplexed teenager. Then returned the paper change to the wallet and the wallet back into the pants, leaving whatever coins for a tip. How had the wallet found its way into Amit's trousers in the first place? Had he put it there before the start of Shabbat? Ziv shook his head over his brother's self-justifications. It was bad karma to contort Jewish law for one's own power agenda.

"Your friend Jerome," continued Amit, as they sat down with their drinks. "Who said all humankind was ashamed of me. I don't know how you come to decide that."

Ziv shrugged. "Maybe that was a bit sweeping."

"*You* are ashamed of me, Ziv. You and no one else." Amit stared over the rim of his cup. "Did you hear that statement last week? Your beloved prime minister? He's predicting big advances in the peace process. He's predicting this. The man is a clairvoyant. You know how he knows? Because he plans to give the country away. So, maybe next election, no country for me to vote in."

"There will be a country," said Ziv, forcing himself to match his brother's gaze. "And you will break your word if it suits you. Because my regard means so little."

"That's not true. But I do put my principles over your regard for me."

"Principles," said Ziv, eyes suddenly moist.

Amit tossed back the rest of his juice. "You want another?"

Ziv pictured going through that dance with the wallet again and shook his head. Said he had to lead a class in an hour.

"You're working on Shabbat now?"

"For you work maybe, but for me still a calling." Silently he wondered if the "other Debra" might be there.

"Whoever made you such a high horse?" His brother crumpled his napkin and frowned. "I don't want to discuss business on Shabbat."

"Who's making you?"

As though unable to stop himself, Amit leaned forward and murmured, "I'll give you one last chance to put this whole stupid thing behind us and be partners again. We can have two studios growing successfully, instead of each tearing the other one down."

Ziv pretended to concentrate on the last sip of his juice, but inside felt such an enormous hunger he became light-headed. If only the "whole stupid thing" could indeed fall aside so easily. Something was still missing from the offer, however, some essential repair to his pride, and the sad fact remained: it would not likely be forthcoming.

"Do you remember," Ziv asked wistfully, "why we became yoga instructors?"

"Let's not discuss business."

"We were just discussing business. You don't remember, do you."

Amit scowled. "Because you were sick of teaching high school civics and I was sick of clerking in the morgue."

No, thought Ziv, *the real reason, the noble reason*. It had to do with leading people to peace. And this peace would spread, throughout Israel, throughout the Middle East, and beyond. How ludicrous that sounded now. Staring at the wheat grass scum rimming his cup, Ziv smiled with rue at his own naiveté and shook his head.

Amit stood abruptly. Jamming his arms through his coat sleeves, he said, "If you try again to hurt my studio, I will strike back. I will knock the hyphen right out of your sign. No more 'Go-Yoga,' for people on the go."

In designing his new sign, Ziv had succumbed to a base commercial impulse, and he cringed now to hear himself mocked.

"Instead, everyone will know you are offering 'goy yoga,' " his brother barreled on, his cheeks reddening. "For goyim from goyim."

When exactly had Amit become so hateful? His reactionary descent seemed to Ziv as mysterious as it was deplorable. Halfway out the door now, Amit glanced back over his shoulder and said, "You no longer need a ride?"

Speechless with humiliation, Ziv slunk off his stool and followed.

On Monday afternoon, Garrett looked up from his computer screen and saw his assistant, Adriane, standing in the doorway, hand on slightly cocked hip.

"Will there be anything else, Mr. Hughes?" she asked.

Garrett blinked, dumbfounded. This nonsense had been going on too long.

"Do you have to call me Mr. Hughes?" he said. "Why call me anything? We're the only people in the room."

"Because," she said, taking a step inside. "I made a New Year's resolution. If I was going to keep working here, a few principles of decorum needed to be upheld."

"Decorum is fine. Decorum is *great*. But we've known each other too long for that kind of formality." He made himself look at her when he said this.

"I'm reestablishing boundaries."

You seduced me, he wanted to remind her. But that would have sounded ungentlemanly, and *seduction* wasn't even the right word. Neither was *affair,* which connoted a dark glamour or at least the idea of pleasure and, more technically, consummation. Their little "lapse," small and sad, was more an urgent grab for comfort at a time when comfort had been scarce.

"It feels like I'm being punished," he blurted.

"You *are* being punished. We both are." She sighed, adding, "I'm going home."

"But it's only three-forty-five." The winter sun angled low through his window.

"Well, is there something you need me to be working on?" she asked with mounting irritation.

He thought about it and there wasn't. There was barely enough work for one person in their little department.

"I guess not." Watching her turn toward the door, he murmured a small attempt at amends: "Have a good evening."

"What's that supposed to mean?" she called over her shoulder.

"Nothing." He cradled his face in his hands, and wondered glumly if he should find himself another job. His wife had insisted it wasn't necessary, but did she secretly want him to?

For fifteen years, he'd been with the Mayor's Office of Neighborhood Enhancement, a department so low on the political radar he'd managed to duck the cycles of retribution that governed most other appointments. As for the private sector, he'd never set foot in it, but he'd heard stories, always on the theme of upheaval, rude awakenings, and the cutthroat struggle to survive. Every man for himself. It was disheartening just to think about.

Garrett decided to head home a little early himself. He'd agreed to meet May-Annlouise at her yoga class later that evening and, as he drove now, he noticed a mounting sense of dread. After pulling into his garage, he entered the kitchen, where he found his stepson standing before the refrigerator, his halo rig matching the stainless steel door. Garrett recalled the boy's house-arrest gizmo from the year before; it seemed the kid was always getting yoked to some restraint or other. As though his adolescent chaos were otherwise in danger of bursting from the orbit of civilized daily life.

"How was your first day back at school?" Garrett asked.

"Pretty good." Turpin carried a casserole of leftover lasagna to the breakfast nook.

"Your classmates didn't give you a hard time, I hope. About that contraption."

"I got three offers on it already."

"What do you mean, offers?"

"To buy it."

"But it's, it's keeping your head on!" Garrett stammered. No matter how hard he tried to keep his cool around his stepson, the boy always knew just how to zing him. To soften his outburst, Garrett now added, in as gentle a voice as he could muster, "son."

"I meant when I'm all better, but I think I want to keep it anyway." Turpin chewed cold lasagna. "You want some of this?"

Garrett loosened his tie and found himself a plate. "Sure," he said. "Thanks."

"You've been calling me *son* a lot lately," Turpin noted.

Garrett hadn't wished to be so obvious, but he had been sprinkling a few *sons* into his conversation, like breadcrumbs that might lead them closer to one other.

"Have I?" he asked.

His stepdaughter entered the kitchen, a rare appearance from her room, to return a bowl of grapes. Ever since calling off her wedding, she'd become kind of a hermit. Entire days could pass when Garrett didn't even see her.

"Lynn," he asked, "why don't you come with me tonight?"

"Yoga is a venerable Indian tradition," she said, pouring herself some water. "And it's being marketed to people who only care about tight buns."

"He doesn't care about tight buns," his stepson put in. "I think it's cool he's trying something new."

She turned to Garrett and said, "He thinks you're cool. You must be relieved." Eyeing their plates of lasagna, she added, "You're having a big meal?"

"Not a meal," Garrett insisted. "Why? It's not like I'm going to play basketball."

His stepdaughter smiled cryptically and kissed his cheek.

"Are you sure you won't come?" he pleaded.

"Good luck," she told him, before retreating with her water.

Garrett ate more than he should. The lasagna was delicious cold, and more important, it was comfortable in the kitchen. He could not remember his stepson ever defending him on any point, and frankly it *was* a relief. He wanted to linger, eating in peaceful silence.

When the lasagna was at last finished, he put their plates in the dishwasher and ran some water to soak the pan. Turpin began reading his chemistry textbook, and Garrett excused himself to go change.

After putting on his gym clothes—a baggy pair of shorts and ancient Terrapins T-shirt—he bounded back downstairs, slowing when he felt a twinge in his leg. He grabbed his parka and would have said good-bye to his stepson, except the boy was no longer in the kitchen. Garrett felt disappointed, as though he'd merely imagined that earlier moment of harmony.

As he backed out of the driveway, he realized he'd left his wife's directions upstairs. But he knew the place was on Reisterstown and so decided to wing it. If he got lost, he'd just have to attend another time. He'd begun to wonder anyhow whether his leg was ready.

He found his way to a strip mall parking lot in front of something called BALTIMORE YOGA WORKS, which seemed a likely candidate. Getting out of the car, he took a few steps forward, but now the name sounded wrong. The name of the place he wanted was catchier, cheesier; he stood still, trying to remember it. Feeling a winter wind on his shins, he looked at his bare legs disappearing under his parka. He had dressed like a flasher. Unzipping the coat helped a little, but still his wife would have something to say about this. He heard a rustle and turned just as a small dark figure finished placing something under his wiper.

Garrett walked to his car and pulled off the sheet of paper, which read:

"WHAT HAST THOU DONE [AMIT MITZNA]?
THE VOICE OF THY BROTHER'S BLOOD CRIETH UNTO ME."—GEN. 4.
GO-YOGA, 4 BLOCKS EAST. FIRST TIME FREE W/COUPON BELOW.

Who was Amit Mitzna? Garrett wondered. And what had the guy done to provoke biblical condemnation?

"Are you here for class?" a deep voice called out. "We start in ten minutes."

Garrett looked up and saw a man, wearing loose pants and a muscle shirt and standing in the doorway of BALTIMORE YOGA WORKS.

"Thanks, but I'm supposed to meet my wife at this other place." Garrett waved the sheet of paper and climbed back into his car. Turning onto Reisterstown Road, he glanced in his rearview mirror and saw the man storming through the parking lot, yanking flyers from windshields. It made no sense to Garrett; still the scene added to his trepidation. After parking in front of GO-YOGA, he stayed in his car a while, collecting his resolve. Rereading the flyer and its coupon, he thought: at least it's free.

The front door of the place opened into a warm antechamber. Two incense coils burned atop a small table next to a box with a slotted lid and a sign saying, PLEASE MAKE CHECKS PAYABLE TO GO-YOGA. There was a clipboard with forms for those who preferred to pay by credit card, and everything seemed to depend on the honor system. Garrett wrote his name on the coupon part of his flyer, tore it off, and put it in the box.

Passing through a door to the main studio, he felt a cloud of hot air, easily ninety degrees, and thick with the odors of exertion. It would have been nice of May-Annlouise to warn him, though it wasn't the kind of thing you prepared for. He edged his way deeper into the dim studio, whose walls were paneled with mirrors.

A dozen students had shown up already. Garrett noticed two other men in the class and felt a spark of irrational gratitude. As the early birds stretched out, perspiring cheerfully, they chatted in hushed tones; most everyone seemed to know each other.

Garrett found one of the mats people were using and spread it near a wall, lay on his back, and felt like he was in kindergarten again. He could easily drift into a nap in this heat, and to keep himself awake he decided to stretch his legs. They were both stiff but the bad one especially. Wondering again if he was ready for this, he caught his wife's reflection, her auburn hair, entering the room, and behind her, Dorothy the boss, whose tall red beehive seemed the very hallmark of danger. For a long moment, Garrett wished he'd suggested the couples counseling.

But the thing about couples counseling, as he imagined it: the therapist always took sides. How could she not? The triangular relationship seemed fundamentally unstable. And Garrett couldn't for the life of him see how the side taken would be his. So, yoga class had felt like a bargain. Also, something about his wife's request had sounded nonnegotiable.

"Hello," said Dorothy Fiske, suddenly towering above, looking at him through a pair of rhinestone-framed glasses. She wore a T-shirt that said READY across the front. Garrett stood and offered his sweaty hand.

"People, please," said his wife, urging the two of them into a social embrace. "You've known each other how many years?"

Dorothy gave him a quick no-nonsense hug—the way men often hugged one another—her hand patting his back as though she were burping him; it was impossible to tell from such a hug how much reproach she harbored.

May-Annlouise excused herself to use the restroom, leaving Garrett and Dorothy alone in each other's company. She looked him up and down, mostly down, and seemed to dwell on his legs, or was it his crotch, before she said, her voice raspy and coy, "So, Garrett, you managing to stay out of trouble?"

His lips parted slightly, but no words came out; the heat seemed to push any thought he might have voiced back into his head. He stood paralyzed by a fear that had been germinating below ground but now bloomed before his eyes: His wife would never forgive him, not completely, without the blessing of her beloved friend and mentor.

From somewhere chimed a musical tone, and over Dorothy's shoulder, he saw a barefoot man wearing a pair of bicycle pants and holding a tuning fork. Its sound continued to float across the room as students—at least thirty now—quickly finished spreading their mats and sat down, assuming an identical meditative pose. Dorothy encamped directly behind Garrett. His wife, returning from the bathroom, quickly set up in front of him. For the first time, he noticed her outfit; ankle-length leotard that clung like paint, with a sexy low-cut back. Did she usually wear this? he wondered. The last sound waves of the fork disappeared, and the instructor put it aside.

"For the next ninety minutes, this will be a place of refuge," he said, strolling among them. "Our time together shall be all about the breath. With each exhale you are erasing whatever you may have brought with you tonight. We will dwell in the honesty of the body. Listen to what your body is telling you. The body never lies."

He spoke with only the slightest accent, and his placid good looks suggested an urbane poise. His frame seemed muscular but padded with a little baby fat. Garrett couldn't tell for sure, but he bet the man got weekly pedicures; his body looked like it was paid a lot of attention.

"Alternating nostrils now," he said.

This came as news to Garrett, who'd never deliberately inhaled through one side of his nose and out the other; he couldn't fathom the purpose of such a thing but gave it a sporting try. At the very least he could describe it later for Turpin.

The instructor sat cross-legged on his own mat at the front of the class and leaned forward, so that his torso folded nearly parallel to the floor. "Bending from the hips, not the spine, keep your spine in alignment," came the directive, which was going to be a problem, Garrett could tell already, a parmesan lump in his throat. If he was going to bend from the hips and only from the hips, he could angle his torso forward maybe a few inches. He glanced at the other students to his right, his wife in front, and saw no one who remained at nearly the seventy-five-degree angle that he did. It was going to be a long hour and a half, he could tell already, full of physical and emotional discomfort and probably humiliation. All of which, it just now occurred to him, might not be entirely beside the evening's point.

The instructor aimed his rump in the air and led everyone into something he called Downward-Facing Dog. Garrett rearranged himself and looked through the gap of his slightly bowed legs. He could see right behind him the swath of Dorothy's beehive, a red exclamation point.

"Rise up on the balls of your feet," urged the instructor's voice. "Focus on what is going on in the body. Focus on the breath. Everything else, let it go. Let us step outside the wheel of desire, gratification, and frustration, shall we? All desire, let it go. Let go of all thought beyond the breath."

As he flexed the balls of his feet, Garrett felt a spasm in his recovering leg and had to immediately lower his knee to the mat. He wondered if he was risking rebreaking the bone, his muscles not yet strong enough to support it.

"Lunge through into Half-Warrior," said the instructor, and everyone but Garrett seemed to know what this meant. He looked at his fellow students in the mirror, at Dorothy to his reflected left, and tried to imitate her lunge while putting most of his weight on the good leg.

"Reach for the sun!"

Garrett pointed toward the ceiling with both arms along

with everyone else. The instructor walked over and placed his hands on Garrett's shoulders and tried to get him to distribute his weight more evenly.

"Got an iffy leg here," Garrett whispered. "Trying to take it easy."

"There are no iffy legs," the teacher reassured him. "Only iffy thoughts *about* legs. Do whatever you feel comfortable."

The instructor let go of him and moved on to May-Annlouise, where he found cause to give her shoulders a little squeeze.

Garrett noticed Dorothy Fiske looking at him in the mirror. *So, Garrett, are you managing to stay out of trouble?*

He smiled and waved a sun-reaching hand, but she did not wave back.

The class now torqued into a pose that made Garrett think of crucifixes, a singularly unsettling thought, not to mention that it was a thought at all and therefore off limits. But that only made him think even more, pondering Dorothy's question, trying to recall her exact emphasis and tone.

"Maybe some of you are worried about pressures in your daily life," said the teacher. "Acknowledge that anxiety, then set it aside and concentrate only on your breath. Over which you have total control."

He picked up a plastic bottle and began to spray a fine mist toward each student's face, two squirts of water per. As he made the rounds, most all of the women presented their faces, like plants to the light, and Garrett's wife was no exception. The male students seemed to draw the line here, and Garrett passed as well, even though he was broiling by now. Dorothy demurred too, maybe because of her carefully set hair, or her glasses. Or because she still had yet to perspire; her READY shirt remained dry and crisp, whereas Garrett's T-shirt sagged under the weight of a tortoise-shaped sweat stain.

The class moved into something called Triangle Pose, which seemed to involve spreading the legs followed by a deep sideways bend at the hip, one arm touching the ground and the other reaching up. Garrett found he could do only the grossest approximation, flexing at every joint, so that he resembled less a triangle than a crude fertility figure. Blood rushed to his face.

Although the instructor had said to go only so far as he felt comfortable, Garrett hated having to "cheat," especially in front of Dorothy, whose gaze now seemed to absorb his inadequate reflection. He tried to make eye contact with her, hoping for a moment of connection, but Dorothy appeared to focus again somewhere in the vicinity of his gym shorts.

He noticed suddenly that her head and his were a mere dozen inches apart. And looking in the mirror he realized the whole class was triangle-ing east except for him; he'd gotten turned around somehow. Too locked into his westerly pose to consider moving any time soon, he tried to make the most of it, his head so close to Dorothy's, a rare opportunity:

"I was a stupid jackass!" he whispered urgently. He could feel the lasagna pressing against his gullet. "Believe me, I know!"

Dorothy raised her eyes to his in the mirror and blinked.

"You're backwards," she mouthed.

From the far corner of the room, the instructor said, "Remember: yoga is a *personal* journey."

His pulse throbbing in his ears, Garrett felt compelled to use this moment of Dorothy's attention and went for broke:

"I swear," he murmured, loud as he dared, "it'll never happen again!"

He balanced there, squat-triangle-ing, his fertility-figure legs spread to an utterly vulnerable degree, and yet his stance now seemed more sure and balanced, as though he'd been able to shift an awkward, top-heavy burden. He felt a euphoric flutter at the thought of having made peace with Dorothy Fiske, who, still blank-faced, turned from the mirror and settled into her next pose. As he turned as well, however, Garrett saw his wife staring at him with profound exasperation.

"Yoga is a *personal* journey," said the instructor, right behind him now. "Let's face front, gently drop to the knees, and move into our Locust Pose," he said, guiding Garrett, who allowed himself to be arranged into a kind of flying insect. Together, the class looked capable of razing entire crops.

He noticed the instructor glance ahead toward May-Annlouise, lying on her stomach, arms and legs pointed back, buttocks pursed—a model student. The teacher squatted behind her and cupped her feet in his hands, tinkering with their angle. For her part, she seemed to take an extra-deep in-breath. Garrett wondered if he was meant to absorb all this, the special care their instructor seemed to be giving her, their rapport. These displays were surely also part of the evening's point.

He had it coming, really. Maybe he didn't deserve to be forgiven, hadn't yet managed to behave like a man *worthy of forgiveness,* a much more daunting standard, it pained him to realize, than any he'd been expected to meet before.

As he lay on his stomach, impersonating a locust, Garrett began to wonder what forgiveness even *was*. He'd hoped for a palpable healing, like a knitted leg or spine. Something he could feel and recognize and tell apart from its opposite— clearly and reliably. But maybe forgiveness was more like soap bubbles from a wand. Something his wife might float his way from time to time.

"Yoga is a *personal* journey," May-Annlouise heard the instructor say from across the room.

She looked in the mirror and saw her husband mouthing something toward Dorothy's reflection.

What on earth was he doing? Did he have no grasp of why he was here? Maybe it was a mistake to bring him tonight, but May-Annlouise had thought the session would do them good, would provide a quiet moment in which the roiling events of the past few months could be banished, her own jealousy banished, and they could just spend an hour and a half together in stillness without bumping against all their painful *knowledge*.

"I swear," he seemed to be saying to the mirror, "*something*, never happen again."

Oh, for goodness' sake, he was apologizing to Dorothy.

The instructor strode over and, with an emphasis bordering on anguish, repeated, "Yoga is a *personal* journey."

Now she would have to explain everything after all. Who knew when her boss would again be able to look Garrett in the eye. How unhelpful, how ridiculous of him. With all his turmoil, he'd even managed to fluster the yogi.

And the worst part, it slowly dawned on her: how was she going to look Dorothy in the eye herself? Stretching deeper into her Locust Pose, May-Annlouise tried to unclench her jaw. *Am I a fool?* she wondered. *Am I a fool to forgive him?* That apology of his, something about it was just a little bit sweet. Was she stupid to think so? Would anyone but her be able to see the truth of the matter? Sweat puddled in the small of her back and her stomach began to cramp.

The instructor knelt behind her and took hold of her feet, trying to bend them inward. "Whatever you are preoccupied with, set those feelings of desire aside and take a deep cleansing breath."

She thought of her husband, pictured him trying to exhale all desire of his own, and felt a pang. When she'd said she wanted him to cultivate greater mindfulness, what she'd really meant was greater mindfulness of *her*. What if each exhale, each shedding of desire, was a betrayal of their marriage? Yearning, distraction, even suffering, these were passion's substance. Was she supposed to deny this? she wondered, her arms and legs reaching behind her with such force they trembled. What if a marriage without suffering was no marriage at all?

"Let go," the instructor whispered, trying to bend her, but she would not.

As Ziv wandered between mats, a small commotion at the studio's far end: that fellow, the newcomer, saying something vaguely but urgently remorseful. The class was getting away from Ziv, and he hurried over to the newcomer and reminded him, "Yoga is a *personal* journey."

Ziv guided the man toward the next asana, got him quiet and lying down, then brought his arms back, and lastly the feet raised off the ground, suspended in midair—subduing him.

Next, Ziv turned to the woman in front—the other Debra—even though her form was near perfect.

"Whatever you are preoccupied with," he said, "set those feelings of desire aside. . . ."

The more he tried to adjust her pose, the more she resisted. A sense of worthlessness nipped at him. *Let go,* he whispered. *Please.* He heard what sounded like the tinkle of glass in the parking lot, and felt a crack in his own chest.

Several students groaned from their efforts, and Ziv went to fetch his spritz bottle to give them relief.

"Maybe you long for justice," he said, keeping one ear open for trouble. "Maybe you anxiously await peace between nations. Let go of all of this for now. Think only of the breath, the cleansing power of the breath."

One woman in a leopard print yogatard looked especially wilted. Just as Ziv moved closer to spritz her, the fire alarm began to jangle. Then the ceiling sprinklers commenced showering—on his studio and everyone and everything in it.

The class gasped, and people quickly abandoned their poses. A growing murmur quickly turned to one of panic.

"Please stay calm," said Ziv, but inside, his blood simmered with suspicion and rage. "It's most likely a false alarm. Take deep breaths, unless you smell smoke, and begin slowly exiting the building. *Namaste,*" he added. "The divine in me recognizes the divine in you."

He waited, captain of his sinking ship, till all the students had charged from the studio, then, draping a towel across his bare shoulders, Ziv followed.

His class milled about the parking lot, looking at the building, which divulged no flame or smoke, nothing that would explain this emergency. The other Debra stood next to that talkative newcomer. Were they together? he wondered. An older woman wearing a READY T-shirt, her sodden hairdo leaning to one side, waved to them and said, "I'm gonna scram. You're riding with him, right?"

So, there is a husband, concluded Ziv, disappointed. *A boorish, disruptive husband.* The cry of fire engines grew louder.

Ziv looked at his neon sign, expecting to see a broken hyphen. He was confused then to see it still lit, with a pulselike flicker. What then, he wondered, had broken? Was all this chaos just dumb accident?

Two fire trucks arrived, their brakes heaving a sigh, a police car along for good measure. Ziv approached the ladder truck and introduced himself. When asked, "Where's the fire?" he honestly couldn't say.

Four firefighters jogged toward the building, as a police officer took down Ziv's rambling statement.

"Any idea what might have set off those sprinklers?" the officer asked.

Shivering under his towel, Ziv became distracted by that talkative husband, who was holding one of the yoga flyers, its coupon casually torn out, and showing it to his wife. "Who's Amit Mitzna?" the man asked her. "And what has he done that's so bad?"

They stood with their backs to Ziv, who suddenly broke away from the cop and darted toward them. "I'll tell you what Amit has done!"

The couple turned and looked at him with anticipation. As though he were about to deliver some last kernel of spiritual enlightenment for the evening. A little parting bonus from the harmless guru. But he was in no mood to share abstract wisdom, only the cold harsh facts of the real world. His rage felt cosmic in its radiance. They must have seen this in his face; before Ziv could even begin the tirade that had been rising inside him, the woman recoiled, leaning into her husband, who in turn put an arm around her shoulder. The two of them seemed to balance against each other.

"We have to be getting home," said the husband.

"We're tired and cold," she apologized.

As Ziv watched them walk away, he felt someone rap on his shoulder.

"We're not done here," said the cop. "You sure you don't know how this started?"

Ziv noticed the officer's gun, primed in its holster, his ebony nightstick, gleaming. The bullet-studded belt encircling his thick waist.

And where was all of this to end? Ziv wondered.

"Come," he told the cop. "I'll show you where he lives."

ten

Lynn, Raving

As Lynn tried to find her way back through the warm, teeming warehouse, some guy with a pacifier lodged between his lips began dancing against her left hipbone. His cheeks puckered in and out, as if he were smooching with himself, and over his heart he wore a large metallic button proclaiming I LOVE MY MIN PINS. He seemed hardly aware of Lynn as he reached for the hem of her sweatshirt.

"Hey!" she said. "Cut it out!"

She slipped away into the mob of strangers: some writhing, others jumping, or spinning like dervishes—more than one colliding against her. *What on earth,* she continued to wonder, *is a Min Pins?* At last, she spotted the top of her brother's blond head.

My tall baby brother, thought Lynn, and her breathing began to calm down. *My tall, know-it-all, lucky-to-be-alive baby brother.* In the time she'd spent in line at the Port-a-Pot, he'd met a girl. Girls often were drawn to his gentle indifference.

"What took you so long!" he shouted over the music. "This is Meg!"

The other girl took hold of Lynn's hand and began undulating the length of their two arms like a Chinese dragon. She looked maybe eighteen or nineteen, younger than Lynn, older than Turpin, and had coffee-colored skin, like Lynn, but wavier hair.

"Meg goes to Hopkins!" said Turpin, accepted there himself for the coming fall.

"Nice!" said Lynn, who took classes at Towson State, part-time. She had a psych test Monday morning she really should be studying for. Uncoupling her hand now, she checked her watch.

"You guys don't look so related!" Meg observed, raising her arms over her head and waving them slowly back and forth.

"She's my *half* sister!" Turpin said, still dancing.

"My father's Indian!" said Lynn, trying to move to the rhythm, but she found it hard to dance and talk at the same time. "He lives in India. With his, um, second wife!"

"Awesome!" Meg said. "My mom's black! She lives in New York with her new girlfriend!"

Lynn nodded, smiled amiably, but it seemed strange bonding over their mixed backgrounds and broken homes.

The girl named Meg now glanced to her right and left, then

reached under her silk camisole and produced a strip of tape with four pills stuck to it. "Refreshments anyone?" she offered.

Turpin's face lit up with that Christmassy expression he got around drugs. "Thanks!" he said, "but we brought our own!"

"We did?" asked Lynn sharply.

From his pants pocket, he withdrew a few white pills and a tuft of lint.

"It's just a little Ecstasy!" he said. "You've been wanting to cut loose!"

"I never said that!"

"Well—" He pressed a pill into her hand. "You've been thinking it!"

Lynn had agreed to come here tonight as a gesture toward her brother, to ease the recent strain between them and get back to something approaching normal, and because he'd assured her: no drugs. But now that she thought about it, he'd promised only not to *buy* drugs tonight. Out of habit, she tried to recall Islam's words on the subject, but she hadn't read her Qur'an in over a year and couldn't remember anything beyond the general sense that intoxicants were off limits. It was hard to concentrate with the music pounding, which was probably the point of the music, the point of the rave itself.

"You have no idea what I've been thinking!" she said. An elbow knocked into her shoulder. "Besides, I have to drive!"

"I'll be designated driver!"

"A gentleman!" said Meg, reaching into a leather shoulder sack and pulling out a bottle of fluorescent-green Gatorade.

Lynn regarded her brother skeptically. She didn't believe his offer would endure. He'd start feeling left out and would end up indulging, and then they'd be without a sober driver. She gave him back his pill, had never really considered taking it—not seriously—and watched him down it with long gulps of Gatorade, his Adam's apple a pogo. Meanwhile, Meg had begun unscrewing the cap to a small glass jar.

"This stuff'll smell great when you're rolling!" she said, and smeared a little Vicks Vapo-Rub underneath her nose, then applied some under Turpin's.

"I'll try some of that, I guess," said Lynn. She used to look forward to colds, when she could stay home from school and her mother would smooth Vapo-Rub on her chest.

Meg dabbed some on the cleft under Lynn's nose, and the menthol brought with it the memory of her mother pampering her and granting her a pass from the pressures of the outside world. Sometimes Lynn would just pretend to have a cold.

She began to dance again, mincingly. Turpin hopped up and down and flailed his arms, and Lynn pictured him, as she often did, a year and a half earlier, falling off the roof of their house on her wedding day. On what would have been her wedding day before he'd made such a terrible scene and brought everything to a halt. He could be such a cocky brat, so sure he knew best what was right for her.

That was an unkind way to put it, considering how badly he'd been injured.

Turpin hadn't tried to hook up with this Meg girl. She'd smiled at him from afar and gradually begun dancing closer and closer to him. Fine. Cool. Though he didn't want his sister to think he was ditching her, especially since they were getting along for the first time in a while. But at a rave you weren't dancing with just one person anyway, you were dancing at large. You could even be dancing with your sister, and it was okay.

"Good morning, Baltimore!" shouted someone from the stage. The DJ had been replaced by a band called Blood Brain Barrier.

"These guys are supposed to be—incredible!" Meg shouted toward Turpin's ear.

"You have to hear these guys!" he in turn shouted at his sister.

If only she'd loosen up a little. It would have been nice to see what Ecstasy could release in her, but he should've known that wasn't going to happen. Amazing really that he'd gotten her to come in the first place. Just a year and a half ago she was wearing robes and engaged to a stranger from India, some mechanical engineer her father had picked out. Even now she still hid herself under baggy clothes, which was a waste of her good looks. She definitely needed to have her mind blown a little.

The crowd cheered as the band launched into its first song, characterized by the spiky interplay of two electric guitars. Turpin could see a commotion in the distance. Near the exit, a girl was screaming at two police officers who'd handcuffed her wrists behind her back.

The band stopped abruptly, except for the tapping of unamplified drums, and then that also stopped. A policeman walked over to the lead singer's microphone, which began to squeal with feedback.

"Good morning, Baltimore," said the cop and waited for all the booing to fade. "Party's over."

"Come on!" someone shouted. "One more song!"

"*Say—no—to—drugs,*" the officer sang, before stepping down from the stage.

About half the people at the rave, which was a lot of people, began reaching into their pockets or underneath their shirts or down into their underwear and flinging whatever they'd stashed onto the floor, and this made a soft, fluttering, but greatly multiplied sound like a flock of birds landing. The crowd moved toward the exit.

"Stay close!" Turpin told his sister. As he was shuttled forward, he could glimpse the floor below littered with little packets of powder and pills. How tempting to scoop some up, like Halloween candy. But the crowd pressed together so tight, he couldn't bend down if he'd tried.

At the exit ahead, six police searched people at random—a symbolic gesture to everyone else. Turpin wiped the Vicks from under his nose and held his head straight, ready to meet any cop's gaze with the calm, assured nod of the blameless. But it hardly came to that; the police had their hands full without him.

A few yards into the parking lot, he turned to find Meg at his heels.

"Where's my sister?" he asked.

He looked around the lot, saw her detained at the exit. She was leaning, arms and legs spread, against the outside wall of the warehouse, as a policewoman frisked her, pulling the pockets of her baggy jeans inside out.

His sister's long dark hair fanned across her sweatshirt.

"I should go help her," he said.

"You'll just make trouble for yourself," said Meg, touching his forearm.

"She needs the moral support," he argued, which was a strange expression when you thought about it. As he ambled back toward the exit, he felt almost knightly, like he was defending his sister's honor; it was a nice little rush, layered overtop the Ecstasy.

"Excuse me," he said to the policewoman. "Is there some problem here, officer?"

The cop, a broad-shouldered woman with robust thighs, cast Turpin a sour look and shined her flashlight in his eyes.

Squinting now, he added, "I can vouch for this young lady."

"You can?" said the cop. "You her lawyer?"

He realized too late that the phrase *vouch for this young lady* might have sounded stoned. "I'm her brother. I've known her my whole life."

"Turpin, just drop it. We're almost done," his sister said.

"You don't look like her brother," said the policewoman, still shining her light in his face.

"She's innocent," muttered Turpin, hands jammed into his own pockets now, fingering the pills there. "She's, like, the most innocent person here."

"Turpin, wait in the car!" Lynn shouted over her shoulder. "You're making it worse."

"I'm just saying anyone who knew you would understand you're the least likely person—"

"You want to come over here and join her?" asked the policewoman.

Turpin suddenly felt wobbly, tried to remember if the number of pills he was carrying constituted an intent to distribute.

"Do you want to come over here and join her?" the cop repeated.

He couldn't see the expression on her face and he couldn't read the tone of voice.

"Is that," he ventured, his left knee beginning to shudder, "a rhetorical question?"

"Is that a what?" the cop snapped.

"Rhetorical," said Turpin weakly. "It means—"

"I know what it means, you smart-mouth," said the cop. "Tell your client here to wipe her nose." She waved them both along.

As they scurried toward the parking lot, Turpin reeled with adrenaline, Ecstasy, and that chivalry thing. What an amazing feeling! His sister crammed her pockets back inside, then, like a kid with the sniffles, used her sleeve to remove the glistening Vicks, which she'd neglected before the checkpoint. He should have reminded her. She was so completely guileless, his sister. She was! She was! You just had to love someone that guileless.

"What in the world is a Min Pins?" she demanded.

"They're toy-sized Dobermans," he told her. "They're, like, adorable."

She turned toward him with an uncomprehending scowl, and he noticed one little spot of Vapo-Rub still shining above her lip.

Turpin reached over to wipe it off, but suddenly his arms grew heavy.

And then he blacked out.

As her brother collapsed against the trunk of a parked car, shoulder clapping sheet metal, Lynn envisioned him falling from the roof of their house. So reckless, so cocky. She imagined him parading across the shingles like a town crier—

"Wake up!" she yelled in his ear, slapping his face, probably harder than needed.

He opened his eyes, looked back and forth between Lynn and Meg, smiled blearily and said, "I'm starving."

"Me, too," said Meg.

"What just happened here?" said Lynn, trying to downplay her alarm. "Is this an overdose?"

He laughed and said his blood sugar was low. "Let's go empty the fridge."

Somehow Meg had been included in this invitation and was now climbing into their mother's car with them.

"You didn't drive here?" Lynn asked her.

"Nah. I can take a cab home from your place."

Lynn started the engine, her hands sweating against the steering wheel, and she recalled the roughness of brick against her palms from the warehouse wall. So it turned out she had that jelly on her lip, but at the time it seemed totally arbitrary, her being picked from the crowd and frisked. How obnoxious: to be so intimately misjudged.

She glanced at her brother now, and he seemed mesmerized by the traffic jammed in front of them.

"Are you sure you're all right?" Lynn asked.

"Oh yeah."

"I think someone fainted is all," said Meg from the backseat.

Lynn couldn't tell if her brother blushed or that was just the glow of taillights.

It took them twenty minutes to get home, during which no one spoke until Lynn pulled into the garage and unlocked the kitchen. As promised, Turpin went straight to the refrigerator and began raiding it, loading the countertop with cold cuts, cheese, the leftover pork loin, a jar of grapefruit cocktail. . . .

"Why are you guys so hungry?" Lynn asked. "Is this 'the munchies'?"

"Because we were dancing, like, five hours!" said Meg, shucking an ear of corn and stroking the silk against her eyelids. "Aren't you?"

"No," Lynn said, heading for the den. "I've got studying to do. Excuse me."

Behind her, she heard Meg's muffled voice ask Turpin, "Where are your parents?"

"Some country inn," he replied. "It's their anniversary."

Lynn sat down on the den couch and arranged her three highlighters (orange for material she believed would be on the test, yellow for material she thought *might* be on the test, and blue for material that probably wouldn't be on the test but interested her anyway). She opened her textbook—*Our Human Psychology, Third Edition*, much of which had been highlighted in blue—to the module on emotions.

There was a lot of test-likely stuff she still didn't know, and she was starting to stress. An emotion, she read, began with a stimulus that a person assessed "in terms of his or her well-being."

"Butter is super smooth," she heard her brother say in the distance.

Lynn closed her eyes and tried to concentrate, but it was hard over the guffawing from the kitchen, where stimuli seemed to abound.

She overheard something about a chicken. And then she heard her brother say "kind of shy," and she assumed they must be talking about her, but when she tried to overhear more, they'd moved on to talking about salad. She felt a spike of annoyance, but truth be told, Lynn *was* a chicken. She feared a lot of things, like the unknown, and change, as well as the prospect of change. These were potential stimuli she judged dangerous to her well-being. She feared the fragility of marriage and the volatility of passion. Heartbreak, rejection, and good-byes, she feared. Also dating and the social pressure to have a boyfriend, and keep him. There had been a boyfriend at photography camp, who would worshipfully fondle her breasts under the modest glow of the darkroom safety light. In that darkroom, she made love for the first time—intrigued by the blood on her thighs and fingertips and how the safety light seemed to leach away most of its color. She and her boyfriend returned to the darkroom often that summer, until one time she must have inhaled too many fumes from the developer, hypo, and stop-bath trays, and she threw up. The expression on his face—she had never seen such naked contempt before, as though he blamed her for everything that was unromantic in the world.

On the drive home from camp, Lynn was barely able to hold back her tears, but she kept the inglorious details from her mom, who had to content herself with dispensing generic heartbreak advice. She said Lynn was bound to move on soon and would forget about it. But if that was her mother's method—the one that got her through two divorces and into three marriages—Lynn preferred to look elsewhere. One might think, with such a track record, her mom would have shown a little more support about Lynn's spiritual path. Instead, Lynn's decision to become a Muslim seemed to threaten her, as though Lynn had taken sides with her birth father. Turpin was even worse about it. He gave her a very hard time and showed no cultural sensitivity whatsoever. And even after she eventually changed her mind and admitted she'd made a mistake, he still couldn't stop teasing her. It infuriated her, his teasing, but it was better than that other thing he sometimes did, like when she first returned from photo camp and was moping around the house. Then he'd offered to help with her chores and her homework, as though he'd presumed, more fully than their mother, the secrets of her summer and decided to pity her. That freaked her out and surely ranked high on her list of fears: she was afraid, truly afraid, of being pathetic.

She opened her eyes now and startled at the sight of her brother standing in the doorway. He held a glass of water and smiled shyly—almost coyly.

"You'd get better grades if you read with your eyes open," he said.

Lynn was in no mood to be teased for her study habits, or her slow progress toward a college degree, or her desire to live at home, or her lack of a focused life plan.

"Fuck off!" she said, preemptively.

He scowled and examined his thumb. "Seriously, you want to know why your grades suck?"

"Because I'm not as gifted as you?"

"It has nothing to do with smart or stupid," he said and began pacing. "You're just trying to punish Mom."

"Punish Mom."

"You know, for the divorces."

"That's ridiculous."

"You know you're angry at her," he said. "You've told me so yourself."

"That doesn't mean I'm out to punish her—by punishing myself!"

Turpin nodded toward her psych book. "Why not open your mind to new ways of thinking?"

"Like new drugged-out ways?" An easy cheap shot, scolding him on the drug point—her signature argument.

"By the way, I saved yours." He smiled again and reached into his pocket.

Her jawed dropped. "You kept it?"

"You don't have to drive anymore," he said, holding his remaining pills plus the ball of lint.

"You could have been arrested!"

"But I wasn't."

"You stupid idiot!"

Her brother cringed a little as he laughed.

"How can you be so reckless!" she groaned; she really wanted to understand.

He shrugged. "I took a medium-sized risk so you could take a small one."

Holding out the pill and the glass of water, he then set them on the coffee table and backed off, as though she were a wild animal who might approach the bait if it could be made to appear indigenous. He acted so sure of himself. Even if she was curious to try Ecstasy, she wouldn't give him the satisfaction. *But maybe he's betting I'll say no*, it occurred to her, *and he's just waiting to call me a geek*.

As she pondered the less predictable course of action—the choice least like her, or least like his idea of her—she reached for the pill. Turpin was leaning against the wall, picking at his thumbnail with questionable concentration. Her own hand, she noticed, shook as she held the Ecstasy in her palm. What was a drug trip, if not an invitation to confront some of her fears?

Her brother continued to pick at his thumb, and it struck her that maybe he wasn't so sure of himself after all. Maybe he was even more nervous than she was. The idea appealed to her greatly.

In the background, she heard the flush of the hallway toilet, its final swallow and belch, and she hoped the timing wasn't ominous, that she wasn't about to flush away anything irretrievable like, for starters, her integrity. She placed the Ecstasy on her tongue and took a long, defiant gulp of water.

"Okay, I did it," she said, setting the glass back onto the coffee table. "Now scram. I have studying to do."

He looked stunned, then disappointed. Heading for the door, he mumbled, "It's supposed to be a group thing."

Lynn understood that but couldn't stop fuming over his earlier diagnosis about her bad grades. Couldn't he just accept that she tested poorly? Why did it have to mean she was punitive and self-destructive? He was her baby brother, not a psychotherapist.

She tried now to make herself pay attention to the sections of her book she'd underlined in orange, but it soon became impossible to concentrate when someone put on her mother's Bessie Smith CD. Her mom always claimed listening to the blues made her happy. This confounded Lynn, who'd usually leave the room rather than have to hear about yet another love gone south, at least not in front of her mother, who often sang along.

Lynn picked up her orange marker and began drawing on the palm of her free hand, squiggly henna lines that grew more and more absorbing to her. In the background, Bessie Smith was singing how she'd killed her unfaithful man.

When Lynn finished with the right hand, she began hennaing the left, which was more difficult and took longer, but if she really tried, she could draw the lines close together without having them touch. Her hands hadn't looked this beautiful since her wedding day, when she'd had them drawn professionally. She closed her book, admitted to herself that she was done studying for the night, and drifted into the living room, where Meg and Turpin sat on the floor nodding to the music.

For the first time in her life, Lynn was stoned.

"I guess I'm just a hypocrite," she announced, then threw her highlighters and watched them bounce off her brother's chest.

He smiled broadly and stood up. "I guess you are!"

She walked to him and punched his shoulder. He spread his arms, gawkily, in what must have been an invitation to hug. Lynn couldn't recall the last time they'd hugged—certainly not since he'd grown this tall; she had no memory of hugging him in his current body. She leaned toward him, paused, and punched his other shoulder instead.

"I'm proud of you," he told her, dropping his arms.

"I kicked him in the side," sang Bessie Smith. *"I stood there laughing o'r him. While he wallowed 'round and died."*

"So, your folks are into the blues?" asked Meg.

"My mom," said Lynn, sitting on the floor. "She's into drama."

Her brother sat again, and the three of them formed a triangle.

"I love your hands," said Meg and immediately uncapped a highlighter. She leaned toward Turpin now, and drew a short line from his temple to his cheekbone. "You're so pale," she told him. "You're like a fresh canvas."

She turned his chin and drew a matching line on the other side.

Turpin picked up the yellow highlighter and, while Meg continued drawing on him, he began pressing moist dots of color across Lynn's forehead.

Lynn was busy studying her hands, but after a while, she uncapped the third highlighter and reached toward Meg and, beginning with her chin, accented the fissure below her lip, extending a line toward her throat. Lynn could feel the kiss of Turpin's highlighter across her own cheek now. After a while, the three of them switched colors.

"Dirty two-timer," sang Bessie Smith; different song, same idea. *"You ain't coming clean."*

"You two ain't coming clean either," said Meg and began to laugh.

"This is pretty neat," said Lynn, appraising her work on Meg. "It's like a mask."

"Nuh-uh, it's the opposite," said Meg, "It's an X-ray soul portrait."

"You guys look great," admired Turpin. "You should see yourselves."

"You should see yourself."

They stood before the mantel mirror—tall, pale Turpin between the two darker women, like Gauguin run off to Polynesia, painting the natives; with their faces marked, Lynn noticed, she and the other girl resembled one another even more.

"Do you have a swimming pool?" asked Meg. "We could go skinny dipping."

"We don't," said Turpin. His eyes drifted across Lynn's in the mirror, then darted downward. "Does your family, um, have a pool?"

"Not a big one," said Meg. "Let's skinny dip on the rug." She reached over to the wall switch and blinked all light from the room. "Carpeting is awesome against your bare skin."

Lynn felt the breeze of Meg's camisole flying past. Heard her brother's footsteps retreat to a corner of the room near the window and glimpsed the dim outline of his arms raising his shirt over his head. Heard the stripping of pants on either side of her. Wasn't there supposed to be a vote or something? She sat down on her own plot of carpeting, peeled off her socks and rolled the legs of her jeans as though preparing to walk on the beach. Pulled the sleeves of her sweatshirt elbow-high.

"Oh, man!" Meg was flouncing against the carpet in her underwear. "It's like a thousand caterpillars crawling over me."

"Yeah, I feel 'em," said Turpin.

Lynn gamely rubbed her calves and forearms back and forth across the carpet. She did feel something tingly, but it wasn't exactly pleasant.

"Hey, Sis," Turpin called out, "do you feel that?"

"Um-hmm," she said. "Amazing."

Turpin began sniffing the air, and Lynn picked up on it as well, another mysterious smell from her childhood.

"I think our chicken's ready," he said.

"Perfect," said Meg. The two of them leapt to their feet and skipped toward the kitchen. Alone now, Lynn took off her sweatshirt and raised her undershirt a few inches.

"I'm a lone bo'weevil," sang Bessie, attacking her subject from yet another angle.

Lynn wriggled her sensitized skin against the carpet and tried to feel the pleasure the others had claimed; maybe it was caterpillars she felt, maybe simply the tickle of exposure; it was nice, but a little creepy. She couldn't completely give herself up to it. She tried concentrating on the song now, hoped to get whatever it was her mother got—some kind of consolation from Bessie Smith's anguish—but this still seemed beyond her as well. Ecstasy, Lynn started to fear, was wasted on her.

She groped her way to the stereo and shut it off. Wandered now into the kitchen, where she found most of the refrigerator's contents lying across the counter in a kind of suspended state, like exhibits at a food museum.

As Turpin, wearing just his boxer shorts, slid the chicken

from the oven, Lynn picked up the bottle of *samsa* pepper puree—that's what she smelled—and saw it had been emptied.

"Yeah, what is that?" Meg asked. "I used it on the chicken. It smells great."

"It's from India," Lynn explained.

"This man in the picture—" Meg tapped the refrigerator. "Is this your father holding you? Looks like he's standing in this same kitchen. Oh, cool!" she said, peering closer now, "he's standing in front of the same refrigerator that his picture is on."

"That's only a year and a half old," Lynn said. "He was visiting with his new daughter."

"That picture," added Turpin, taking the electric carving knife out of its box, "is from Lynn's wedding."

"Excuse me?"

"It never happened," murmured Lynn, crossing her bare arms in front of her chest. "I backed out. We don't need to talk about it."

"She was going to have an arranged Muslim marriage!" shouted Turpin, over the carving knife's clatter. "Some mechanical engineer she'd never met! It was her idea, too. It drove our parents crazy. Even her Indian father thought she'd gone overboard, and he arranged it!" Her brother hacked off a drumstick.

"You could put on some pants, please," said Lynn.

She turned to the kitchen window and looked outside, was unnerved to see the sky already dawning. Just eighteen months ago, in that same backyard, her intended's family meandered gingerly across the lawn, jet-lagged from their delayed flight—

they were supposed to have arrived earlier, not on the wedding day itself. Her father, wearing his best Harrods suit, chatted them up, as though he were hosting, even though it wasn't his house. From the little he'd spoken of it, Lynn always pictured his divorce from her mother, no matter whose fault, as a deep gash to his confidence, and his traditional marriage to Nazar a healing balm. But pumping hands with the first, early guests, he seemed taut with bravado, his wounds still unhealed, and it gave Lynn an ache in her stomach as she watched from her window. Over in the gazebo, the groom, Hafiz, sat by himself, elegant in his white *sherwani*, tapping his foot on the cedar planks. There was a bench knothole just to his left, and he idly poked his fingers into it. Lynn kept waiting for him to show enough curiosity to peer through it, but he stared straight ahead. She wondered with creeping distress what assumptions he'd made about her purity, and she began to consider the many ways she might disappoint him. Lynn herself had assumed that with time she would come to love him, but suddenly she felt a rising panic that he would never return the favor, and she'd be married without knowing whether anybody in the world could ever fall in love with her. She recalled her mother's not-so-innocent remark that Hafiz must surely be looking forward to receiving his green card, and Lynn chastised herself for allowing such an unworthy thought to take root in her mind. Such a profane thought! On the day of her wedding, her mind was a bee's nest of profanity! She'd been sincere about Islam, Lynn realized just then, but not devout. She meant it, but she didn't feel it. Before she could fully grasp what she was going to do about any of this, however, her brother began screaming from the roof—possessed by some arrogant compulsion to disrupt her wedding. Then losing his balance and falling, his recklessness catching up with him on the ground. Buying time for her, as it turned out. Allowing her to call things off. She was furious with him and secretly grateful—and furious with herself for being grateful. So now here she stood, exposed and vulnerable, with all her existential fears restored—just another infidel in the suburbs. She thought: *I'm a lone bo'weevil.*

Turning now from the window, she said, almost a whimper, "That sweet boy came all the way from India."

"Sweet boy?" Turpin scowled as he carved deep into the white meat. "You don't know anything about him! And he knew dick about you!"

"I'm just—"

"You have a lot of quirks. You're a very quirky person."

Meg piped up: "Let's hear an embarrassing one."

"She, like, wraps brand new oranges and bananas in cellophane."

"They keep longer," argued Lynn.

"I'm not saying there's anything wrong with it. It's just not the kind of thing a stranger might understand."

"It's not so quirky."

"You smash Ping-Pong balls with a hammer and take pictures of them."

"That was an art project. I got an A!"

"Good for you. I'm just saying it could raise some eyebrows. What about how you make all your greeting cards out of old *Newsweeks*, or never ever hang up on a telemarketer. And you sleep with a stuffed animal under every part of your body—"

"You've been watching me sleep?"

Meg guffawed, her mouth full of fruit cocktail. "Man, you got a crush on your sister."

"No—" he sputtered. "I just mean that guy, that engineer wouldn't have understood her."

Lynn brought her fingertips to the side of her jaw and bent forward to get a better look at herself in the toaster oven, her striped-and-dotted face bouncing off the silvery metal like an electrically charged projection, like an X-ray soul portrait. Suddenly dizzy, she held on to the countertop, turned toward her brother, and said, "You have a crush on me?"

He was shredding the white meat any which way with the out-of-control carving knife. She looked back and forth between his clenched jaw and Meg's laughing mouth, which appeared to be dancing.

"Do you? Is that why you wanted me to take Ecstasy?"

"No!" he said, almost a moan.

"Maybe she's thinking of that date-rape drug," Meg put in.

"Are you *kidding*? I'd *never* take advantage of her," he said to Meg, as though Lynn had left the room. "Never in a million years."

He turned off the carver and stepped away from it.

"That chicken," mumbled Meg, "looks like it tried to cross a freeway."

They all stared at the chicken, and Lynn pictured her brother on the roof, this time not cavorting. Not reckless. Not careless at all.

"Oh my God, you didn't fall," she said, "you jumped."

He mumbled, "That's nuts."

"You jumped," said Lynn. She continued to envision him: willful, driven. Obsessed. It was far worse this way.

"Fell," he insisted. He seemed to glance toward her chest. Even under his face paint she could see him flush.

"What is wrong with you?" she said, heart racing. "You don't have a normal bone in your body!" She'd harangued him before, but always in a big-sisterly way; this time sounded personal and cruel. "You're . . . hopeless!"

Turpin hung his head, frowning at the mangled animal before him.

The phone rang, but no one moved, and eventually the answering machine began to record.

"Lynn?" her mother's voice reached out. "Lynn, pick up, would you? I turned on the news. There were arrests last night? At a concert? Turpin wasn't there, was he? Turpin, pick up if you can hear me."

Turpin began to reach for the phone, but Lynn put a hand on his arm.

In the background their stepfather was saying, "It's seven in the morning!"

Her mother continued: "Well, I hope you two are just sleeping? We'll see you tonight?" Then she muttered hurriedly to Lynn's stepfather, "I don't know, Garrett—" before hanging up.

The three ravers stood quietly around the kitchen island for maybe a full minute, glumly picking at the chicken, before Turpin said, "She sounded worried."

"Well, we couldn't talk to her like this!" Lynn meant, she supposed, high.

The long night had caught up with her. She announced she was going to bed, said it was nice having met Meg, and told Turpin he could leave the dishes for later.

After gathering her textbook and highlighters, she climbed the stairs to her bedroom and closed the door. Took off her undershirt and jeans and pulled her nightgown over her head before removing her bra, the way she always prepared for bed. She lay down and closed her eyes.

Coming up the stairs now, Meg's muted voice said something like, "Can I see?" And soon their footsteps padded down the hallway to Turpin's room, and then his door closed behind them. Had they been waiting for Lynn to say good-night so they could be alone together? She wondered what was going on behind her brother's closed door and held her breath trying to hear, distressed to note the tingle of betrayal that felt, strangely enough, like caterpillars across her skin.

Turpin and Meg lay down on his bed, her cheek against his chest. He could almost imagine taking a nap like this with his sister. What harm that would unleash he wasn't sure, but she seemed, back there in the kitchen, not so happy with him.

The worst part was he couldn't just tell her: "I take it back, I didn't mean it." Because he hadn't admitted anything in the first place. She'd simply glimpsed the overfondness in his heart, and it revolted her. In fact, he had pretty much intended to jump off the roof. But before he could go through with that part of his wedding protest, he fell—making him a freak and a fuck-up. Fine. Fair enough. He could own up to that. But an incestuous, sister-drugging pervert? Turpin shuddered.

"Is my head heavy?" Meg asked.

"No," he lied. He was exhausted, and the newly risen sun shining brightly through his bedroom window made no sense to him. "Is college different than high school, Meg?" he asked into her sprawling hair. "Has it changed you?"

"Mmm," she said drowsily. "Not different enough. I'm taking some time off to go to Africa. Volunteer relief work. That'll change me."

"Your parents don't mind?"

"Oh, they might." She paused. "But they'll have no moral argument."

He felt her eyelid blink against his skin. Was he supposed to make some kind of move toward her? Would she be insulted if he didn't? If he did? As Turpin pondered this, she began snoring lightly.

At some point he, too, fell asleep and eventually he heard in his dreams the churning of a garage door. It dawned on him as he opened his eyes that his parents were back. Outside the sun poised high in the sky, which meant they'd come home early.

His jaw ached from grinding his teeth. His eyelids felt chafed, his guts knotted. The comedown from Ecstasy, he reminded himself, was never a picnic, but this time was shaping up to be brutal.

He pulled on some clothes, saw the phone number Meg had left on his desk, and stumbled down the stairs. If shit was about to hit the fan, he should point himself to take the brunt of it, since the rave and the drugs were his idea. But he found his sister already dressed and in the kitchen, tossing corn and lettuce into the fridge, without pausing to wrap them in cellophane.

They didn't speak or even look each other in the eye, just hurriedly put away food, and a moment later their parents entered from the garage, carrying a bulky antique chair between them.

"Hey, Turp, grab your mother's end, would you?" asked his stepfather.

"No, no, that's okay," said his mom, still paranoid about his injury.

Turpin went to her side and hefted part of the chair. "It's light. I got it."

His mother, he noticed, was gawking at the *National Geographic* sight of him. She gazed now, almost pleadingly at Lynn, as if to say, *You too?*

Although his parents expected good grades from Turpin, they made allowances for his behavior, ever since he . . . tumbled. You break one neck and people start tiptoeing around you. Of his sister, they'd always demanded more solid citizenship.

"I'll take care of the dishes," Lynn murmured, approaching the sink.

As they made their way into the den, Turpin and his stepfather tried to coordinate the chair like a hook-and-ladder truck. Turpin chipped the doorway a bit, and Garrett grimaced, but didn't criticize. They set the chair down.

"Thanks, son." His stepfather lightly clapped him on the shoulder. "So what do you think?"

"About what?" Turpin said.

"Your mom's anniversary present. Try it out."

"Nah," he said. "I'll mess it up."

His stepfather looked surprised. "What kind of talk is that?"

"You first," said Turpin.

Garrett carefully sat down and reached underneath the chair, sliding a rickety footrest forward along its wooden tracks. He then leaned back and pushed a button on the chair's right arm that allowed him, after some effort, to recline. He beamed with satisfaction over the mechanical ingenuity of this.

"We looked in a dozen shops before she found what she wanted," he said, proud to have made Turpin's mom happy.

And with such an everyday item, too, a chair. So normal, so ordinary. Turpin gazed at the dent he'd made in the doorway, and his eyes began to water.

"What's the matter?" said his stepfather. "What's going on over there? Inside."

"Nothing," said Turpin, who thought, *you wouldn't want to know. I don't even want to know.* Forcing a smile he said, "That's a cool anniversary present, dude."

As she washed dishes, Lynn felt as if she were standing under a waterfall—still a little stoned. She hadn't gotten a wink of sleep, which left her exhausted and edgy.

Her mom stroked a dishtowel across Lynn's temple, rubbing at her brother's designs.

"Don't worry," said Lynn. "It'll fade." She sounded almost cynical to herself.

"All this wasted food," her mother said wistfully, hefting the empty bottle of *samsa* pepper. "You always hated to waste food. You used to scold your brother for it."

She never yelled, their mother, just unnerved you by pointing out the contrast of your own former goodness. She began to help load the dishwasher and asked, "Don't you have a test tomorrow?"

"Yes, I do!" Lynn snapped. "I'm almost ready!"

"My God, I was just asking." Her mother gazed at her appraisingly, the way she used to when trying to tell whether Lynn should stay home from school.

"Sorry," Lynn mumbled and bowed her head. Truth be told, she wasn't all that ready. As usual she'd managed to study the wrong things.

Her brother, she supposed, had a point: floundering at school was probably her way of punishing Mom for the divorces. Her flirtation with Islam and her betrothal—maybe that all belonged to this other program. She began to wonder if it was possible to punish her mother without punishing herself. And even if it wasn't, might she do it anyway?

Behind them, Turpin slouched wretchedly toward the garage as he carried out the trash, then back through the kitchen on his way to his room. The stairs creaked under his pitifully large feet, and Lynn felt god-awful guilty for having been so unkind to him last night—or this morning—whenever.

Her mom hung the dishtowel on its hook and announced she and Garrett were going to take a nap.

In the kitchen alone now, Lynn poured herself some water. As she drank, she viewed her hand, looming eerily large, through the glass; the henna lines had smeared from dishwashing and now looked bloody to her. She heard a scrabbling sound waft through the open window. It seemed to come from the roof, the slipping of feet across shingles. Lynn let go of her glass, which hovered in midair a long time before breaking. Instinctively, she called her brother's name.

She raced to the backyard and looked up, expected to find him teetering with passion and despair. It was hard to see into the noonday sun. She called his name again, loud and hoarse, before she could make out a pair of squirrels racing along the rain gutter. They chased one another into the arms of an overhanging oak and disappeared.

Her brother loped through the kitchen doorway now, brilliant with color. Her tribesman, the person who knew her best in the world. He walked toward her across the flagstone path and said, "What?"

Lynn dropped to her knees and ran her hands through the grass. Sun spots continued to dance across her eyes. She grabbed hold of her brother's feet and pressed them against the safe solid ground. One of his sneaker laces hung loose, and as she retied it for him now, Lynn could not remember ever feeling so deliriously happy.

eleven

Garrett in the Wild

"I'm on my way," said Garrett.

"No need to rush." His wife's voice sounded calm over the phone, almost dazed. "Darcy's already here."

Without bothering to shut his office door behind him, Garrett soon was speeding toward home, running yellow and red lights, committing illegal left turns and U's—ready to shout righteously at any Baltimore city cop who stopped him: "My wife is having a baby!"

He pulled into his driveway—that is, pulled in as far as Darcy Albright's Volvo allowed. A faded bumper sticker announced: MIDWIVES DO IT NATURALLY! She was a little intense, this Darcy Albright. But he and his wife had interviewed a dozen candidates, and this one seemed the most competent; plus she shared many of his wife's convictions about birth.

Chiefly, May-Annlouise had grown weary of episiotomies. What her perineum needed, she'd made very clear, was oversight, not surgery. "I need a perineum spotter," she'd said, more than once.

Garrett now stood on the front step to his own house and, without thinking, rang the bell. He shook his head at his own dumbness and was reaching for his keys when the door swung open. He found himself staring into the lens of a video camera. Behind it: his stepdaughter, Lynn.

"Garrett!" she squealed.

"Sweetie. I didn't know you were coming down."

"Are you kidding? This is great material!" Without lowering her camera, she gave him a quick hug.

His stepdaughter, having abandoned her brief flirtation with Islam, now labored as a performance artist in New York. Her most recent piece involved sitting naked in a glass box during the four days of her menstruation. Garrett could not bring himself to attend the gallery opening, though he did send roses.

"Enter the expectant father—inseminator, helpmate, and birthing coach," she narrated as he loosened his tie. *"How will he acquit himself?"*

"Is your mother all right?" he asked, draping his jacket across the nearby banister.

"She's fine. There's plenty of time still." Lynn set aside her camera for a moment. "Hey, I got a rave review from the *Village Voice*. Can I read it to you?"

"Sure," he said, glancing beyond her shoulder and straining to hear any word or sound from his wife.

Lynn was already unfolding a worn piece of newspaper

from the back pocket of her jeans. "OK, it says: '*Period Piece* tenders a neo-Darwinian critique of an entrenched taboo.'"

Garrett waited for her to continue, but apparently it was a brief review. "That's wonderful, sweetie." He searched for something else to say. "Are you going to perform it again next month?"

"Hoping to." She sounded distant and a bit melancholy all of a sudden.

He touched the banister's newel post. Hadn't he once caught her, kept her from tripping, on these stairs? Not so very long ago. He wondered if she remembered, considered asking her.

"Hey!" she said suddenly. "I got a postcard from Turp. Did he tell you he delivered this package of antibiotics? And the villagers carried him around on their shoulders?"

"He never told us that. Amazing." His stepson, his wife's other child, now a LifeCorps volunteer in Cameroon—no one saw *that* coming. The boy had finagled, perhaps fraudulently, early admission. But give him credit: he'd been a pill-popper; now, apparently, he was a healer.

It baffled Garrett, how people ended up the way they did; their lives took the most sudden turns, and if you weren't present at just the right moment to go through it with them, you became . . . less.

"We should go check on your mother," he said anxiously.

They crossed the living room into the den: there his wife reclined in the Morris chair he'd bought her last year for their tenth anniversary. How strange to see her dressed only in a UMBC sweatshirt, naked from the waist down, in the presence of other people.

"Hello, Garrett," said Darcy Albright, glancing up from his wife's vulva. The midwife wore a barbecue apron over a nylon jogging suit and had clipped back her hair with a pair of barrettes. Garrett didn't normally register things like barrettes, but these were made of lime green plastic in the shape of butterflies. "Someone you know could use a shoulder rub," she suggested.

"Oh, sure," he said, rolling up his sleeves. He stood behind May-Annlouise and began kneading her shoulders like a boxer's cornerman.

"That feels good," said his wife, reaching to pat his hand. Just then she gave an urgent little yelp. A trickle of fluid seeped out of her and onto the tarp someone had been wise to lay.

"Let's double-check your pulse," said Darcy, taking May-Annlouise's wrist and glancing at her own. "Oh, shoot. I've stopped ticking. Hand me your watch, would you, Garrett?"

"I could do it," he offered.

"We need you to keep rubbing those shoulders. And help Mother with her breathing like we talked about. Don't worry, I won't break it."

Garrett carefully handed over the watch—a present from his wife—to Darcy Albright, who quickly strapped it on.

"Everything's looking good," she soon announced in her singsong midwestern twang.

May-Annlouise's eyes narrowed and she let forth a muted howl. Her body quivered like a single muscle in spasm.

Darcy now folded a compress, one of the washcloths Garrett had brought home years ago from India, and laid it across his wife's forehead.

"Jasmine oil," explained Darcy, "for stamina and elasticity."

Embroidered with an image of the child Krishna stealing a glob of butter, the frayed washcloth was another totem from Garrett's life that Darcy commandeered with apparent ease.

"Can I boil something?" he asked, a bit desperately.

"Everything's taken care of," said Darcy. She reached for a foot-long tube and placed its flattened end against her ear and the flared end against his wife's distended belly. Made of wood, this oddly plain object looked like the kind of stethoscope the Amish might craft.

May-Annlouise yelped, and her womb wept again. She sucked in a breath and let it hiss out between her teeth. Almost immediately another contraction took over and filled the room with shuddering urgency.

"We're almost there," said Darcy, checking the dilation now. "If your little girl could talk, she'd say: 'I'm ready to come out! I'm so excited, Mommy! Thanks for giving birth to me!'"

Hovering in the background, Lynn trained her video camera on Garrett: *"At what point,"* she narrated, *"did Primitive Man come to understand the causal link between sex and childbirth?"*

Primitive Man? he wondered.

"Dearest," beckoned May-Annlouise. A rill of sweat ran down her temple and under her chin. Garrett dabbed her face with the washcloth. She gazed up at him curiously—as though she just now remembered something that had been eluding her. "Good of you," she panted, "to . . . to be here."

"Where else would I be?" He tried to smile. "Bowling?"

"You know. What I mean. Much nicer when . . . father is there."

Eyes suddenly bulging, she screamed, voicing a pain so raw

that all the possible layers of her disposition seemed to emerge, connecting her to the very root of the species, all the way back to Lucy herself. Cavewoman pain. It scared the daylights out of Garrett.

He rushed around front to see what was happening and nearly fainted at the sight of her gaping vagina. Feeling an involuntary tug across his ribs, he watched her perineum vibrate, as though it were a taut span of lawn-chair webbing being asked to support a great weight. Slowly its fascia seemed to fray, teasing out the red threads of a million capillaries. And now, another scream, more helpless and abandoned than her most violent orgasm, signaled that his wife had been wrenched into the spiraling center of the universe, as ply after ply of tissue separating her birth canal from her rectum appeared to disintegrate.

"I am so never going to do this," murmured Lynn from behind her viewfinder.

"I'll call 911!" Garrett shouted while hunting for the phone. "They'll be here in a second."

"We've got it all under control," said Darcy Albright, calm as soap.

Having finally found the receiver, Garrett now looked over his shoulder to check on his wife's progress and felt a clench of heartache to realize that his baby, in the blink of his eye, had emerged in her entirety, and was already being held aloft by the competent hands of Darcy Albright.

"Oh!" May-Annlouise was sobbing, while Darcy cleaned the infant's nose and led her toward her first breath of the new, outside world. "Oh," trembled May-Annlouise, and Garrett moved to her side and swabbed her brow and tears and helped raise her sweatshirt, revealing her plum-tipped breast, as Darcy lay the infant on his wife's soft belly. "Oh," said May-Annlouise, taking the child to her breast. Darcy, meanwhile, kept a lookout for the afterbirth.

"My God," whispered Garrett, gazing at his infant daughter, "she's so *perfect*." He glanced guiltily toward Lynn, afraid she might have mistaken his remark as a comparison.

"Oh, yes," said his wife, "most perfect. Perfect. Perfect Anne."

Garrett cupped the child's warm head with trembling fingers, as she began to nuzzle against her mother's breast. He bent forward to kiss the damp tufts of hair and let his lips linger on their salty wetness. Finally—to have become a bona fide seed-sowing father! After trying for years, then giving up, and then out of the blue! He kissed the infant's head once more and thought, *So this is what real fatherhood tastes like*. May-Annlouise murmured that she wanted to switch Anne over to the other breast.

"I'm seeing just a tiny tear down here," Darcy called up from her post.

"Really?" wondered Garrett in amazement. "It looked so— huge."

Darcy laughed. "Mr. Squeamish! No, I doubt we'll even need any stitches."

"Good," said May-Annlouise.

"Are you sure?" he asked.

"Sorry, Garrett. No husband's knot tonight."

"That's like, what?" asked Lynn. "Some kind of extra stitch?"

"You're so clever," said Darcy, winking at the girl.

"In this manner, the midwife subverts another patriarchal reconfiguration of women's bodies," Lynn told the camera.

Garrett's thoughts turned to Husband's Day, the holiday his wife had coined early in their marriage as an excuse to pamper him. Third Sunday of each month. Sure, they'd had to skip it now and then; distractions came up, especially in the last trimester—which was *completely understandable,* Garrett told himself, if a little disappointing.

"I wasn't asking for a husband's knot," he insisted, but no one seemed to hear him.

Darcy Albright spent that first night in Turpin's old room, should anything medical come up, though, mercifully, nothing did. And the following afternoon, she was relieved by her nursemaid sister, Daphne. The Albrights often worked in tandem like this—Daphne postpartum, Darcy pre- and during. Even though her official duties were now over, Darcy continued to drop by with herbs from her garden or to share a cup of tea with her sister. On several mornings Garrett woke to find the two Albrights in the breakfast nook with his wife and the baby—all of them still in pj's; well, Darcy wore jogging clothes but they certainly looked like pj's. Lynn remained on the scene as well, to document her infant sister's first weeks and also lend a hand. The house seemed bursting with neonatal attendants. Having cared for two earlier newborns with hardly any involvement from her prior husbands, May-Annlouise made it clear that this time she was going to have plenty of help.

"But now you have a husband who does want to pitch in," he pointed out. "Me, I mean."

"Yes, thank God for that!" she said, clutching his arm. "But you can't be around *all* the time."

This lust for staff, Garrett told himself—well, she was merely overcompensating. But there seemed no sense in pointing it out. She'd gone through all that labor, which, he could tell already, was going to give her a real edge in any argument.

One morning during the baby's first week—the fourth day of her worldly life—Garrett was walking past the den when he saw Lynn without her shirt. She was sitting in the Morris chair, holding the baby to her bare bosom and staring into the tripod-mounted video camera.

Garrett averted his eyes and went searching for May-Annlouise. He found her in the kitchen.

"Lynn," he reported, "is dry-nursing our baby."

"I told her she could," said his wife, perched above a sitz bath.

"You did?"

May-Annlouise raised herself out of the water; Daphne had a towel ready and set to work patting her dry. A pair of neon hummingbirds clamped Daphne's blond hair.

Darcy, meanwhile, stood at the kitchen counter in her jog-wear. "We're out of Cheerios," she said, rattling the empty box.

"Garrett, what is the problem?" asked his wife. "Lynn's experimenting with a natural body function."

He wondered if May-Annlouise could really be so sanguine about her daughter's bodily experiments, or whether she was just putting up a united front.

"I think I preferred it when she was experimenting with pur-dah," he said.

"Don't even joke about that," she said. "I'm so glad that's behind us."

"Amen to that," chimed Daphne, even though she hadn't known Lynn then. "No young woman should have to hide her-self in robes."

"Amen," echoed Darcy, reaching for the Corn Flakes.

After Garrett's paternity leave ended—the fastest two weeks of his life—he grudgingly resumed his place in the Bal-timore city bureaucracy. He spent most of that Monday passing out chocolate cigars, showing snapshots of the baby, and de-scribing the miracle of home birth. He glossed over the fact that he'd missed the climactic moment and had instead been squinting at it over and over again through the eyepiece of his stepdaughter's video camera.

Every other hour, he called home, and by four o'clock, he couldn't stand to be away any longer and left early. He arrived to find May-Annlouise cradling Anne on the living room couch, while the Albright sisters knelt before them, adjusting some kind of yellow headpiece on the baby.

Daphne turned to him. "These sunbonnets your mother sent are adorable."

"She sent sunbonnets?" At least he hadn't interrupted a se-cret rite.

"That was very sweet of her, Garrett," said his wife. "She wants to know when she can come visit her granddaughter."

"My mother?" His stomach tightened; ever since his par-ents' bitter divorce, visits and even phone calls stressed Garrett.

He glanced at the dining room table, covered with a Monopoly game that Daphne, Darcy, and Lynn had been playing for more than a week. "Where will we put her?"

"In the baby's room, as long as Anne's staying in ours."

"Um, sure. We can invite her. Sometime." He set down his briefcase. "Listen," he said. He had a proposal of his own to make. "I was thinking of bringing Anne to the office. Show her around. Give her the tour."

An awkward silence followed.

"It might be a little early for that yet," said Darcy Albright. "The workplace is a very life-hostile environment."

"How do you mean?"

"All those harsh, manmade products," said Darcy. There was a slight emphasis, as Garrett heard it, on *man*. The petroleum in the carpets, she said, the asbestos around the heating ducts—all of a sudden Darcy was a chemical engineer.

"We're talking about City Hall," he argued. "It's not like I work in a coal mine."

"The average office is a cesspool of toxins." This from Daphne now.

"What about me?" He tried not to sound petulant. "I mean, why aren't I dead already?"

Darcy took a step toward him. He'd never noticed before, but she stood nearly as tall as he did. "You're an adult, Garrett," she explained. "You've built up some resistance to all those industrial irritants. But to an infant, they're like napalm."

"OK, OK," he said, backing away from her, backing out of the living room altogether. "I wouldn't want to napalm the baby."

"Soon, dear," his wife called after him. "When Anne's a little older, we'll swing by your office and you can show her off."

Another week passed. May-Annlouise rented a breast pump in order to stockpile some milk in case she got sore or so that someone else could feed the baby if need be. Which was great! "Pump away!" he told her. Garrett *loved* feeding Anne—guiding that tiny bottle toward her minuscule mouth—the one time he'd gotten to do it. Even that was short-lived, because as soon as she began to cry, her mother reached for her. Okay, so he'd let the baby's head flop a little, but that didn't mean he should have to give her back, did it? Surely he could have gotten her to stop crying on his own, but May-Annlouise said something about a "steep learning curve," which put an end to that conversation.

During the weekdays, Garrett could barely concentrate at work, then would rush home and try to participate in whatever infant tasks remained before bedtime. He found it nearly impossible to so much as change Anne's diaper without someone—usually Daphne Albright—hanging around, offering guidance.

"Front to back," she reminded him one evening, as he wiped.

"I remember."

"No month-old little girl should have to suffer a bacterial infection," she said, leaning against the doorway to the master bedroom.

"Yes." Garrett sighed. "I do remember."

He fitted Anne into a new diaper and a fresh pajama suit. Through the cotton fabric, he traced a finger along her ribs, counting them up one side and down the other, savoring the calm this produced in him—as luxurious as any he'd ever known. As he carefully lowered her over the railing of her crib, he cooed, "Watch your head."

"*You* watch her head," said Daphne, in the Albright singsong twang.

Garrett's arms and fingers tensed, and the baby began to cry just as he was putting her down.

Daphne strode into the bedroom and over to the crib, nudging him slightly with her hip, and lifted Anne out again. "There, there," she said, "do you want to stay up a little longer?" She turned to Garrett. "I can watch her for a while."

Later that night, as he and May-Annlouise were getting ready for bed, she asked him, "Could you pick up a box of Cheerios on your way home tomorrow?"

"No," he told her.

She looked at him, puzzled. "Why not?"

He took a deep breath and said it: "I hate the Albrights."

"Why?" she whispered. "They've been a godsend!"

"I want to fire them. Her. They're rude and underfoot."

"When were they ever rude?"

"Daphne told me I should watch the baby's head as I was lowering her into the crib." In his telling of it, the moment lost some of its bite.

"So?" said his wife. "You should."

"Of course I should. You don't think I know that?" he asked, approaching the tender heart of his grievance.

"She was just trying to be helpful."

"We don't need her help," he insisted.

"Are you going to stay home from work when I have to go in?"

"You can bring her with you," he said, gazing at their sleeping daughter. "Or I can take her with me."

"I don't think you've thought this through," said May-Annlouise. She retrieved her sleep mask from the drawer in her bedside table. "And you heard what Darcy said about toxins in the workplace."

"Where does she get her information?"

"I've never met anybody as dependable as those two."

"I'm dependable."

"They're super-dependable."

"Just because my predecessors—"

"Garrett, please," said May-Annlouise. She slid the mask down over her eyes, then turned off her bedside light and told the suddenly dark room: "If they're doing things you don't like, we'll talk to them, but we're not firing anybody."

Garrett groped his way into bed. As he lay awake, he could feel the strands of his patience fray, like his wife's perineum a month earlier, and he suppressed a grunt from deep within his gut.

Overcompensating! he thought.

Sometime in the middle of the night, a full moon streamed through the bedroom window; its blue rays framed his face so squarely they seemed to be searching for him, prodding him awake.

He stepped into his slippers and stood, looking out at the backyard. The late spring grass glowed.

As his wife slept, her lips slightly parted, Garrett tiptoed toward Anne's crib at the foot of their bed. He looked down at her, so peacefully asleep. She was a sound sleeper. A good baby, May-Annlouise said. A good baby, the Albrights agreed.

Feeling agitated, he shuffled downstairs, in need of something to do. He poured himself a bowl of Shredded Wheat—the only remaining cereal in the house—and brought it to the dining room table, where he squeezed into the one empty corner not covered with Monopoly. Atlantic City had undergone a dramatic buildup: most of the houses and many hotels crowded the board. Ownership had been carved up almost evenly, and the players all possessed deep cash reserves; the game, he realized grimly, could last years.

The air inside his house suddenly felt gummy and barely breathable. He headed for the kitchen door and stepped into the cooler garage. Filled his lungs. When his head cleared, he eyed the two cars—same reliable make and model—each outfitted with an infant seat in back. So far, only May-Annlouise had taken Anne anywhere: to her one-week and three-week checkups. The infant seat in Garrett's car seemed to taunt him with disuse.

He opened the storage closet in a back corner of the garage and began to rummage around. There, behind years of junk, he glimpsed what he'd instinctively been drawn toward. He pulled out a long cardboard box, containing the three-person tent he'd bought years before but had never inaugurated. Never even opened the box!

He regarded the front picture: a father and mother and toddler camping in a flowering meadow. The father, who sported a puffy 1980s hairstyle, was splitting logs with his ax while the mother and child watched indulgently from a safe distance. *That child,* Garrett realized, *must be in high school by now.*

Impulsively, he loaded the tent into his car trunk, next to a parka he kept for the unexpected.

He then found a storage bag of old wool blankets. And a plastic tarp. Spying the laundry hamper, he pulled out a pair of jeans and a T-shirt and put them on, dumped a few other items in his trunk. Made sure to fish out one of Anne's sunbonnets.

He returned now to the pantry for a bale of disposable diapers, and a large plastic garbage bag in which to dispose of them. A box of cornstarch. A flashlight. A book of matches. A cooking pot. Two gallons of drinking water. A citronella tiki torch.

In the refrigerator's light, he grabbed a few bottles of pre-pumped milk and packed them into a foam cooler. He hastily added a package of frozen hot dogs, a bag of marshmallows, a jar of cocktail olives. A box of graham crackers. A carton of orange juice. A bag of pretzels. A few carryout packets of mustard. Clutching the squeaky foam, he shambled to the garage and crammed the cooler into his trunk.

He now tiptoed back upstairs, holding on to the banister tightly, his palm damp against the wood. On the second-floor landing, he paused. Wiped his clammy hands on his jeans. Then glided toward to the master bedroom; there the shaft of moonlight, having drifted down his side of the bed, now lingered over his baby's crib.

Easing his hands beneath Anne, he raised her to him, amazed at her near weightlessness, the utter lack of resistance, as though his hands were holding lightness itself. A pleasant tingle crept up his fingers, along his arms and into his chest. He felt the baby's lightness transfer to himself as he tiptoed downstairs. Into the garage now.

Without waking her, he carefully buckled Anne into the infant seat of his car.

"I'll be right back," he whispered.

He stepped into the kitchen, found a pad of paper and a pen. His hand trembled as he wrote. He kept the note brief. Left it in the middle of the counter, anchored under a rubber pacifier. Breathing deeply, he tried to slow his thudding heart.

He then, once again, tiptoed upstairs.

Sitting on the edge of the bed, he traced a finger along the length of his wife's arm. She sprang upright.

"What is it?" she asked, ripping the sleep mask from her eyes. "What's wrong?"

"Nothing," he assured her. "Nothing's wrong."

She looked at him blurrily.

"Come with me," he said.

"Garrett, I'm exhausted!"

"Just come," he pleaded, taking her hand and gently pulling her to her feet.

"Where's Anne?" she demanded, glancing at the empty crib.

"Shhh," whispered Garrett, as they passed Turpin's old room, where Daphne now slept.

"Where is she?" hissed May-Annlouise.

Garrett led his wife downstairs, through the kitchen, to the garage. Cupping her hands around her eyes, she leaned forward and peered inside his car at their sleeping baby.

"Explain this," she said.

"We're going on a small outing. We want you to come."

"Outing? Where?"

"You'll see." Garrett opened the garage, then unlocked the driver's door and climbed in. He started the car. Unlocked the passenger-side door. May-Annlouise continued to stand on his side of the car, and he rolled down his window. "Please get in," he said.

"This is nuts, Garrett. It's four A.M." Her expression was hard to read in the flickering utility light. "Bring her back upstairs, and we'll talk about this in the morning."

Garrett put the car in reverse. "Trust me."

"I don't!"

It stung, how quickly she said this. The ugly declaration echoed through their garage, stirring what few wisps of rancor had settled into the corners of their marriage. May-Annlouise scrunched her mouth, as though tasting the sourness of her own words. Cruelty had always seemed against her nature. She started to say something more—something gentler, he hoped—before stopping herself.

Instead, she walked around to the passenger side, climbed in, and softly closed the door behind her.

"Buckle your seat belt, please," Garrett said.

She did so.

"Garrett?" she asked, as he backed the car into the driveway.

"Yes?"

"I'm wearing pajamas."

"That's all right. So is Anne. Why don't you take a little nap?"

She sniffed. "You think I can sleep?"

But soon the car grew warm, and the small rhythmic burp of the pavement seams became hypnotic, and his exhausted wife closed her eyes. Occasionally, she would rouse with a start and look around and ask again where they were going, but Garrett would say only, "soon," and she drifted off again.

They were headed west, toward Garrett County—there seemed a rightness to that. He'd never been to his namesake county and wondered for the first time in his life what it might be like.

With the day's first sunlight rising behind them, he maintained their westward course into the Allegheny foothills. They passed a pair of grazing cows, then a green tractor pulling a line of plowing disks. The highway flowed beneath his car, carrying them toward the crest of each next hill, as the terrain became rounder, fuller.

Eventually, they arrived at the entrance to a state park, represented in his road atlas as a green spot no larger than his baby's thumb. He drove past an empty ranger booth, then along a winding lane into a forest of pines and oaks. He soon came upon an unmarked dirt road and felt moved to follow it, deeper into the forest—the trees taller now—until he found yet another turnoff, a swath of flattened leaves and pine needles. As the car bounced over a large stick that lay across this path, May-Annlouise opened her eyes. "Where are we?" she asked dreamily.

Garrett stopped the car before the mouth of a small clearing.

He rolled down his window and shut off the engine. Morning sunshine slanted through the pine boughs, and the day's first currents of warmth floated through the air. In the distance, he heard the brisk rap of a woodpecker.

"Where are we?" she asked again, her voice soft with awe.

She opened her door and took a deep breath. Garrett did too. The air here smelled simpler, not crowded with the perfumes of garden flowers and the cloying musk of fertilizers. He'd become unused to seeing any greenery without the *thrum* of lawn mowers somewhere in the background. Here things were allowed to grow as they might.

May-Annlouise looked back toward Anne, who was still asleep, and whispered, "She likes the car."

"Let's stretch our legs," he proposed.

The two of them climbed out, then took a few steps into the glade, its floor covered by several inches of brown pine needles. Garrett felt an urge to lie down in them. He watched his wife stroll across the small clearing in her cotton pajamas and ratty slippers, like some character in a fairy tale who has mysteriously awakened in the forest. Birds were flirting tunefully with one another. Somewhere a stream trickled, out of sight.

"It's beautiful," she said. "How long have we been driving?"

"A couple hours," said Garrett, understating it slightly.

May-Annlouise raised an eyebrow. "How did you know this spot was here?"

"It had to be," he said. "Something like this had to be around here somewhere."

She seemed to be considering this statement of reckless faith—so unusual for him—when Anne began to cry. May-

Annlouise scurried to the car, climbed into the backseat, and within a quarter minute had managed to unbuckle the baby and begin breast-feeding her.

Cradled securely in her mother's arms, Anne fed hungrily, while May-Annlouise murmured something that Garrett couldn't quite make out. He moved closer to them and watched his daughter eat; she sucked with her eyes closed, her hand squeezing then letting go of the air around her, in what seemed to Garrett a gesture of utter fulfillment.

His wife shifted Anne upright against her and began to rub small circles along the length of the baby's back. "She's wet," May-Annlouise determined, telepathically it seemed to Garrett. "Do we have anything?"

He went to the trunk and retrieved the changing gear. Together he and his wife gentled Anne out of her pajamas and old diaper. May-Annlouise cleaned her with the washcloth and distilled water. Then Garrett patted her dry, sprinkled the lightest dusting of cornstarch between her legs.

"You packed well," May-Annlouise said suspiciously. "How long were you planning to stay?"

"Overnight," he said, trying to sound matter-of-fact. "I brought the tent."

May-Annlouise glanced out the rear window at the tranquil, deserted woods, then cast a good long look at him, perhaps taking the measure of his conviction.

"I see," was all she said. Then added: "What about Lynn and Daphne? They must be——"

"I left Lynn a note."

"I see," his wife said again.

Garrett brought out one of the wool blankets and began to spread it across a cushion of pine needles. Still holding the baby, May-Annlouise took hold of a blanket corner and pulled it smooth. He and his wife then breakfasted on graham crackers and orange juice, which tasted good to him and felt surprisingly filling. They consumed only half, and Garrett chose to believe this meant they were deliberately saving the rest for tomorrow's breakfast. Fortified, he set to work on the tent.

That it remained sealed in its box all these years mocked his credentials as an outdoorsman. But May-Annlouise was good about not saying so. She watched patiently, bouncing Anne on her knee, as Garrett read the instructions, which seemed to address a different tent than the one before him.

A trio of butterflies, palest yellow, hovered over his shoulder, as though contemplating the instructions with him, then silently moved on. After tinkering with rods and sleeves and stakes and ropes for the better part of an hour he managed to erect something reasonably shelterlike in a shady spot under the tallest pine.

May-Annlouise handed him the baby and crawled inside their tent and began to spread the remaining wool blankets from corner to corner.

Sitting on a log that lay at the center of the clearing, Garrett held Anne on his lap. A beam of sunlight warmed the back of his neck, and his head shaded her face. He began introducing her to whatever bits of landscape caught his eye.

"Leaf," he said, twirling a tan one between his fingers. "Log," he said, patting its bark.

There was something fundamentally gratifying about naming each item for her.

A small gray lizard lay sunning itself farther down the log, its back toward them. Garrett reached over and plucked it by the tail and held it for Anne's inspection. "Lizard," he proclaimed.

Just then the creature broke free of its tail, fell to the ground, and scampered under the thatch of pine needles.

"Oh shit!"

Anne began to cry, more likely at his reaction than the sight of the wriggling tail in his grasp. He tossed it far behind him, tried to downplay his revulsion.

"Nothing to be alarmed about," he murmured. "Daddy just broke the lizard."

May-Annlouise began to laugh. She was watching them from the tent. "He'll grow a new one," she called out.

"Really?" This struck Garrett as a most hopeful quirk of nature.

"Come inside." She sat cross-legged on the blankets; the tent glowed greenly around her.

He handed Anne ahead, through the parted flaps, and crawled in behind her. He and May-Annlouise lay down and nestled Anne between them. His wife yawned widely.

"How are you feeling?" he asked.

"I told you, dear, exhausted! I haven't done this in ages!"

"Camping?"

"Having a baby. My poor old body!"

"So it's not like riding a bicycle?" Her recurring bicycle

dreams—a light joke between them over the years; he wondered now if she caught the reference.

"I find it's much, much harder than riding a bicycle." She smiled sleepily at him. "But that's just me."

"I mention the bicycle—"

"You know, that joke always seemed slightly at my expense."

"I'm sorry," he said, surprised. "I won't make it any more."

"Thank you," she said and then drowsed off to sleep.

He watched his wife and baby nap, and when Anne squirmed on occasion, he let her play with his fingers, and this soothed her enough that she'd fall back asleep for another few minutes. When he wasn't gazing at his family, he studied the shadows swaying against the tent.

May-Annlouise eventually awoke, and she reached across Anne to give him a lingering kiss. She touched a hand to her pajama top.

"I've been leaking," she said.

How amazing that his wife could lie still, asleep, and milk would spontaneously flow from her, as though from an underground spring.

"I brought some clothes from the hamper," he said, "if you want something else to wear."

She wrinkled her nose. "What's for lunch?"

"I didn't pack the most nutritious fare for a nursing mother," Garrett admitted.

"It's only for a day."

They ate pretzels dipped in mustard, and afterward May-Annlouise fed Anne again.

"Did you happen to bring some paper towels?" she asked, looking down at her damp pajamas.

Garrett shook his head.

"How about toilet paper? I have to pee."

"Um," he said, "hang on a sec." He went to the car, where the only paper he could find was the road atlas; he ripped out Alaska, deciding they could do without it—though a family road trip to Alaska: that might be nice someday. He'd like to show Anne a moose or a glacier—add them to her repertoire of leaf, log, and lizard. He handed the map to May-Annlouise.

"No, thanks," she said.

"A diaper maybe?"

She shrugged. "I'll improvise." She gave him the baby and wandered toward a thicket of berry bushes.

"Your mother's being modest," he said to Anne, who began crying again. He reached into the cooler for one of the bottles of breast milk, dabbed a drop on his pinkie, and offered it to her. She accepted the pinkie and shifted idly against the soft shelf of his stomach, her eyes seeking out his. Every day her eyes seemed to focus more sharply. He wondered how much of this, her first time in the real outdoors, she actually perceived. Surely she wouldn't remember any of it, and yet, it had to affect her somehow. Didn't it? Maybe, years from now, she would walk through a pine forest, and the brisk scent of rising sap would gratify her in ways she could not explain.

"Is there anything you want to tell me?" he whispered in his baby's ear. "Anything at all?"

A small bird—bright red spot on its breast—glided past them and perched on the berry thicket, beyond which May-

Annlouise began to appear. First her auburn hair. And now the rest of her, naked except for her slippers, emerged into the glade. In one hand, she held her pajamas, wringing wet. As she walked past Garrett, she blew him a kiss. She began to drape her pajamas across a tent rope so they might dry in the warm breeze.

"I found the stream," she said over her pale, freckled shoulder. She turned to face him, crossed her arms, then uncrossed them. "I feel a little empty-handed."

"Do you want her?" he asked, nodding toward Anne.

"That's all right." May-Annlouise sighed. "You two seem very comfortable."

❧

The moon, full plus a day, bathed the woods in blue light.

The three of them sat around the campfire Garrett had built. Dry pine needles made for ready kindling, and he'd used large handfuls of them to ignite the twigs and larger sticks. Finally, he'd been able to light the first of a half-dozen small logs he'd found just beyond the clearing.

Over her clean pajamas, May-Annlouise wore Garrett's parka, open in front so she could snuggle Anne against her. Garrett was warm enough by the fire. He asked May-Annlouise if she wanted another hot dog.

"No, thank you." She brushed a marshmallow against Anne's cheek then let the baby lick it.

"Marshmallow," said Garrett, naming it. "Do you want a cooked one?" he asked his wife, reaching into the bag.

But instead of answering him, his wife posed a question of her own: "What would you have done, if I hadn't gotten into the car?"

Garrett speared a marshmallow on his stick. "You think you might not have gotten in the car?" A tongue of flame poked between the logs.

"Would you have gone without me?" she asked. "You were acting like you would."

He fidgeted against the stone he was sitting on, which suddenly felt cold. "It's hard to say for sure what you'll do until you're doing it," he said.

"You mean what *you'll* do, or what *I'll* do?"

"Me." He smiled. "I guess both."

"There's a scary thought," she said. Looking at the fire, she added quietly, "for a daddy."

The marshmallow was burning, and he removed it from the flames and blew on it, then offered it to May-Annlouise, who barely shook her head. He didn't want it either, so he propped the stick against one of the rocks ringing the campfire.

"So *do* it, now I mean. Close your eyes," she urged him, "and tell me what's happening."

She sounded serious about this, almost solemn.

"Okay," Garrett said. He closed his eyes, stroked the stubble that had sprouted on his chin during the day. "Well," he began cautiously, "the car is turned on." He took a moment to locate himself behind the wheel. "And I guess it's moving, slowly. I'm pulling out of the driveway. And looking out the rear window. Anne is asleep. And I turn onto the street. . . ."

He paused, confused. The campfire felt hot against his face, as though it had inched closer to him.

"And?"

"Well—" The car was idling in front of their house now. The transmission in neutral. "It depends," he said. "If I look back toward the house. I mean, if I look up the driveway—and see you—standing outside—"

"I'm standing outside?"

"I think you would be, don't you?"

She thought about it. "Probably."

"Outside," he forged ahead, "in all that moonlight, seeing you there—then I—" This was coming out wrong, he thought; it sounded so *up to chance*. . . . "I couldn't—"

"Hmmm?"

"Go without you."

They were silent for a while. The only sound was the crackle from the fire. And then a twig snapping, or was that also the fire? Garrett wondered if his wife was still seated next to him.

He waited for her to make some kind of sound. Any sound, just so he would know she hadn't tiptoed away, with Anne, that she wasn't about to drive off. Leaving him behind in the woods.

As he listened for that sound, he kept his eyes closed; he hadn't fully answered her, it seemed, and he felt he should. He should answer her completely.

A breeze rustled the treetops, traveling from one end of the camp to the other.

"So," she said at last, her mouth surprisingly close to his ear. "Are you looking? Up the driveway? Seeing me there?"

These questions, a rope back to her in that moment. A life-line.

"Yes," he answered truthfully.

"Yes?"

In that wash of blue light, her face, bright with care. Honest, natural face that he loved.

"Yes. I am."

"All right," she said. "You can open your eyes now."

READERS GUIDE TO

Garrett in

Wedlock

Discussion Questions

1. In the book's first story, "Garrett in Wedlock," a nervous Garrett tries to calm himself by thinking: "so many other men had summoned the courage to wed before him" [p. 5]. Nonetheless, his wedding day is filled with omens including strange sound bites from the television and radio, a lost and loose-fitting wedding ring, and an oncoming solar eclipse. What do these things symbolize to Garrett? Are his fears justified?

2. In "The Explorers," Garrett and May-Annlouise welcome her dying second husband into their home, where he shares stories of his exotic adventures as a world traveler—and his belief that "Everything eats everything else. Eventually" [p. 46]. How does Garrett perceive all

this as a threat and, ultimately, a comfort? What role does sex play in his mixed feelings? Why do you think the story ends with a sexual conquest rather than a death?

3. In the story "Pendant," Garrett and his stepdaughter, Lynn, meet a young woman in India who longs for a "love marriage" but is afraid it will curse her to a series of progressively worse marriages in her reincarnated lives. How is this fear similar to Garrett's fear of repeating the mistakes of past relationships? Can these patterns be broken, or are most of us trapped in a never-ending cycle of our own making?

4. In spite of the repressions of arranged marriages (shown in the story "Pendant") and the restraints of social status (in the story "Parni's Present"), Lynn decides to embrace her father's religion and traditions. Why? Personal rebellion? Spiritual seeking? Or something else?

5. In the story "Changeling," May-Annlouise contemplates the active-passive roles of her relationships, deciding that "this seemed the choice all married people made: one either took charge or was taken charge of" [p. 118]. Do you think this is a universal truth? How does it apply to May-Annlouise and her three marriages?

6. After the car accident in the story "Several Answers," Turpin hears his dead father explain that the concept of reincarnation "in which one whole being returns as an-

other . . . was an invention of human ego" [p. 149]. How does ego play a role in Garrett's feelings about his wife's ex-husbands? In May-Annlouise's interactions with Parni's wife, Nazar—and her desire to donate her eggs? In the shifting attitudes and lifestyles embraced by Lynn and Turpin? What role does ego play in our religious beliefs? In our personal relationships?

7. In "The Omelet King," Lynn prepares to marry a stranger selected for her by her natural father. Why is the idea of an arranged marriage so disturbing to Turpin, to her mother and stepfather—and to most Americans? Is there a deeper fear involved? Why doesn't anyone (except Turpin) try to stop her? Is there any truth to her mother's feeling that "If May-Annlouise were any kind of saint, she'd have been willing to risk her daughter's love to ensure her daughter's happiness . . . To be a saint . . . was to suffer an intense loneliness" [p. 169]?

8. In the story "Virtue," we meet Garrett's coworker Adriane, a "Conscientious Seducer" with a unique vision of God as a giant ear and an equally unique view of ethics and morality. Garrett tells her the story of his wife imagining a cat's eye marble as a sign that the universe is watching them. Throughout the book, most of the characters explore a variety of personal and religious beliefs. Do any of them find true comfort in their spiritual quests?

9. In "Yoga Is a Personal Journey," an instructor with personal problems of his own urges his students to "step outside the wheel of desire, gratification, and frustration" [p. 229]. May-Annlouise feels a pang upon hearing this and thinks: "Yearning, distraction, even suffering . . . were passion's substance. Was she supposed to deny this? . . . What if a marriage without suffering was no marriage at all?" [p. 234]. Do you agree with her generalization? Or is it simply an opinion born of May-Annlouise's own personal journey?

10. In the story "Lynn, Raving," the Islam-dabbling daughter experiments with another kind of spiritual trip when Turpin talks her into trying Ecstasy. Before the drug kicks in, she reads in her psychology book that an emotion begins with a stimulus that a person assesses "in terms of his or her well-being" [p. 247]. How does this textbook definition of emotion pertain to Turpin's feelings toward Lynn? To Lynn's reaction to his "crush" on her? To her eventual perception of her half-brother as "her tribesman"?

11. In the final story, "Garrett in the Wild," the new father finds himself entrenched in a nearly all-female household and—inspired by comments of "Primitive Man" and sights of "cave woman pain"—flees to the wilderness with his wife and newborn child. What does this symbolic return to the Garden of Eden represent in the overall scheme of the book? What does it reveal about

the characters' spiritual paths? What does it imply about the family's future? And, from what we've seen in the book, what are the real reasons Adam and Eve were banished from the garden?

12. *Garrett in Wedlock* is very much a novel of our times. The stories are like snapshots of the new American family—a social dynamic redefined by multiple marriages, cultural diversity, global awareness, and spiritual choices. The personal journeys of the characters in the book reveal some of the individual challenges of this new family dynamic. Has your life been affected by similar changes and challenges? Can these changes be used as an opportunity for growth?